THE KIND BROTHERS

(KIND BROTHERS SERIES, BOOK SIX)

SANDI LYNN

SANDI LYNN ROMANCE, LLC

THE KIND BROTHERS

The Kind Brothers
(Kind Brothers Series, Book Six)

New York Times, USA Today & Wall Street Journal
Bestselling Author

Sandi Lynn

The Kind Brothers

Copyright © 2022 Sandi Lynn Romance, LLC

All rights reserved. No part of this publication may be reproduced, distributed, or transmitted in any form or by any means, including photocopying, recording, or other electronic or mechanical methods, without the publisher's prior written permission.
This is a work of fiction. Names, characters, places, and incidents are the products of the author's imagination or are used fictitiously. Any resemblance to actual events, locales, or persons, living or dead, is entirely coincidental.

Photographer: Wander Aguiar
Models:
Sam
Zakk
Travis
Soj
Pat

✺ Created with Vellum

MISSION STATEMENT

Sandi Lynn Romance

**Providing readers with romance novels that will whisk them away
to another world and from the daily grind of life – one book at a time.**

CHAPTER 1

Shaun

"Shaun, Barb is here to see you," Selena spoke as she poked her head through my office door.

"Does she know I'm here?"

"Yes. She's downstairs, and she can see you through the glass."

"Shit. Send her up. But if you don't see her leave my office in ten minutes, I want you to come in and tell me I'm late for a meeting."

"You don't have a meeting scheduled," she said.

"Duh, Selena. She gets ten minutes. Understand me?"

She rolled her eyes.

"Don't roll your eyes at me." I pointed at her.

She did it again and shut the door.

The door opened, and Barb stepped inside.

"Hello, Shaun."

"Barb, it's good to see you." I faked a smile as I stood up from my chair. "Please, have a seat. To what do I owe the pleasure?" I sat back down.

"Julia told me that you're throwing my sons a birthday bash."

"I am."

"Well, I was going to do the same." Her brow arched in a disapproving way. "There's no sense for them to have two birthday parties. So, you can cancel whatever plans you've made."

The nerve of this woman.

"Sorry, Barb. No can do. Everything is already set." I took great pleasure in saying that to her.

"They're my boys, and I'm their mother. It's my responsibility to give them a birthday party."

"They're my brothers, and this is the first birthday I'm celebrating with them. So, I'm throwing them a big birthday bash."

"And where is this event taking place?"

"Casa di Pietra."

"That stone house on the water in Malibu?" she asked.

"Yes. Don't worry, Barb. It will be exquisite, and I promise you'll have a good time. Listen, I know you still resent me, and I was hoping by now you would have found it in your heart not to hold my mother's actions against me. After all, I've forgiven you for keeping my existence a secret for thirty-three years." I cocked my head.

The door opened, and Selena stuck her head inside my office. "Excuse me, Shaun. Everyone is waiting for you in the conference room for the meeting you're late for."

"Thank you, Selena. I'll be right there."

I stood up from my chair and buttoned my suit coat.

"I'm sorry, Barb. I have to run. It was nice seeing you again. Don't worry. You'll be getting your invitation to the party soon."

She stood up with a scowl and headed for the door.

"Um, Barb?" I called out.

She stopped, turned her head, and looked at me.

"Remember, this is a surprise party. Can I trust you won't tell my brothers about it?"

"Don't worry. I would never ruin a surprise for my sons." She turned and walked out the door.

I grabbed my briefcase and walked out of my office.

"I'm headed out for the day," I spoke as I stopped at Selena's desk. "When I come in tomorrow morning, we'll go over the final details for the party."

"Okay. Enjoy the rest of your day."

"You too. In fact, you can leave for the day as well."

"Really?" Her face lit up.

"Yeah." I grinned.

"Why are you being so generous today?" Her eye steadily narrowed.

"In two seconds, I'm changing my mind, and you'll be here until seven o'clock." My brow arched.

"Have I told you that you are the best boss in the entire world?" Her lips displayed a wide grin.

"Enjoy your freedom." I gave her a wink as I walked away.

I climbed into my car and headed to Jenni's studio. When I stepped through the door, I walked up the stairs and saw her standing in my old office, looking at the bridesmaid dresses that hung on the headless mannequins. Quietly stepping behind her, I placed my hands over her eyes and whispered in her ear.

"I've been stalking you because you are the most beautiful woman I've ever seen."

"I'm flattered, but I have a boyfriend."

"I don't care. Get rid of him. You're mine now."

"The only way I'd get rid of him is if you're better in bed than he is."

"I guarantee I am. I will take your body to places it's never been before."

"Done. He's gone." She smiled as she turned around and wrapped her arms around my neck.

"Hi." I grinned as I placed my hands on her hips and brushed my lips against hers.

"Hi. What are you doing here?"

"I decided to leave the office for the rest of the day, and I wanted to see you. I miss you."

"I miss you too. The dresses are done. What do you think?" She turned around and stared at them.

"They're beautiful, and I can't wait to see you in it. Perhaps you can bring it home tonight and try it on for me."

"I could. I guess the new lingerie I bought can wait for another night."

"You bought new lingerie?" My brow raised.

"I did." The corners of her mouth curved upward.

"The dress can stay here." I kissed her again. "Barb paid me a visit earlier."

Jenni's brows furrowed. "Why?"

"She wanted me to cancel the birthday party so she could throw one. She is their mother, and it's her responsibility."

"What are they? Five?" Jenni rolled her eyes, and I let out a chuckle. "I hope you didn't give in to her."

"Do you think I did?"

"No. But I'm just double-checking."

"Oh. Hey, Shaun," Wes spoke as he poked his head into the office. "Jenni, there's a problem with some of the fabric that just came in."

"Ugh! What now?"

"Go deal with your fabric." I kissed her forehead. "I'll see you later at home. I love you."

"I love you, too." She let out a sigh.

When I got home, I changed into a pair of gray sweatpants and a Nike t-shirt. Grabbing a beer from the fridge, I took it out to the patio. As I was sitting on the lounger, Ruby came walking over.

"Hey, girl." I patted her back as she laid her chin on my lap. "How's your day going so far? I'm sure it's great since you can sleep whenever you want, play all day, and always have a full belly."

She lifted her head and stared at me.

"What a life. You have no idea how you have it made. I sure hope you don't take it for granted." I ran my hand across her head.

"Really? Isn't Jenni giving you enough attention that you have to resort to carrying on a conversation with a dog?" Simon walked over and fist-bumped me.

"Very funny. Beer?"

"Sure." He sat down.

"You know where the refrigerator is." I brought the bottle to my lips.

"Dude, I'm a guest."

"You're not a guest. You're my brother." I smirked.

He smiled as he shook his head and went inside the house. Ruby took it upon herself to lay down next to my chair as I stroked her soft fur.

"What are you doing home already?" Simon asked as he walked back out. "Aren't there billions to be made?"

"Trust me. As I sit here drinking this beer, billions are being made." I cracked a smile as I held my bottle up to him.

"Touché, bro." He tapped his bottle against mine.

"What you are you doing home already? Aren't there drug dealers and murderers to be caught?"

"Grace and I are doing a stakeout tonight, so we thought we'd come home for a while."

"Sounds like fun."

"If you call sitting in a car for god knows how many

hours waiting for a suspect to leave the house so you can follow him, fun, be my guest and join us."

"I'm good, bro." I chuckled.

Ruby quickly got up and ran to Sebastian as he stepped on the patio.

"Hey, girl." He bent over and petted her. "What's going on over here?"

"Shooting the shit. Care to join us?" Simon asked him.

"I'd love nothing better, but Emilia and I are meeting with the minister to go over a few things for the ceremony."

"Same guy who married Dad and Celeste, Sam and Julia, and Stefan and Alex?" he asked.

"Yep."

"Wow. Does he give family discounts?" I chuckled.

"Why? Are you planning on asking Jenni to marry you?" Simon cocked his head.

"No. We're still adapting to living together. I came home the other day, and when I walked into the bedroom, there was a pile of her clothes lying on the bedroom floor."

"And?" Sebastian's brow arched.

"I called her and asked her what happened. She said she was trying to find the perfect outfit for a meeting she had, and she would put them all away when she got home."

"Did she?" Simon asked.

"No. I put them away because I couldn't stand seeing them lying there. I mean, who does that? All she had to do was hang each piece back up the second she took it off. Am I right?"

Simon and Sebastian both started to laugh.

"This is a conversation you should have with Sam," Sebastian spoke.

"Yeah. We don't really care." Simon laughed.

"I have to run. Come on, Ruby. Let's go home."

"Bye, bro." I waved.

"I should go too. Grace and I are heading out soon. Thanks for the beer." He held out his fist.

"You're welcome." I bumped my fist against his.

I finished my beer and went inside. I couldn't stop thinking about how Simon asked if I was planning on asking Jenni to marry me. I loved her more than life, but I wasn't ready for marriage. Did two people who were madly in love need that piece of paper? Because that's all it was. Jenni knew how much I loved her and would do anything in the world for her, and I knew how much she loved me. Our relationship was perfect the way it was, and there was nothing else we needed to do to solidify it.

I was outside throwing a couple of steaks on the grill when the sliding door opened, beautiful arms wrapped around me from behind, and her head laid against my back.

"I missed you, but my girlfriend will be home soon. If she catches you here, I'm a dead man." I flipped the steaks.

"Get rid of her."

"I'm not sure I can do that. She's sexy, incredibly talented, selfless, generous, extremely talented in bed, and I love her more than anything in the world."

"She sounds amazing." Her grip tightened around me.

"She is."

I closed the lid on the grill, turned around in her arms, and softly kissed her lips.

"Welcome home." I smiled.

"It's good to be home. It's been a long day." She laid her head on my chest.

"Okay. This is what we're going to do. The steaks will be done in a couple of minutes. We'll eat dinner, take a relaxing bubble bath together, and then I'm going to give you the most amazing body massage."

"Sounds wonderful. Can we skip dinner?" Her brow arched.

"No." I shook my head as I scrunched my nose. "I'm starving. So, go inside, grab me a plate for the steaks, and we'll eat."

"Did you make anything else to go with the steaks?" she asked.

"Baked potatoes are in the oven, and I made that salad you love. Now, get me that plate before the steaks overcook." I slapped her ass.

CHAPTER 2

Stefan

"Here's the contract for the Leeds project." I walked into Sam's office and handed him the file.

"Thanks." He sighed, set the file down, and leaned back in his chair.

"What's wrong?"

He ran his hand down his face. "Nothing. I'm just tired. The girls were up all night."

"It gets better, Sam. Just hang in there. You know we're all here to help. Feel free to drop the girls off with any of us if you need a break. Have you and Julia discussed what you're going to do when she goes back to the shop full time?"

"We're going to hire a nanny."

"That's a good idea. If you can find someone like Nanny Kate, you'll have it made without worries."

"Nanny Kate was a rare find. Julia said she'll call a couple of agencies and set up some interviews."

"Maybe Alex can help out and watch the girls," I said.

Sam let out a chuckle. "Don't you think she has her hands full with Lily, Henry, and bartending a couple of nights a week? I dare you to ask her." The corners of his mouth curved upward.

"You're right." I sighed. "It's probably safer if I don't even mention it."

"Good idea." He pointed at me.

I glanced at my watch. "I have to run. Alex asked if I could pick up Lily from school today since Henry has a doctor's appointment with Emilia."

"This is her last week, right?"

"Yep. Bro, I don't know what I'm going to do."

"About?"

"She starts middle school in the Fall. You know what that means." I ran my hand down my face while letting out a sigh.

"Boys. Fucking boys." He shook his head. "Don't worry. Between the five of us, those boys don't stand a chance."

"You remember what we were like in middle school," I said.

"I remember." He grinned.

"Don't forget we're having an end-of-school-year party on Saturday."

"I haven't forgotten. Julia and I will be there as always."

"Okay. I have to go. I'll talk to you later."

I was sitting in the pickup line listening to some music when Reece walked over. Letting out a sigh, I put the window down and smiled at her.

"Hey, Reece."

"Hello, Stefan. I haven't seen you around here in a while." She flirtatiously smiled.

"Alex took Henry to the doctor this afternoon, so she asked me to pick up Lily."

"The ladies and I are looking forward to the end of the school year party on Saturday. Is there anything I can bring?"

"Nope. We've got everything covered."

"Is your brother, Shaun, going to be attending? We haven't met him yet."

"Yes. Shaun will be there." I grinned.

"Great. I look forward to meeting him."

The bell rang, and I was saved.

"It was great talking to you, Reece. I'll see you on Saturday."

"Bye, Stefan." Her smile widened as she strutted away."

"Hi, Dad." Lily grinned when she climbed into the car.

"Hey, baby girl."

"Guess what?"

"What?"

"No more homework!" She beamed.

"Yes!" I held up my hand for a high-five.

When I pulled into the driveway, Lily climbed out and said she was going over to Julia's to see the babies. I grabbed her backpack and took it inside the house. A few moments later, Alex stepped inside with Henry.

"Hey, babe." I walked over, kissed her lips, and took Henry from her arms. "How is my baby boy?" I held him up in the air, and he laughed.

"He was a very good boy for Emilia."

"Of course, he was." I threw him up in the air a couple of times.

"Where's Lily?"

"She went over to Julia's to see the girls." I walked over to where she stood and wrapped one arm around her waist with Henry in my other arm. "How about we put this little one down for a nap and have some fun." My lips pressed against the flesh of her neck.

"I think I'm pregnant, Stefan." She blurted out.

"What?" I took a step back as my eyes widened.

She walked over to the diaper bag, unzipped it, and took out a pregnancy test.

"I stopped on the way home and picked up a test."

I let out a sigh as I rubbed the back of my neck.

"Okay. Let's go find out if we're having another baby." I held my hand out to her.

She placed her hand in mine, and we went upstairs. I laid Henry down in his crib while Alex went to pee on the stick. When I walked into the bedroom, I found her lying on the bed with the pregnancy stick sitting on the nightstand. Climbing on the bed, I laid down and faced her. Bringing my hand up, I softly stroked her cheek as our eyes stayed locked on each other.

"Maybe I'm not," she quietly spoke.

"Maybe you are." I smiled. "Either way, it'll be okay."

"Are you sure?"

"Of course. I want a dozen babies with you."

She let out a laugh. "Let's not be dramatic. If I am pregnant, though, I think three children are perfect, and it completes our family."

"I agree, babe." I leaned in and brushed my lips against hers.

The timer on her phone went off, and my heart started to race.

"Here we go," she said as she reached over and grabbed the stick from the nightstand.

She held it in front of us, and the word "pregnant" appeared in the window.

"Look at that. We're having another baby." I smiled.

Her eyes filled with tears. "I can't believe it. Oh my God, Stefan. We're having another baby."

"We sure are, and I couldn't be any happier." I pulled her into me.

"You both know you're supposed to shut the door, right?" Lily spoke as she stood in the doorway with her hands on her hips.

Alex and I laughed as I held out my arm.

"Come here, baby girl. We have something to tell you." I smiled.

"You're having another baby, aren't you?" she asked as she climbed on the bed.

"Yes, Lily. I'm pregnant." Alex smiled as she showed her the pregnancy test.

"Okay. But it better be a girl this time. I love my brother, but I want a sister. Then Dad can stop calling me baby girl." She narrowed her eye at me.

"I already told you that you'll always be my baby girl." I pulled Lily into me and kissed the top of her head.

"And that's okay, Dad. But for the love of God, please stop saying it out loud. I'm going into middle school. You can't keep calling me that. It's embarrassing."

Alex laughed as my brows furrowed.

"Well, I'm going to keep calling you that until we find out the sex of the baby. Deal?"

"And if it's a boy?" she asked.

"We can talk about that when the time comes. But for now, you can't tell anyone. Not yet."

"You're not telling the family?"

"Of course. But don't mention anything to your friends about it."

"Okay. I won't. I'm going to grandma and grandpa's house to play with Nora." She climbed off the bed. As she reached the doorway, she stopped and turned to us. "I think the two of you need to be more careful in the future. Two siblings are enough. I can't guarantee I'll be happy if more come along." She turned and walked out of the room.

Alex and I looked at each and laughed. I pulled her into me and held her tight.

"Life is about to get crazy," she said.

"I know. But it'll be a good kind of crazy." I pressed my

lips against the top of her head. "I saw Reece today when I was picking Lily up."

"Oh yeah?" Alex lifted her head.

"She said she can't wait to meet Shaun." A hint of a smile played on my lips.

"I bet." She shook her head. "Poor Shaun. We better warn him before Saturday."

"Nah. Don't say anything. He's the new victim. Let's watch those women sink their claws into him." A wide grin crossed my face. "Besides, they wouldn't dare go near Simon. They're all too afraid of Grace."

Alex laughed.

"You're bad, Mr. Kind."

"You love me when I'm bad." I placed my hand on her belly. "And this little peanut proves it."

CHAPTER 3

Sam

When I walked through the door, the house was quiet. I didn't dare say a word because I woke the girls up the last time I did, and Julia just about killed me. I set my briefcase down and walked up the stairs. When I reached the bedroom, I saw the light on in the bathroom. Stepping inside, I saw my beautiful wife covered in bubbles.

"You are a sight for sore eyes." I smiled as I walked over, bent down, and kissed her lips.

"Welcome home."

"Are the girls sleeping?"

"Yeah. I just laid them down about ten minutes ago."

I took off my suit coat, rolled up my sleeves, knelt next to the tub, and grabbed the loofah.

"Pour some body wash on this, and I'll wash your back."

She did as I asked and sat up as she hugged her legs.

"Oh my God. That feels amazing. I set up nanny interviews."

"For when?"

"Two of them are tomorrow, and the other two are the following day. Can you be here?"

"Of course, I'll be here. What time?"

"Three o'clock and five o'clock. I tried to schedule them as late in the day as I could to make it easier for you."

"I appreciate that. I'll be here." I pressed my lips against her shoulder.

"I'd been thinking about something, and I want to talk to you about it."

"Okay. What were you thinking about?"

"I love you and our girls so much, but I think we're a perfect family of four."

"Are you saying you don't want any more children?"

"Yes, Sam." Her eyes stared into mine. "There's a great possibility that it could be twins if I got pregnant again. That's why my mom and dad didn't have any more after she had Jenni and me. We always talked about having two kids, and we just happened to have our two children at the same time. They have us and each other, and I think we should be done having children."

"Thank you." I kissed her lips. "I was thinking the same thing."

"You were?" she asked with surprise.

"Yes. But I didn't want to bring it up just in case you wanted more."

"So, we're on the same page?"

"We're on the same page, babe." I smiled as I leaned in and kissed her.

My phone rang, and when I grabbed it from the bathroom counter, I saw my cousin Jackson was calling.

"Babe, it's Jackson. I have to take this. I'll be right back."

I walked out of the bathroom and answered his call.

"Hey, Jackson. What's up?"

"Sammy. Are you busy?"

"No. I just got home from work."

"Conner, Nathan, and I are coming to L.A. in a couple of days."

"That's great. I can't wait to see you three again. How long are you staying?"

"We're not sure yet. Probably about a week."

"Are you guys on vacation?" I asked.

"Not really. We're coming in for business. I'll tell you all about it when I see you."

"Okay. Don't think you're staying in a hotel. Between all of us, we have plenty of room."

"Thanks, Cous. We appreciate that, but we don't want to disrupt your lives."

I breathed out a laugh. "You wouldn't be, and right now, we'd welcome it. Trust me. Does my father know you're coming?"

"No. I haven't spoken to him."

"I'll let him, and my brothers know. Speaking of brothers, you'll finally get to meet Shaun."

"I know, and I can't wait. That's some crazy shit right there, Sammy."

"It is, but you're going to love him. He's a great guy."

"Of course, he is. He has the Kind blood in him. Listen, I have to go. I have to cut out a tumor in a sixteen-year-old's head soon that I have to scrub in for."

"Take care, Jackson. I'll see you in a couple of days."

"Thanks, cousin. You too."

I ended the call and tossed my phone on the bed.

"What was Jackson calling about?" Julia asked as she stepped into the bedroom with a towel wrapped around her.

"The three of them are coming to Los Angeles in a couple of days."

"That's great. It'll be good to see them again. We haven't

seen them since Stefan and Alex's wedding. Is there a particular reason all three of them are coming together?"

"He said business, and he'd tell me more when they arrive."

I walked over, gripped her hips, and my tongue trailed along her neck.

"You smell delicious, and you're getting me very hard."

"Maybe we should do something about that." A smile graced her lips as she let the towel fall to the floor.

"Damn, you're sexy." I grinned as I pushed her down on the bed.

My mouth devoured her beautiful breasts, and as I went to dip my finger inside her, a screeching cry came through the monitor. Then another cry came through. I dropped my head and slowly closed my eyes as we waited and prayed the girls would go back to sleep. They didn't.

"I'll go get them while you get dressed." I kissed her lips.

I walked into the bedroom and looked at my girls. The moment they saw me, they stopped crying.

"Hello there, Lorelei. Hello there, Lena. Fifteen more minutes. That's all Daddy needed." I scooped up Lorelei first and handed her to Julia when she walked into the room. Reaching over, I picked up Lena.

"Did you just tell our babies you needed fifteen more minutes?"

"I did." I smirked. "There's breast milk in a bottle, right?"

"Yes. In the refrigerator."

"I'll take Lena and feed her the bottle out on the patio. I want to call my brothers over and tell them about our cousins while you feed Lorelei."

"Okay." She smiled as she brushed her lips against mine.

Walking to our bedroom, I picked up my phone and walked downstairs. Grabbing a bottle from the refrigerator, I took it outside with Lena and sat down in one of the loungers as I sent a text message to my brothers.

"My house. Patio. Beer. Now."

Within a few minutes, the four of them walked over.

"What's up?" Sebastian asked.

"Go grab us some beers, and I'll tell you."

Sebastian went inside, grabbed five beers, and brought them out.

"Thanks, bro. Jackson called me, and he, Conner, and Nathan are coming to L.A. in a couple of days."

"Awesome. Why?" Stefan asked.

"All he said was that they're coming in for business."

"That's strange." Sebastian's brows furrowed. "What business would all three of them have here?"

"Medical conference, maybe?" Simon spoke.

"He would have said. Anyway, they'll be here for about a week, and I told them between all of us, they can crash at our houses instead of getting a hotel."

"They can stay with Grace and me."

"They're welcome at my house," Sebastian spoke.

"I have plenty of room at my house," Shaun said. "I know I haven't met my cousins yet, but it would be a great way to get to know them."

"Jackson said they can't wait to meet you."

"If they're here for a week, they'll be around for Lily's end-of-year party," Stefan said.

"I'm surprised they're coming since they're coming in for the wedding," Sebastian spoke.

"I guess we'll find out more when they get here." I held Lena over my shoulder to burp her. What's wrong?" I asked Stefan.

"Nothing. Why?"

"You're being oddly quiet."

"Yeah, bro." Simon smacked his arm with the back of his hand. "What's going on?"

"Talk to us, bro," Sebastian said.

"You have to promise me that you won't say anything to the girls. Promise."

"We promise. You know we always keep our word," Sebastian said.

"Alex is pregnant."

"Whoa. What?" Simon placed his hand on Stefan's shoulder.

"Congrats, bro." Shaun grinned.

"Baby number three. Wow. I'm happy for you," Sebastian said.

"Congrats, Stefan. How do you feel about it?" I asked.

"I'm happy. I really am. But Alex and I agreed that this is the last kid."

"Funny you should say that. Julia and I had a discussion earlier that we aren't going to have any more kids either," I spoke.

"Why?" Shaun asked.

"There's a chance we could have another set of twins, and that's a chance we don't want to take. We're happy with our two little girls and our family of four. You could be next in line for twins." I smirked as I pointed at Shaun.

"Jenni and I never talked about kids. I'm not even sure if I want kids."

"I can relate," Stefan said.

"Excuse me, douchebag?" Sebastian spoke. "You have two and one on the way. What the fuck do you mean?"

"Shit. That came out wrong. I meant that's how I felt years ago. And don't any of you sit there and say you can't relate. We all felt the same way at one time. But, bro, when you love someone so much, and she's your entire world and the air you breathe, all you see are children in your future. Right, Sam?"

"He has a point. I never wanted kids until I met Julia."

"I never wanted kids either until Emilia. It's up to us to keep the Kind name going."

"Unless you all keep making girls." Simon smirked. "You better hope this kid is another boy, Stefan."

"What about you?" Stefan cocked his head. "Your douchebag sperms might be girls."

"Nah. My sperm are strong, powerful boys."

"Why are you guys talking about sperm?" Julia walked out and took Lena from me.

"Just guy talk, Jules." Simon smiled. "Kind of like how you women talk about penises."

She breathed a laugh and shook her head as she walked back into the house.

"That was close." Stefan reached over and smacked Simon in the back of the head.

CHAPTER 4

Simon

"Grace," I shouted when I walked into the house.

"I'm upstairs in the bathroom," she shouted back.

Walking up the stairs, I stepped into the bathroom and found her brushing her wet hair.

"How are your brothers?" she asked.

"They're good." I came up from behind and planted my lips against her neck. "You took a shower without me?"

"You weren't here, and it was getting late. What did Sam want?"

"My cousins are coming to L.A. in a couple of days," I spoke as I walked out and into the bedroom.

"The doctors?" Grace followed behind.

"Yes. Jackson told Sam it was for business. Would it be okay if all of them or one of them stayed with us?"

"Yeah. Of course. They're coming to the wedding, right?"

"Yeah. That's why I'm surprised they're coming now."

"It'll be great to meet them finally." She smiled as she climbed into bed.

THE KIND BROTHERS

I took down my pants, lifted my shirt over my head, and climbed in next to her.

"Anything else you have to tell me?" she asked.

"No. Oh, wait. Sam and Julia decided not to have any more kids. Don't say anything to her until she tells you herself."

"Wow. Really? I guess having twins would quickly change one's mind. Anything else?"

"No. That's it." I furrowed my brows.

"You sure about that?"

"Grace, what is going on? I said that was it. Now, come here." I placed my hand in between her legs, and she tightened them.

"You're lying. I know when you lie, Detective Kind."

"Oh, my freaking God! I am not lying."

"You are. And until you tell me what you're keeping to yourself, the sex gate is closed for the evening." She rolled over and away from me.

I lay there and stared at her in disbelief.

"Fine. Keep it closed. I don't care." I rolled over and pulled the sheet over me.

My cock was aching to be inside her. Suddenly, I heard her let out a moan. I lay there for a moment, and she did it again. I quickly sat up.

"Are you—"

She let out another moan.

"Okay. Okay. Alex is pregnant. I swear to God if you let on you know, you'll be taking care of yourself for a long time."

She laughed as she rolled over and looked at me.

"I already know." She pushed me on my back and climbed on top. "After you left to go to Sam's, she Facetimed us. She knew Stefan couldn't keep it a secret until we were all together and they could announce it."

"Why would you put me through that if you already knew?"

"I was just checking to see if you could keep your promise not to tell. But obviously, sex is more important to you." A grin crossed her lips.

"Damn right it is." I pulled her down and smashed my mouth against hers.

~

Sebastian

The alarm went off and jolted me from my sleep. Emilia stirred as I reached over and shut it off. My arm tightened around her as she snuggled her body against mine and moaned.

"Time to get up." I kissed the top of her head as it rested on my chest.

She pulled the covers over her head, and I chuckled.

"Do we have to?" she sleepily asked.

"Unfortunately, we do. You have sick kids to treat."

She threw the covers back and lifted her head.

"Are you making breakfast?"

"Don't I always?" My lips formed a smirk. "Is there something you want me to make?"

"Eggs Benedict, please." Her soft lips pressed against my chest.

"Eggs Benedict it is. Go get in the shower, and I'll take Ruby out and get breakfast started."

"I love you." She reached up and pressed her lips against mine.

"I love you, too."

We climbed out of bed and stared at Ruby, who was sound asleep on her back in her dog bed.

"Come on, Ruby. Let's go outside."

She didn't move.

"See. She doesn't want to get up either," Emilia said as she headed into the bathroom.

"Ruby! Come on." I pulled on a pair of sweatpants.

Ruby jumped up and followed me down the stairs. Opening the front door, I let her out and watched as she did her business on the grass. After feeding her, I started breakfast.

"Morning, Uncle Sebastian," Lily said as she opened the sliding door and walked in.

"Good morning, your royal highness. What's up?"

"Can you make me breakfast?" She sat on the floor and played with Ruby.

"Of course. I'm making eggs benedict."

"Ew." Her brows furrowed.

"Is there something else you would like?"

"Waffles with strawberries and bananas?" A grin crossed her lips.

I stood there and stared at her with a raised brow.

"Have I told you that you're my *favorite* uncle?"

My eye narrowed at her.

"What? You are." Her smile widened.

"Waffles with strawberries and bananas coming right up."

"Hey, Lily." Emilia smiled.

"Hi, Aunt Emilia. Uncle Sebastian is making me waffles with strawberries and bananas."

"Actually, that sounds good, babe." She walked over and kissed my cheek.

"So, you don't want eggs benedict?"

"We can have that tomorrow." She smiled as she brewed a cup of coffee.

The sliding door opened, and Shaun walked in.

"Good morning, Kind fam." He grinned.

"Hi, Uncle Shaun." Lily ran over and hugged him.

"Morning, Shaun. Coffee?"

"No, thanks, Emilia."

"Hey, bro," I said.

"Do you have some Kale I can steal from you by any chance?"

"Yeah. I have a bunch of it in the fridge."

"Thanks. I ran out, and I'm in the middle of making a green smoothie." He walked over to the refrigerator and took some out.

"Do you want to stay and have waffles with us?" Lily asked.

"As delicious as that sounds, I'm afraid I don't have time. Why isn't your mom or dad making you breakfast?" he asked her.

"They're too busy having sex."

Emilia spit out her coffee, and I dropped the spoon in the waffle batter.

"Oh," Shaun said.

"They weren't up, so I went to open their bedroom door, and it was locked. My dad said they'd be out in a minute, and I heard them giggling. I know what they were doing."

"Where was Henry?" I asked.

"He was still sleeping. I checked on him before I came over."

"There you are!" Stefan exclaimed as he walked in. "I went to Uncle Sam's first, and when you weren't there, I knew you'd be over here conning your Uncle Sebastian into making you breakfast."

"Having a good morning, bro?" Shaun smirked as he patted Stefan's shoulder. "I'll see you guys later."

"What did he mean by that?" Stefan's brows furrowed.

"I told them you and Mom were having sex."

"Lily!"

"What?" She shrugged. "He asked why you or mom

weren't making breakfast, so I told them the truth. You always tell me not to lie."

Stefan ran his hand down his face while Emilia and I stood there smiling at him.

"You better hurry up and eat. It's your last day of school, and you don't want to be late."

"I will, Dad. Don't worry."

After breakfast, Lily took Ruby home with her, Emilia left for work, and I cleaned up the kitchen. I had to go to the grocery store to pick up a few things for tomorrow night's barbeque before heading to the restaurant.

I couldn't wait for my cousins to arrive because the last time we saw them was at Stefan's wedding. The seven of us had always been close and grew up together until we all went off to college. We still kept in touch almost daily and saw each other as much as our studies and life would allow.

CHAPTER 5

Shaun

"Has the guest list been confirmed?" I asked Selena as she sat across from my desk.

"Yes. There will be approximately one hundred people there."

"Excellent. And the—"

"Shaun. Everything is taken care of. This isn't the first party I've put together for you."

"I know, but I just want everything to be perfect for my brothers."

"It will be. Have I ever let you down?"

I arched my brow at her.

"That was one time, Shaun. One time." She held up her finger. "And if you recall, I had just started working for you. I wasn't yet aware of your overly controlling and OCD ways."

I rolled my eyes and let out a sigh as I leaned back in my chair. Looking at my watch, I would be late for a meeting if I didn't get going.

"I need to leave for my meeting with Raphael," I spoke as I

stood from my chair. "Keep up the good work, Selena." I smiled as I walked past her and patted her shoulder.

"I want a bonus when the party is over!" she shouted as I walked out of my office.

I gestured a wave as I walked down the stairs and to the elevator.

Walking into the Four Seasons, I made my way to Culina Ristorante, where I met Raphael Lumens of Lumens Ltd. When I stepped inside, the hostess took me to the table where Raphael was already seated.

"Raphael." I smiled as I extended my hand.

"Shaun. Good to see you again." He shook my hand.

I took the seat across from him, and we started talking business.

"I looked over your five-year business plan, and I think it's good. The question is can you deliver?" I arched my brow. "And I think the answer to that is yes. I rarely invest in start-up companies."

"Didn't you just invest in some fashion designer's company?" Raphael asked.

"I did." I smiled. "But that's different. She's my girlfriend, we live together, and I love her more than anything. If you'll excuse me, I need to use the restroom. We will finish our discussion when I get back."

I stood up from my seat, and when I approached the restroom in the restaurant, there was a sign on the door stating the bathroom was out of order. Sighing, I headed to the lobby and the restroom, to the right and down the hall from the concierge desk. After I finished, I stepped out of the bathroom and headed back to the restaurant. As I reached the lobby, I saw my father and a woman, who was not Celeste, walk into the hotel. He hooked his arm around her with a smile and headed towards the elevator. I stood closer to the wall and out of sight. Slowly peeking around the corner, I saw them in a lip lock while they waited for the elevator to come down. I inhaled a deep breath as my heart started to pick up its pace. The elevator door opened, and the two of them stepped inside. Looking up at the number of floors lighting up, the elevator stopped on the fourth floor. But that didn't mean anything. It could have stopped to pick up other guests.

Walking over to the check-in desk, I was greeted by a young gentleman in a dark blue suit.

"Welcome to the Four Seasons. How may I assist you today?"

"I'm meeting my father, and I cannot remember which room he said he was in for the life of me. I tried calling his cell, and he didn't answer."

"What is your father's name?"

"Henry Kind."

"I'll need to see your I.D."

I pulled out my wallet, removed my I.D., and handed it to him.

"Thank you, Mr. Kind." He nodded. "Your father's suite is 1622."

"Yes. That's right. I can't believe I forgot that. Thank you."

"You're welcome. Have a nice day."

As I turned and headed in the restaurant's direction, I heard the young man call my name.

"Excuse me, Mr. Kind?"

"Yes." I turned and looked at him.

"The elevators are over there." He pointed.

"Yes. I know. I'm just going to grab a drink before I head up."

I finished my meeting with Raphael and was tempted to go up to my father's suite and ask him what the fuck was going on. I was enraged that he would do something like this to Celeste and Nora. I restrained, walked out to the valet, and handed him my ticket. Confusion and rage blew up inside me, and I didn't know how I was going to tell my brothers what I'd seen. Instead of going back to the office, I went to Jenni's studio.

"Hey." A big grin crossed her lips. "What are you doing here?"

"I missed you." I smiled as I wrapped my arms around her and kissed her lips.

"I missed you too."

"I need to talk to you, Jen. Can we go up to your office?"

"Yeah. Of course. You're scaring me, Shaun."

"Don't be scared. It has nothing to do with us. Well, in a sense, it does."

We walked up the stairs and into her office, where I shut the door behind me.

"Do I need to take a Xanax before you tell me whatever you have to tell me?"

"No." I chuckled.

"Then spit it out, Kind. You're killing me here."

"I was at the Four Seasons meeting with a client, and I saw Henry with another woman."

"WHAT?" Her jaw dropped. "Who is she?"

"I don't know. They were in a lip lock while waiting for the elevator to come down. After they got into the elevator, I went to the front desk and told them I was there to meet my father, and I couldn't remember which room he was in. The guy was nice enough to tell me."

"Did you go up there and beat the shit out of him?"

"No. I was in shock. I came right here from the hotel to talk to you."

"You didn't call your brothers?"

"No."

"Shaun," she shook her head, "you have to tell them."

"I know. But it has to be after the birthday party. I am not going to ruin that for them."

She sighed and brought her hand to the back of her head as she looked down at the floor.

"You're right. This news will definitely ruin their birthday. Shit. Fuck! Why is Henry doing this? What did she look like?"

"I'd say she was around thirty-five, medium length blonde hair, five foot seven."

"Was she pretty?" Her eye narrowed at me.

"She was okay. Not as pretty as Celeste." I lied.

"I cannot believe it. Do you think Celeste knows?" Jenni asked.

"Probably not." I sighed. "I just feel like saying fuck it and get my brothers all together and tell them."

"Their birthday is next week. We can keep it to ourselves until after the party because we both know Simon will kill him."

"Yeah. That's the first thing I thought of."

She wrapped her arms around my waist and laid her head against my chest.

"Prepare yourself, babe. The shit is going hit the fan in the Kind family."

CHAPTER 6

Sam

"How did your interviews with the nannies go?" Stefan smirked as I sat across from his desk.

"Terrible."

"Shit. What happened?"

"All the candidates just didn't sit well with either of us." I let out a sigh. "The agency is sending over three more women."

"Were they that bad, or are you and Julia just scared to leave the twins in the care of a total stranger?"

"Both." I leaned back in my chair. "I don't know what else to do."

"Excuse me, Sam?" Josh popped his head into Stefan's office. "Is it okay if I leave now to pick up my cousin from the airport?"

"Yeah, Josh. That's fine. I'll see you tomorrow."

"Thanks, boss." He smiled.

Looking at my watch, I stood up from my seat.

"I have a couple of contracts to look over before heading home for another round of interviews."

"Good luck, bro. I hope one of them works out."
"Thanks. I'll talk to you later."

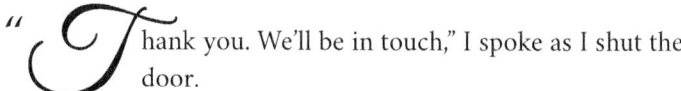

"Thank you. We'll be in touch," I spoke as I shut the door.

I could see the despair on Julia's face as she held Lorelei.

"No. Just no." She shook her head. "None of them were the right fit for our daughters."

"I thought Margie was okay," I spoke as I walked over and took Lena from her bouncy seat.

"Really, Sam?" Julia cocked her head. "Lorelei screamed the minute that woman held her. They know. Our babies know."

"So now what?" I asked.

"How the hell do I know? I guess we just need to forget about it," she spoke with a raised voice.

I walked over to her and pressed my lips against her forehead.

"Everything is going to be okay, babe. I'll put Lena in her swing, and then I'll start cleaning up."

"I'll help you."

"No. I want you to put Lorelei down, pour yourself a glass of wine, sit out on the patio, and relax."

"What about dinner?"

"Don't worry about dinner. I'll take care of it."

"I feel bad, Sam. You worked all day."

"And so did you." I smiled as I kissed her lips. "Now go."

After Julia set Lorelei in her swing, I set Lena in hers, turned them on, and went upstairs to change out of my suit. Pulling out my phone, I called Sebastian.

"Hey, bro."

"Hey. Are you going to be coming home soon?"

"Yeah. I'm leaving the restaurant in about thirty minutes. Why?"

"Can you bring dinner home for Julia and me? It's been a rough day, and we just interviewed three more candidates for the nanny position. Julia didn't like them, and she's stressed."

"Of course. I'll bring the food over in about an hour."

"Thanks, bro. I owe you."

"I'll see you soon."

After I changed into some casual clothes, I went downstairs and saw the girls had fallen asleep in their swings, so I started picking up the living room and then moved into the kitchen, where the dishes were piled up in the sink. I took a deep breath and tried not to let the anxiety get to me. As I was unloading the dishwasher, Shaun walked in.

"Emergency help is here." He grinned.

"Hey, bro."

I looked out the sliding door and saw Jenni sitting next to Julia.

"Julia texted Jenni and said the interviews were a no and that you sent her outside so you could clean up. I figured you needed the help."

"You are a godsend." The corners of my mouth curved upward.

"Wow. It kind of looks like a tornado blew through here."

"Tell me about it." I sighed. "There's shit everywhere."

"I'll finish cleaning up the kitchen if you want to clean up somewhere else," Shaun said.

"Are you sure?"

"Yeah, bro. Go."

"Thanks." I placed my hand on his shoulder.

I wouldn't lie. It had been tough since the girls came into our lives and trying to find the perfect balance. Our girls were our world, and we wouldn't trade this life for anything.

We just needed a little more time to figure it out. Julia was struggling with a touch of postpartum depression, and I tried to be there and help her as much as I could. The most important thing was not to let my OCD get in the way, which was a difficult task. Our families helped as much as they could, and we were grateful. It was just so damn hard to catch a breath sometimes.

The following day, I kissed Julia goodbye, kissed my girls, and headed to the office.

"Morning, Josh," I spoke as I walked past his desk.

"Morning, Sam. You look like you could use a cup of coffee."

"That would be great. Thanks."

I set my briefcase down, took out some files, and sat behind my desk.

"Here you go." Josh set a large mug filled with coffee down.

"You are amazing. Thank you."

"Tough night again?"

"Yeah." I let out a breath. "The girls were up every two hours again, but at different times. Just when one would fall back asleep, the other would wake up. Did your cousin arrive safely?"

"He did. He's coming in around noon for lunch."

"Great. I look forward to meeting him. By the way, Julia is bringing the girls up for lunch, and then I'll be leaving for the rest of the day. We're taking the girls to their doctor's appointments, and my cousins are flying in today."

"The doctors?" Josh asked.

"Yes." I chuckled. "The doctors."

"Morning, Josh. Morning, bro."

"Good morning, Stefan," Josh spoke before walking out of my office.

"How did the nanny interviews go?"

"I liked one of the women, but Julia didn't. She's finding every little fault she can. We talked last night, and we're going to put the brakes on trying to find someone."

"Why?" Stefan furrowed his brows.

"In all honesty, I don't think we'll ever like anyone enough to help with the girls. Nanny Kate spoiled it." A smirk crossed my lips.

"Yeah." Stefan sighed. "I can understand that. She was the best."

"Julia is bringing the girls up, and we're having lunch in the conference room before we take them to see Emilia. You can join us."

"Thanks, bro, but I have to meet Carl at the site around noon. What time are Jackson, Conner, and Nathan, flying in?"

"Jackson said their plane is scheduled to land at two-thirty."

"Okay. I'm just going to head home after I meet with Carl."

"Sounds good."

CHAPTER 7

Julia

I pulled into the parking garage, and the second I put the car in park, the girls woke up and started crying. Grabbing my phone, I sent a text message to Sam to come down and help me.

"It's okay, girls. Daddy is on his way down."

I climbed out of the car, threw the diaper bag over my shoulder, and began to unbuckle their car seats while they continued to scream. Taking Lorelei's seat out, I set it on the cement while grabbing Lena's.

"Where the hell are you, Sam?" I spoke with irritation as I placed their pacifiers back in their mouths, and they quieted down.

Pulling my phone from my purse, I checked my messages and noticed the one I'd sent him wasn't delivered.

"Ugh!"

"Excuse me. It looks like you could use a little help," A young man with dark hair walked over. "Are you going into the building?"

"Yes. Thank you, but my husband is on his way down to help."

"You aren't by any chance, Julia, are you?"

I looked at him with confusion.

"Yes. I am."

"Wow. It's so nice to finally meet you. I'm Lucas, Josh's cousin." He extended his hand.

"Cousin Lucas from New York?"

"The one and only." A grin crossed his lips.

"Oh my gosh, it's so nice to meet you too." I shook his hand with a smile.

"I'm going up there now to have lunch with him. Is your husband coming down?"

"Apparently not." I glanced at my phone. "My message didn't go through."

"Let me take one of these beautiful babies for you." He picked up Lorelei's car seat and took the diaper bag from my shoulder.

"Thank you. I really appreciate it," I spoke as we walked into the building and over to the elevators.

"No problem. They're gorgeous. They have your eyes."

"Thanks. They're a handful."

"Do twins run in your family?" he asked as we stepped into the elevator.

"Yes. I have a twin sister."

"Cool. I'm the oldest of eight, so I know how tough it can be."

The elevator door opened, and we stepped into the lobby.

"Hey, Julia!" Francine's eyes lit up as she stepped from behind her desk. "Let me see those babies." She walked over and smiled at the girls. "They are growing way too fast."

"I know. Is Sam in his office?"

"Last time I checked, he was."

"Great. Thank you."

Lucas and I walked down the hallway until we reached Josh's desk, where Sam was standing.

"Who's this, and why does he have my daughter?" he asked.

"This is my new boyfriend, Lucas. He saw me struggling in the parking garage and was kind enough to help me with the girls. Unlike their father, whom I sent a text message to over ten minutes ago." I pursed my lips and cocked my head.

Josh let out a chuckle.

"Shit." He pulled his phone from his pocket. "It's dead again. Josh, after lunch, I need you to go to the Apple Store and get me a new phone."

"Sure thing, Sam. Same one or the new one that just came out."

"Get me the new one. I'm going to assume you're Josh's cousin?" Sam extended his hand.

"It's nice to meet you, Sam." Lucas shook it.

"Nice to meet you too, Lucas. If you don't mind, I'll take my daughter."

"Of course." He smiled as he handed him Lorelei and the diaper bag.

"Thank you for helping Julia."

"It was my pleasure."

Sam and I walked into the office, and we set the car seats on the table.

"I'm sorry, babe. You know my phone has been having major issues lately."

"I know. At least you're finally getting a new one today."

He walked over to the charger and plugged his phone in. After we finished lunch and took the girls to see Emilia, we headed home.

"Why don't you take a nap while the girls are sleeping," Sam spoke as his lips pressed against my forehead.

I glanced at my watch.

"Why don't we make better use of the time we have while the girls are sleeping," the corners of my mouth curved upward as I ran my finger down his chest.

"Have I ever told you how intelligent I think you are?" He grinned as he swooped me up and carried me upstairs to the bedroom.

∽

Sam's fingers interlaced mine as he held my arms above my head while thrusting inside me, and our lips locked as we enjoyed each other. Sex was just as incredible as it was before the twins were born. As tired as both of us always were, we were never too tired to make love. It was our time to reconnect with each other after the chaos of the day ended. I loved my husband more now, and I didn't think that was possible. My heart melted when I saw him feeding the girls, rocking them in the nursery late at night, or sitting on the floor playing with them.

There was nothing worse than when you're just about to have an earth-shattering orgasm and the cries of two babies come through the monitor.

"Focus on me, babe," Sam breathlessly spoke as he thrust in and out of me. "They can cry for a few more minutes." His mouth smashed against mine, and suddenly, I was in another world. I cried out in pleasure as my body shook. Sam slowed his thrust and let out a satisfying moan as he exploded inside me. His body dropped on mine, and I could feel the warmth of his breath against my ear. My fingers softly stroked his back as we both lay there and listened to the screams of our children.

He lifted his body off mine and smiled. "At least we got to finish this time."

I laughed, and his lips met mine. Climbing off the bed, we quickly threw on our clothes and ran to the nursery to fetch the girls.

CHAPTER 8

Sebastian

"Sebastian, my man." Jackson smiled as he, Conner, and Nathan stepped onto the patio, and Ruby ran over to them.

Setting down the tongs, I walked over and gave them each a hug.

"It's good to see you guys again."

"Good to be back in L.A." Conner grinned. "Hey, Ruby." He ran his hand across her back.

"Have you figured out where you're staying?"

"I'm staying here," Nathan spoke. "I'm no fool." He smiled as he patted my back.

"We're going to crash at Simon's place," Jackson said.

"Probably a good idea. I know Stefan and Sam would like you to stay with them, but it's kind of chaotic with the kids. Grab a beer or a scotch. You know where it's at."

Emilia opened the sliding door and stepped onto the patio.

"There she is." Conner grinned as he held out his arm. "The woman I can't stop thinking about."

Emilia laughed as she walked over and gave them each a hug.

"Watch how you're talking about my future wife, douchebag." I picked up my tongs and pointed at him.

"Can't help it, cousin. I'll try to behave myself." Conner winked at me.

I laughed and shook my head as I flipped the chicken on the grill.

"So, where's Cousin Shaun?" Jackson asked.

"He'll be over soon."

"And Uncle Henry?" Nathan asked.

"He'll be here with Celeste and Nora."

A few moments later, Sam, Julia, Stefan, Alex, Shaun, and Simon walked over.

"There's someone I don't know," Conner said as he walked over to where Shaun stood and extended his hand. "You must be Shaun. I'm Conner, and these are my brothers, your other cousins, Jackson and Nathan."

"It's great to meet you finally." Shaun shook their hands.

"It's great to meet you too," Nathan spoke. "We've heard a lot about you."

A few moments later, Jenni and Grace walked over.

"There she is. The woman of my dreams who was stolen from me by my own cousin." Nathan grinned as he held out his arms.

"In your dreams, Kind." Jenni slapped his chest before hugging him.

"Jackson, Conner, Nathan, I'd like you to meet my girlfriend, Grace," Simon spoke.

"Hello, Grace. It's a pleasure to meet you." Jackson extended his hand.

"It's nice to meet the three of you." Grace smiled as she shook their hands.

Just as dinner was about to be served, my father and Celeste walked over.

"Uncle Henry." Nathan smiled.

"Hello, boys. It's good to see you again."

They all took turns hugging him.

"Celeste, you look stunning." Conner smiled as he took Nora from her. "Hi there, Nora."

∽

*S*haun

I stared at my father as he held Nora on his lap. Keeping what I saw to myself was hard, but I'd tell my brothers what I'd seen at the hotel in one more week.

"Now that we got dinner out of the way, what business do you guys have in Los Angeles?" Simon asked.

"We have decided to open a medical health center," Jackson spoke.

"In Los Angeles?" Stefan asked.

"Yeah," Conner said. "It's something we've talked about since medical school. Now that Nathan finished his residency and is established, we're moving forward with our plans."

"That's wonderful news, boys. Your father would have been very proud," my father spoke. "Let me ask you this. Why Los Angeles and not San Francisco?"

"Well, we know Jackson has his reasons. The truth is that we think Los Angeles would be a better choice. Plus, we want to be closer to family," Conner said.

"Yeah. Since Dad died a couple of years ago, we feel it's important to be near family," Nathan spoke.

"Are you looking at bringing in other doctors?" I asked.

"Yes. We'll have a variety of doctors and different specialties in one building," Jackson spoke. "Along with a lab, radiology department, and a surgical center."

"Federally funded?" I asked.

"No. Privately funded," Conner said.

"Do you have investors already?"

"We did." Nathan sighed. "But the investor unexpectedly passed away three months ago, and the firm pulled out because they're in a state of chaos right now."

"So, we're looking into other options," Jackson said.

"I didn't know you boys were doing this," my father said. "Why didn't you come to me? I'll be more than happy to invest in your medical center."

"We were going to, Uncle Henry, but we didn't want to ask with you being retired and everything."

"Nonsense. We're all family, and family helps out each other. Isn't that right, Shaun?" He looked at me.

"Yes. He's right. In fact, why don't the three of you come over tomorrow morning, and we can discuss it."

"That's nice of you, Shaun, but we didn't come here—"

"I know you didn't. You're family. You're my family." I interrupted him.

"So, Uncle Henry, how is retired life treating you?" Jackson asked.

"Better than I ever expected. I'm married to the woman of my dreams and have a beautiful daughter. I couldn't ask for anything more in life." He leaned over and kissed Celeste.

I could feel my blood pressure rising and anger roaring inside me. Getting up, I walked into the house and poured myself a glass of scotch.

"Are you okay, bro?" Simon asked as he walked over to me.

"I'm fine."

"No, you're not. I can tell. What's going on? I've been

watching you and the way you're staring at Dad. What did he do that you're not telling us?"

I threw back my drink and poured another one for my brother and me.

"Not here. Let's go to my house," I said.

CHAPTER 9

Simon

Something was up with Shaun and our father. I could feel it, and I could see it by the way Shaun stared at him. It was the same look he'd had when he first came to Venice Beach.

"What are you two up to?" Grace asked as she walked in.

"Shaun needs to talk to me for a minute, so we're going to go to his house. If anyone asks, tell them we'll be right back."

"Is everything okay?" Grace's brows furrowed.

"Yeah. I just need to talk to Simon for a minute," Shaun spoke.

We went out the front and walked over to Shaun's house.

"What's going on?" I asked as we stood in the middle of the living room.

"I wanted to wait to tell you this because I didn't want to ruin your birthday."

"What the hell are you talking about?" My brows furrowed.

"First, I need to tell you something about your birthday, but I don't want you to mention it to our brothers."

"Okay. I promise I won't."

"I'm throwing the four of you a surprise party at Casa di Pietra."

"Damn, bro." I grinned. "That's really nice of you. When?"

"Next Saturday. We're all spending the night and leaving the next morning after breakfast."

"Awesome. You are the best brother ever." I patted his shoulder. "So, what news do you have that you wanted to wait until after our birthday?"

He inhaled a sharp breath and tucked his hands into his pants pockets.

"When I was at the Four Seasons the other day having a lunch meeting with a client, I excused myself to the restroom. When I stepped out and headed back to the restaurant, I saw Dad walk into the hotel with some woman."

"Okay. Maybe he was there for a meeting, and they walked in together."

"That's what I thought at first until I saw his arm around her and kissing her while they waited for the elevator. I went to the front desk and told the clerk that I was meeting Dad there, and I forgot which room he was in. Come to find out, he has a suite there."

I ran my hand down my face as I sat on the couch.

"Who was this woman?"

"I have no idea."

"What did she look like?" I asked.

"She was around thirty-five and five foot seven with medium length blonde hair."

"That motherfucker!" I shouted as I stood up.

"Simon, calm down."

"No. I knew he couldn't keep his dick in his pants. I fucking knew it, and I told our brothers from the moment he met Celeste that she wouldn't be the last. Fuck! What is wrong with him?"

"Do you understand now why I didn't want to say anything until after your birthday party? Please, bro. Please don't mention it to Sam, Stefan, and Sebastian. We can all sit down after the party and discuss it."

"Damn it. You're right. This news will ruin everything." I let out a sigh as I rubbed the back of my neck. "Fine. I won't tell them. It stays between us for now."

"I have a guy back in New York I can bring here to follow him," Shaun said.

"No need. I have a guy here who will do it. In the meantime, I think we need to pop over to his house more and get a feel to see if Celeste suspects anything."

"I thought about that, but honestly, I think if she suspects something, she'll probably mention it to the girls. I told Jenni, and I know you'll tell Grace."

"Damn right, I'll tell Grace. In fact, I'm going to need her services."

"Like?" Shaun asked in confusion.

"She's a good hacker, and she can get into anything."

"Oh shit." Shaun chuckled. "Okay. Just make sure she doesn't say anything."

"She won't. If anyone can keep a secret, Grace can."

"Maybe we should tell them to ask Celeste to lunch. That way, they can get a feel for if she suspects something."

"You talk to Jenni, and I'll talk to Grace." I hooked my arm around him. "We better get back before the calvary hunts us down and asks questions. By the way, thanks a lot for the surprise birthday party. I can't wait."

"You're welcome. I'm sorry I spoiled it for you."

"Nah. Don't be. I'm not going to let this ruin my day."

It was a great night to be had. We played a lot of music with our guitars, sang, drank, laughed, and had a really good time. Hanging with our cousins again was amazing, and I couldn't believe they would be permanently moving to Los Angeles.

I took Conner and Jackson's bag to the house and up to the guestroom.

"Thanks for letting us stay," Jackson said.

"Yeah, cousin. Thanks."

"Stop it. You know you're all welcome here anytime. Casa Kind is better than any hotel you'll ever stay in."

"That's for sure," Jackson said. "And we don't even have to pay for the alcohol."

"True. Very true." I chuckled. "I'll see you two in the morning. Six a.m. Make sure you set your alarms."

"It'll be great to surf with you guys again." Connor smiled.

I went to my bedroom and shut the door. Walking over to Grace, who was taking her makeup off in the bathroom, I wrapped my arms around her from behind.

"The boys all settled?" she asked.

"Yeah."

"What did Shaun want to talk to you about?" she asked, scrubbing her face.

Releasing my arms from her, I walked into the bedroom and took my pants down.

"He saw our father and another woman at a hotel. He had his arm around her, and they were kissing."

"WHAT?" She walked into the bedroom.

"I promised not to tell the others until after our party."

"He told you about the party?"

"Yeah. He really didn't have a choice. He needed to talk about it."

"I can't believe this. What the fuck is wrong with Henry?"

"He's the same piece of shit man he always was." I lifted my shirt over my head and pulled back the covers on the bed. "Are you going to wash that off your face?" I asked with a smirk.

51

She went into the bathroom and finished cleansing her face.

"Are you okay?" Grace climbed in and snuggled against me.

"Honestly, no. It makes me sick to think he's doing that shit again. It's taking everything I have not to go over there and beat the shit out of him. We need to find out who this woman is. Can you hack into my father's phone records and possibly some credit card statements tomorrow?"

"You seriously want me to do that?"

"Yeah, and I'm going to call Pete in the morning."

"Really, Simon? You're going to have your dad followed?"

"Damn right, I am. I want any information I can get for when I tell my brothers what a lying, cheating bastard he is once again."

"We have Lily's end of the school year party tomorrow," she said.

"We don't have to be there until the afternoon. That gives you plenty of time to do your hacking." I grinned.

She let out a sigh as she lifted her head and stared into my eyes.

"Fine. Let's get some sleep." She kissed my lips. "You have to be up at dawn to go surfing with your brothers and cousins."

CHAPTER 10

*S*tefan

After the alarm went off, I rolled over and wrapped my arm around Alex.

"Oh, God." She jumped up and ran into the bathroom.

Climbing out of bed, I walked into the bathroom and pulled back her hair as she leaned over the toilet.

"Are you okay, babe?"

"I will be."

After she vomited, I reached over, grabbed a couple of tissues, and handed them to her. Walking out of the bathroom, I grabbed my boardshorts from the drawer and slipped them on.

"Why don't you go back to bed for a while," I said to Alex when she emerged from the bathroom.

"I think I will. Henry shouldn't be up for at least another two hours."

I kissed her forehead. "I won't be gone long. I love you."

"I love you too. Have fun."

I opened the sliding door, grabbed my surfboard, and ran

down to the beach, where my brothers and cousins were waiting for me.

"Bro, you're late," Sebastian said.

"Sorry. Alex was throwing up."

"Is she okay?" Shaun asked.

"Yeah. Morning sickness. It usually passes after a couple of hours."

I fist-bumped my cousins, and we all put our boards in the water. It had been a long time since we'd surfed with Jackson, Conner, and Nathan, and I couldn't be happier than I was in the water with them.

"I can't believe you guys are moving to Los Angeles," I said. "Have you figured out where you're going to live yet?"

"Not yet. We're taking things one day at a time," Jackson spoke. "Wherever we land, it will definitely be a place on the beach."

"Yeah. I'm not giving that up," Conner said.

"It would be great if the three of you could move here and live by us," Sam spoke.

"If any houses go up for sale, let us know," Nathan said.

"We just built some great condos in Pacific Palisades," I said.

"Or maybe you could just offer the three neighbors next to our father triple the value for their house as Shaun did for his." Simon smirked.

"I heard about that." Jackson chuckled. "Bold move, Shaun."

"It all worked out in the end."

We talked some more, caught some waves, and pulled our boards out of the water.

"I need to get back up to the house and help Alex with the party. You three better be there." I pointed at my cousins.

"We wouldn't miss it for the world. We promised Lily last night we'd be there."

"Great. Bro, what time is the restaurant delivering all the food?" I asked Sebastian.

"Around noon."

"Excellent. Thanks. I'll see all you douchebags later." I placed my board under my arm and went back to the house.

When I stepped through the sliding door, I saw Lily feeding Henry in his highchair.

"Hey, Dad."

"Morning, baby girl." I kissed the top of her head. "Where's your mom?"

"She's taking a shower. I told her I'd give Henry his breakfast."

"You are my favorite daughter." I gave her a wink.

"I'm your only daughter. But hopefully, that will all be changing soon."

"You really want a sister that bad, eh?"

"Yeah, Dad. I do."

"Well, we'll find out in a couple of months. I'll take over feeding Henry."

"Okay." She smiled. "I'm going to get dressed for the party. I want to look extra nice for Jace." She walked out of the kitchen.

"Hold up, Lillian. Get back here!"

"Yeah, Dad?"

"Who is Jace?"

"This boy at school."

"And may I ask why you want to look extra nice for him?" I arched my brow.

"Because I think he's hot, and I like him."

My heart started racing at the speed of light.

"Hot? You mean cute, right?"

She let out a laugh. "No, Dad. He's hot." A wide grin crossed her face as she turned and walked out.

I looked at Henry.

"Did you hear that? What am I going to do?"

"About what?" Alex asked as she stepped into the kitchen.

"Do you know anything about a boy named Jace?"

"Lily's friend?" She grabbed a cup from the cabinet.

"Yes. Lily's friend."

"She's mentioned him a few times. I think she likes him." Alex smiled.

"She shouldn't be interested in boys at her age. Did you know she thinks he's 'hot'?"

"She mentioned it." A smirk crossed her lips.

"I'm not okay with that, Alex. Absolutely not." I shook my head. "How does she even know what hot is when it comes to boys?"

"Do you think she lives in a bubble, Stefan? She always hears us women talking about how hot you and your brothers are. You're lucky she didn't say he was sexy. Besides, she's at that age where she will notice boys, and boys will notice her."

"Over my dead body!"

She walked over and clasped my shoulders.

"Relax, babe. She's growing up, and you're going to have to accept it."

"The hell I will."

She leaned over and pressed her cheek against mine.

"You're sexy when you're in panic mode. We'll talk about this another time. We have to get things ready for the party."

CHAPTER 11

Shaun

"Great house, Shaun," Jackson said when he and his brothers stepped inside.

"Thank you. It's way too early for a drink, so can I get you guys a coffee or anything?"

"Coffee sounds good," Nathan said.

While the three of them sat down at the table, I started to make each of us a coffee.

"Cream or sugar?" I asked.

"Just black for all three of us," Conner replied.

"Hey, guys." Jenni smiled when she walked down the stairs.

"There's our little fashionista." Nathan grinned.

"Go sit down, babe. I'll finish the coffees."

I kissed Jenni on the lips and joined my cousins at the table.

"You sure keep an immaculate house, Jen," Jackson spoke.

"Who me?" She let out a laugh. "That would be Shaun's doing, not mine."

"Ah, I see you're a lot like Sammy." Conner smirked.

"Sam and I are on the same level when it comes to organization and cleanliness."

All three of them chuckled.

"You definitely are a Kind," Jackson said.

After Jenni set our cups of coffee on the table, she went over to Alex's to help with the party. Jackson slid a file folder across the table, and I carefully looked over their business plan.

"We have an appointment in about an hour to look at the building we want," Nathan said. "We'd love for you to come with us."

"I'd like to. From what I can see, your plan is impeccable. I also see you're already affiliated with Cedars-Sinai and UCLA Medical Centers."

"Yes. We obtained hospital privileges a few months ago," Jackson said.

"Can you give me a couple of days to look over everything?"

"Of course," Jackson spoke.

"Bro, we better get going. We don't want to be late," Nathan said.

The four of us climbed into the rental car and headed to look at the building.

After I arrived home and walked into the house, Simon and Jenni were sitting at the table.

"Hey, bro," I said as I set my keys down.

"I'll let the two of you talk. I'm going to head over to the party." Jenni walked over and kissed my lips.

"Okay, baby. I'll be over soon."

"What did you find out?" I asked my brother as I walked over to the bar and poured us each a glass of scotch."

I handed Simon his scotch and took a seat.

"Grace was able to pull some credit card statements, and there's a shitload of transactions from a florist, a few from jewelry stores, and of course, the hotel suite charges. I don't know about you, but I haven't seen any fresh flowers hanging around their house lately."

"What about phone records?"

"I was just about to get to that. There are several calls to the same number. What's odd is that there hasn't been one incoming call. So, Dad must have told her never to call him. I assume they're mostly contacting each other through text message."

"You weren't able to pull the messages?"

"Grace is working on it. Are you ready to hear who this woman is?" His brow raised.

"I'm ready." I wrapped both my hands around the glass.

"Her name is Sonya Johansson. She's thirty-five, single, and owns a lash extension place over on Melrose."

"How the hell would Dad meet her?"

"I'm not sure."

I threw the last of my drink down the back of my throat and then slowly shook my head.

"Once we tell the others what's going on, we need to decide if and when we're going to confront him," Simon said.

"What do you mean 'if' we're going to confront him?"

"As much as I want to walk over to his house right now and tell him that we know, we can't. It has to be a group decision. So, don't go getting any ideas." He smirked as he pointed his finger at me.

"I won't." I glanced at my watch. "We better get to Lily's party."

Simon placed his hand on my back. "Are you sure you're ready for it?"

"What does that mean?" I furrowed my brows.

"You'll see." A wide grin crossed his face.

∾

*C*ars lined both sides of the street, and the screams of children could be heard around the block. The moment Simon and I stepped onto the patio, Stefan came running over.

"Where the hell have you two been?"

"Relax, bro. We're five minutes late," Simon said.

"Come over here."

We followed Stefan to where our other brothers were standing.

"Listen up. I want you all to be on the lookout for a boy named Jace."

"Why?" Sam asked.

"Who's Jace?" Sebastian asked.

"He's some boy Lily had to make sure she looked special for. Apparently, she thinks he's hot."

"Oh boy." I chuckled.

"It's not funny, bro. This is serious. You know how boys are at that age. Do you remember what you were like? We sure the hell do."

"Right." I nodded.

"Want me to go get my gun?" Simon smiled.

"What the fuck, bro? Stop it."

"Stefan," Sam placed his hand on his shoulder, "calm down."

"No. I won't, Samuel. This is my daughter. And you just wait." He pointed his finger at him. "Your turn is coming, and it'll be times two for you."

"He has a point," Sebastian said. "Have you discussed it with Alex?"

"Of course. We discussed it this morning."

"And?" Simon's brow arched.

"She thinks it's cute!"

"Dad!" We heard Lily shout as she and a boy headed toward us.

"Guess we don't have to be on the lookout for Jace anymore. She's bringing him right to you." Sebastian grinned.

CHAPTER 12

Stefan

"Dad, this is Jace. Jace, this is my dad, Stefan. And these are my uncles, Sam, Sebastian, Simon, and Shaun."

"It's a pleasure to make your acquaintance, Mr. Kind." He extended his hand.

I shook his hand while my eye narrowed at him. He was —he was nothing as I expected. I stared at the boy my daughter called 'hot.' He was on the shorter side with blond curly hair and green eyes covered with wireframed glasses.

"Jace, it's nice to meet you. What are your goals and ambitions?"

"Bro, seriously?" Sebastian spoke.

"Dad, you're embarrassing me." Lily narrowed her eyes.

"It's okay, Lily. I love science, Mr. Kind. I'm a huge science geek, and I'm going to Princeton to study Biochemistry and Molecular Biology. I'm going to find a cure for cancer. That's my goal and ambition. In the fall, I will be attending Oak Crest Academy and then Princeton, where I will obtain my doctorate."

"That's excellent, Jace. It sounds like you have your life planned out," I said.

"I do, sir." He smiled.

"Come on, Jace." Lily took hold of his hand, and they ran down to the beach.

"Wow," Sam said. "He has some pretty big ambitions."

"Yeah, bro." Simon hooked his arm around me. "You have nothing to worry about. He's a total nerd."

As my brothers and I were talking, Alex walked over.

"I saw you met Jace. I hope you were being nice."

"Stefan grilled the kid." Simon laughed.

Alex cocked her head at me.

"What? I can't ask what his goals and ambitions are? Isn't that what a father does?"

We saw Reece and a few other moms heading toward us, and Alex quickly walked away.

"Hello, boys." Reece's face lit up. "You must be Uncle Shaun?" She extended her perfectly manicured hand. "I'm Reece."

"It's a pleasure to meet you, Reece."

"Trust me. The pleasure is all mine." Her lips formed a flirtatious smile."

Sam, Sebastian, Simon, and I walked away and left our brother standing with the moms we've dealt with for years. It was his turn to experience it.

"You guys are mean." Jenni walked over.

"Why?" I chuckled.

"Leaving Shaun alone with those horny moms."

"He's one of us and should have to endure what the four of us have," Sebastian spoke.

"It's only fair, Jen." Simon smiled.

"What's going on over there." Connor pointed to Shaun as he, Nathan, and Jackson walked over.

"Shaun is getting a lesson in horny moms 101." I laughed.

"That one with the dark hair is kind of hot." Conner smirked. "She's definitely a MILF."

"Knock it off," Jackson slapped the back of his head.

"What? She is."

"How was the building you looked at this morning?" I asked.

"It was great," Jackson replied. "Since it was previously a medical center, it has everything we want."

"We have another one we're looking at tomorrow," Nathan said.

"Hello, boys." My father walked over, holding Nora.

Simon

I took Nora from my father when he walked over and took her over to where Celeste was sitting and talking to Grace and Emilia. I couldn't stand to even look at him, let alone be near him. He lied to our faces when he told us Celeste was the woman of his dreams and how she'd changed him. He was full of shit, just like he always had been. I handed Nora over to Celeste and walked over to rescue Shaun, who was still in the grips of Reece and her friends.

"Bro, I need your help inside with something."

"Sure. Ladies, it was nice meeting you."

We walked away, and he let out a deep breath.

"Why didn't you just walk away?" I asked.

"They wouldn't shut up."

We stepped into Sebastian's house and went into the living room.

"What do you need help with?"

"Nothing. I was rescuing you from them." I grinned as I walked over to the bar and poured us a scotch.

"Thanks. I appreciate that."

"Listen, Shaun. We agreed to keep what we learned about Dad a secret until after our birthday, but I can't. We tell each other everything and always have. You came to me with this because you knew we had the right to know, and you needed to talk about it."

"You want to tell them now?"

"Well, not right this second. But we do need to tell them soon. I know you don't want to ruin our birthday, and I appreciate that bro, but we'll be okay. I promise."

"Okay. When do you want to sit down with them?"

"Let's do it tomorrow night at my house. I think Julia, Alex, and Emilia should also be there. Especially since Grace and Jenni already know."

"I agree."

"What's going on in here?" Sam walked in and laid Lena down on the couch.

"I had to rescue our brother from Reece and her horny mom friends." I smirked. "We were just about to go back outside. What are you and Miss Lena doing?"

"Julia asked if I could change her diaper. Do one of you want to give me a hand?" His brow arched.

"Are we talking just pee?" I asked.

"Nope." He sighed.

"I'm out." I chuckled as I walked out of the room.

When I stepped onto the patio, Grace walked over to me.

"Where were you?" she asked.

"Inside with Shaun. We're going to tell the other three tomorrow at our house."

"I didn't think you could wait." She placed her hand on my back and slowly rubbed it."

CHAPTER 13

Shaun

"Thanks for helping, bro. I need another wipe."

I pulled a wipe from the container and handed it to Sam.

"That is gross," I said.

"Yeah. It's a bad one. I hate when it goes all up her backside. I'm sure Julia packed another outfit in the diaper bag. Can you check for me?"

I dug inside the diaper bag and pulled out a pink floral romper.

"Is this fine?" I held it up.

"Yeah. That's perfect. There should be a matching sunhat in the bag."

I dug through the bag again and found the hat.

"I don't know how you do it, Sam."

"I used to say that to Stefan." He smiled. "And as tough as it is at times, I wouldn't trade my life for anything. Can you take her while I get rid of this smelly diaper?"

"Of course. Come to Uncle Shaun, Lena. I'm going to take her outside."

"Okay. I'll be out in a few."

I walked out onto the patio. The moment Jenni saw me with Lena, she came running over.

"Hello, sexy guy with a baby." She flirted.

"Hello there, the gorgeous woman I want to fuc— hey, Lily." I immediately stopped myself from finishing my sentence.

"Hey, Uncle Shaun. Can I take Lena? Aunt Julia and I are taking the girls down to the beach."

"Sure." I handed Lena over to her.

"Thanks." Lily grinned.

"Now, what were you saying?" Jenni asked as her finger slid down my chest.

I wrapped my arms around her, pulled her into me, and whispered in her ear.

"I want to fuck you."

"Did you see there's cake?" She broke our embrace as a grin crossed her lips.

"I did. Make sure you bring home a big chunk of it." I gave her a wink.

"Alex said she'd make sure to wrap it up for us."

"Good girl." I kissed her forehead. "We're having a family meeting tomorrow at Simon's."

"About?"

I didn't say a word. The look on my face told her.

"Oh." Her eyes widened. "I thought you and Simon agreed to wait until after the party next week."

"Simon said it isn't right to keep it from them, and I agree. It is what it is, Jen."

"Hello, Jenni." Barb walked over and hugged her. "Shaun." She pursed her lips.

"Barb." I gave her a nod.

That woman was never going to like me.

"Do you need me to do anything for the party next week?"

"Nope. Everything is taken care of."

"Of course, it is." She rolled her eyes. "And I'm sure your assistant did it all."

"You know what, Barb? There is one thing that hasn't been done yet. I would greatly appreciate it if you could handle it for me."

"What is it?"

"We haven't ordered the cake yet."

"Oh." Her eyes lit up. "Okay. I'll take care of that." Her tone changed.

"Thank you. I'm leaving it up to you to get whatever you want. They're your sons, and you know better what they like and don't."

"I'll start thinking about it." She started to walk away and then stopped and turned around. "Thank you, Shaun."

"You're welcome, Barb."

"That was nice of you." The corners of Jenni's mouth curved upward.

"I try." I smirked.

"You're just a big teddy bear, and I love you." She wrapped her arms around my neck.

"I love you too." I kissed her lips. "Now, if you'll excuse me, I have to send a text message to Selena."

"Why? Ah, the cake has already been ordered, hasn't it?"

"Yep." I sighed as I pulled my phone from my pocket.

Pulling up Selena's number, I sent her a message.

"Cancel the cake."

"Why?"

"Barb is going to take care of it."

"She finally broke you, eh?"

"Very funny. Cancel it."

"Fine."

"Thank you."

"I still want a bonus."

"Bye, Selena."

~

The party had ended, and everyone left, except for our immediate family. While the girls were in the house, Stefan lit the fire pit, and my brothers and I grabbed a beer and sat down next to our cousins.

"Good job, Stefan. Here's to another successful party," Sam said as he held up his beer bottle.

"Thanks. I'm happy it's over." He let out a sigh.

Lily stepped onto the patio and grabbed a slice of cake.

"Hey, Lily?" Simon said.

"Yeah, Uncle Simon?"

"I like your future husband." He grinned.

"Huh?" Her brows furrowed.

"Jace. That kid is going somewhere in life. He'd make a great husband."

"Knock it off, bro!" Stefan reached over and slapped the back of his head.

"You're silly, Uncle Simon. Dad, Jace is coming over tomorrow, and we're going to build sandcastles. I'm going to go draw mine up now, so it's ready for tomorrow."

"You saw him all day today, baby girl. You don't need to see him again tomorrow."

"I already asked Mom, and she said it's okay, so you two can hash it out." She walked back into the house.

Stefan sat there and shook his head as he brought the beer bottle up to his lips.

"There, you have it. We'll be sitting here one day remembering how it all started with a sandcastle. Next thing you know, she'll be asking you to build her a house for them." Simon grinned.

"Shut the fuck up!" Stefan growled, and we all laughed.

Simon

"Yeah. Yeah. On a more serious note, tomorrow night at my house. Sebastian is going to provide the pizzas and salad."

"I am?" His brow arched. "I just provided the catering for today?"

"That was for Stefan, not me."

He rolled his eyes. "And why are we invited to your house tomorrow?"

"Why not? Do I need a reason to have my family over? I love you guys."

Sam, Stefan, and Sebastian sat there, narrowing their eyes at me.

"I call bullshit," Sebastian said.

"So, do I. What's going on?" Sam asked.

"The three of us even know something isn't right," Jackson said.

"We're all here, so we might as well just tell them," Shaun spoke.

"What do you mean 'we'? What the hell do you two know that we don't?" Sebastian asked.

"Fine. We need to tell you something, but we have to do it inside. Not out here."

We all stood up and went inside the house.

"What's going on?" Grace asked.

"It's time," I said as I walked into the living room, and everyone followed.

CHAPTER 14

Shaun

"Go ahead. Tell them," Simon said.

"Tell us what, bro?" Stefan cocked his head.

"Dad is having an affair."

"For fuck's sake." Sam shook his head.

"How do you know this?" Sebastian asked.

"I was at the Four Seasons having lunch with a client. I went to the bathroom, and when I was on my way back to the restaurant, I saw Dad and a woman walk into the lobby. He had his arm around her, and while they were waiting for the elevator, they kissed."

"Did he see you?" Stefan asked.

"No. He also has a suite there."

"That he pays monthly for," Simon chimed in.

"How do you know that?" Sam asked.

"Grace did some digging."

"I cannot believe this!" Julia said.

"How could he do that to Celeste?" Emilia asked.

"It's what he does," Simon said as he stood up and paced around the room. "He's been doing it since he met Mom."

"Before that," Jackson said.

"What do you mean?" I asked.

"Uncle Henry was nineteen, and our father was seventeen. They both had girlfriends, and Uncle Henry cheated on his girlfriend with our father's girlfriend. It caused a rift in the family, and they had stopped speaking for over a year."

"I didn't know that." Sam's brows furrowed.

"Your father told you that?" I asked.

"No. Our mother did," Nathan said. "Have you found out yet who she is?"

"Her name is Sonya Johannsson. She's thirty-five, single, and owns a lash extension place over on Melrose," Grace spoke up. "Guess who has an appointment next week to get her lashes done?" She grinned.

"You didn't tell me that," Simon said.

"Oh. It's not me. It's Jenni."

I glanced over at Jenni with a raised brow. "When did you do that?"

"During the party after you told me who she was. It just so happened they had a cancellation. I figured I'd be the best one to check her out since I'm the only one with a flexible schedule. Julia and Alex can't go due to their last name, and Emilia and Grace both work during the day.

"What are we going to do about this?" Sebastian asked.

"Besides beat the shit out of him?" Simon smirked.

"As tempting as it is, nobody is beating the shit out of Dad," Sam said. "I think we need to have a talk with him and tell him that we know about Sonya."

"What's that going to do?" I asked.

"Shaun's right, bro," Stefan said. "Maybe we don't tell him we know. Grace has mad skills threatening people. Maybe she can get her to stop seeing Dad after Jenni has her appointment."

"Thanks, Stefan." Grace grinned.

"You're welcome."

"Do not threaten that woman." Simon glanced over at Grace.

She cocked her head and narrowed her eyes at him.

"Please, babe," Simon spoke.

"How are we supposed to celebrate our birthday with him knowing this?" Sebastian asked.

"Do you think we should tell Mom?" Stefan asked. "She always said he'd never change, and he'd do the same thing to Celeste."

"No. Keep Mom out of it," Sam spoke. "We don't need her reveling in her glory."

"I think the main issue here is Celeste," Alex said. "This will destroy her."

"Celeste has a right to know," Emilia spoke. "I would want to know if Sebastian was cheating on me."

"I would never do that, babe. You know that."

"I know. I'm just saying."

"You all want my opinion?" Jackson asked.

"Sure, Cous," we all said.

"It's better to be told your partner is cheating on you than to find them in bed with someone else when you come home early because you wanted to surprise them."

Nathan reached over and placed his hand on Jackson's shoulder.

"There's something else I guess I should tell you." I sighed.

"Now what?" Sebastian cocked his head.

"I'm throwing you a surprise birthday party next Saturday at Casa di Pietra, and you better act surprised!" I pointed at the four of them.

"Damn, bro." Sebastian grinned. "That's nice of you."

"You didn't have to do that," Sam said.

"Sure, he did. He's our brother." Stefan gave me a wink.

"Anyway, the only reason I'm telling you about the party is that Dad and Celeste will be there."

"We were going to wait and tell the three of you after the party," Simon said. "But I couldn't keep it from you any longer."

"When did Shaun tell you?" Sam asked.

"Yesterday. He wasn't going to tell any of us until after the party because he didn't want to ruin our birthday, but he had to tell one of us."

"Bro, that was thoughtful of you," Sebastian said.

"I'm sorry you had to see Dad and that woman," Sam spoke. "But we're okay, and we're going to be okay. We'll figure out what to do about it after the party."

"You know, I don't have time for this shit," Stefan said. "I have two kids and another on the way. Sebastian is getting married in a couple of months, Sam has the babies to deal with, Simon has a lot on his plate with work, and Shaun runs a multi-billion-dollar company. None of us have time for Dad's bullshit. It's his problem, not ours. If he wants to fuck up his marriage to Celeste, let him. It's none of our business."

"Stefan's right," Sebastian said.

"I think you're all forgetting one thing," Julia said. "If Celeste finds out about Henry's affair and finds out we all knew about it and didn't tell her, we can all kiss her friendship goodbye. It's not only her life that will be damaged. Nora's will also."

"So, are you going to be the one to tell her?" Jenni asked.

"No. I don't want to tell her."

"I still say we should let Grace threaten this Sonya woman." Stefan grinned.

"Shut the fuck up, bro," Simon said.

"Let's plan on a family dinner at the restaurant on Wednesday night," Jenni spoke. "I'll get as much info out of her as possible and let you know what she said."

"Sounds good, baby." I leaned over and kissed her lips.

"Great idea, Jen," Sebastian said. "Are you three still going to be in town on Wednesday?" he asked our cousins.

"No. We're heading back to San Francisco Tuesday morning. I have to open up the skull of a fifteen-year-old Wednesday morning," Jackson said.

"And I have to give a twenty-five-year-old woman her breasts back," Nathan said.

"Huh?" Stefan frowned.

"She had breast cancer in both breasts and had a double mastectomy."

"Oh. Poor woman."

CHAPTER 15

Jenni

I drove to Shaun's office to have lunch with him before heading to my lash extension appointment.

"Hey, Jenni." Selena smiled.

"Hi, Selena. Is he up there? I tried to call him, but he didn't answer."

"Yeah. He's up there."

"Thanks." I smiled. "How are you holding up?"

"With the party?" she asked.

"Yeah."

"Aside from him making me want to run him over with my car, I'm fine." The corners of her mouth curved upward.

I let out a laugh. "His OCD?"

"How on earth do you live with that man?"

"I heard that, Selena," Shaun said as he walked down the stairs and over to me. "Hey, baby." His lips met mine. "Are you hungry?"

"Starving."

"Good. Let's go up to my office. I ordered us some Thai food."

"How do you know I want that?" I narrowed my eye at him.

"Because you told me last night during sex." His lips formed a smirk.

"TMI, Shaun!" Selena covered her ears and walked away.

"Ah, I did tell you that, didn't I?"

"You sure did." He hooked his arm around me as we walked up the stairs to his office.

We enjoyed a wonderful lunch together, and it was time for me to head to my appointment.

"I'm off." I leaned over the small round table in his office and kissed his lips. "I love you."

"I love you too, babe. Call me when you're finished."

"I will." I smiled and walked out of his office.

I parked across the street from the lash shop, and when I walked inside, I was pleasantly greeted.

"Good afternoon. Do you have an appointment?" The young auburn-haired woman asked.

"Yes. With Sonya."

"Are you Jenni?" She smiled.

"I am."

"Excellent. I just need you to fill out some paperwork, and Sonya will be right with you."

"Thank you."

I took the clipboard and pen from her and sat down to fill it out. A few moments later, I heard my name.

"Jenni?"

Standing in front of me was a beautiful woman with medium blonde wavy hair and gorgeous green eyes when I looked up. Shaun was lying when he said she was 'okay.'

"I'm Sonya." She extended her hand.

"It's nice to meet you, Sonya."

"If you're done, I'll take that from you, and we'll go back and get your lashes started."

I handed her the clipboard and followed her into a room. After she went over the various styles of lashes with me, I picked the ones I liked best and laid down on the table.

"So, what made you decide to get lash extensions?" she asked. "You have amazing lashes already."

"Thanks. My boyfriend and I broke up, and I'm trying to make myself feel better."

"I'm sorry to hear that. How long has it been?"

"A couple of weeks. They say it's supposed to get easier every day, but it's not." I pushed my bottom lip out.

"I know how hard breakups are. I've been through enough of them. But one day, when you least expect it, you'll find that one special guy who will make you forget about all the other breakups."

"I don't know. I'm so over men."

I took note of the beautiful ring she wore.

"I couldn't help but notice that gorgeous emerald ring you're wearing."

"Thank you. My boyfriend bought it for me for my birthday."

"He must be an exceptional guy."

"He is, and we love each other very much."

A sick feeling settled in my belly, and I wanted to grab this woman and shake some sense into her.

"How long have the two of you been together?"

"About three months."

What the fuck?

"Wow. And he already bought you a ring like that? I think I hear wedding bells in your future."

"I'm not too sure about that."

"Why not?" I asked.

She went silent for a moment, and I knew she was pondering whether or not she should tell me he was married.

"Well, don't judge me."

"I would never. Trust me. I'm the last person who has the right to judge someone else."

"He's married."

"Oh. Does he have any children?"

"He has five sons and a daughter."

"Damn. How old is this guy?"

"He's a lot older than I am."

"Sounds like the situation I was just in," I said.

"Your ex was older?"

"By twenty-four years. He also had a wife and children. It's the reason we broke up. He refused to leave her. Then I realized that he was only using me for a thrill."

"Henry told me that he and his wife don't sleep together, and he sleeps in a separate bedroom. He said they basically have no relationship."

"And you believe him?"

"He's a very charming man, and he wouldn't lie to me. He said he will leave his wife, but he needs time."

"Uh-huh. Same bullshit my man fed me."

As painful as the conversation was, we continued to talk about it.

"How did the two of you meet?" I asked.

"At a restaurant called Emilia's. Have you ever heard of it? It's in downtown L.A.?"

I sucked in a sharp breath.

"Yeah. They have great food."

"I was having dinner with one of my girlfriends, and Henry was sitting at the next table with his friend. I noticed he kept stealing small glances at me, and then he sent my friend and me a round of drinks on him. I thanked him, and after my friend and I left the restaurant, he followed me and introduced himself. We got to talking, exchanged numbers, and we've been seeing each other ever since."

"It doesn't bother you he's married?"

"Yeah. It does. But he's an amazing man, and I immediately fell in love with him. The heart can't help what it wants."

"I guess you're right. So that you know, he's never going to leave her."

"I don't mean this to come off as rude, but all men aren't like your ex. Henry will leave his wife for me. He promised. He just needs time, and I respect that. I told him that I'd wait for however long it took. Okay. Are you ready to see your lashes?"

I sat up from the table as she handed me a mirror. Damn, she was good. The urge to slap her across the face was fierce, and it took everything in me to control myself.

"I love them! Thank you."

"Feel better now?" she asked.

"I do." I smiled.

"It was nice meeting you, Jenni. Thanks for the great conversation. I'll see you in a few weeks for a fill-in."

The hell she will.

I left the shop sick to my stomach. When I climbed into the car, I called Shaun.

"Hey, babe. How did it go?"

"The lashes are fabulous. As for Sonya, I'm just going to leave it as your father is a real piece of shit."

"Oh boy. Where are you going now?"

"Home."

"I'm leaving the office now. I'll see you there in about a half-hour."

"Okay. I'll have the drinks poured."

"Good idea. I love you."

"I love you too."

THE KIND BROTHERS

When I pulled into the driveway, I saw Henry walking toward the house, pushing Nora in the stroller. He was the last person I wanted to see right now, but there was no avoiding him because he was standing in the driveway when I got out of the car.

"Hello, Jenni." A smile crossed his face.

"Hey, Henry." I forced a smile as my stomach tied itself in knots. "Hello there, Nora." I bent down and kissed her cheek.

"You're home from work early today," he said.

"I had an appointment and just decided to take the rest of the day off."

He stood there and stared at me. It was awkward, to say the least.

"You look different," he said.

"I do."

"I can't quite put my finger on it, but your eyes pop more."

"Oh. I bought this new mascara that has been all over the internet, and I'm obsessed!"

"It looks great on you."

"Thanks."

Shaun's car pulled up, and I let out a sigh of relief.

"Hello, son."

"Dad."

Shaun walked over and kissed my lips.

"You're home early as well, I see."

"The perks of running a multi-billion-dollar company," Shaun said.

"Very true." Henry chuckled. "Well, we better get on with our walk."

"Where's Celeste?" I blurted out.

"She's lying down. She has another migraine."

"Oh. That's too bad. Tell her I hope she feels better soon."

"Thanks, Jenni. I will. I'll talk to you both later."

"Bye, Henry."

"See you later, Dad."

We walked into the house, and I set my purse down.

"Are you okay?" Shaun asked.

"Besides having to fake being nice to your piece of shit father, I'm fine."

CHAPTER 16

Shaun

Jenni told me about her conversation with Sonya, and as I sat there and listened, an uneasy feeling settled inside me. I let out a sigh as I looked down at the glass of scotch I held in my hand.

"Why aren't you saying anything?" Jenni asked.

With a slight turn of my head, I stared at her as she sat next to me on the couch.

"I have no words. Plain and simple. The guy is an asshole. I'm really regretting changing my last name."

Jenni reached over and placed her arm around me.

"The Kind name is good. Look at your brothers and your cousins. They're amazing men, just like you are. Henry is just one rotten apple in a barrel full of perfect ones."

"What the hell is wrong with him, Jen?"

"I don't know, babe."

I stared into her eyes as the corners of my mouth curved upward.

"What?" A smile crossed her lips.

"Your lashes look great."

"They are fabulous, aren't they?"

"They're beautiful." I leaned in and brushed my lips against hers.

"Where's Lily?" I asked Stefan as we sat down at the table.

"I asked my mom if she and Curtis would take her to dinner tonight. I didn't want her here while we discussed the situation with our father."

"Good idea."

As soon as Sam and Julia walked in with the twins, they took their seats.

"Sorry, we're late. I had to finish feeding the girls," Julia said.

"Where's Sebastian?" Simon asked.

"Right here." He smiled as he sat down. "Sorry about that. There was an incident in the kitchen."

"Is everything okay?" I asked.

"Yeah. It is now."

Amber and Lucy, two of Sebastian's waitresses, walked over and began setting our plates of food down in front of us. Once dinner was served, all eyes were on Jenni.

"First of all," Sebastian spoke, "your lashes look great. Second of all, what the fuck did that woman tell you?"

Jenni picked up her drink. "Where shall I start? Oh, I know." She stared at Sebastian. "They met at Emilia's."

"What!" Sebastian exclaimed.

"Your father was having dinner with a friend, and Sonya and her friend were at the next table. He bought them a round of drinks and then followed her out of the restaurant so he could introduce himself. They've been seeing each other for three months. He bought her an expensive ass, gorgeous Emerald ring for her birthday, and he told her that he and Celeste don't have sex, and he's sleeping in the guest room." She brought the glass up to her lips and chugged her drink.

All four of my brothers sat there speechless. I glanced over at Simon, who tried his hardest not to lose control.

"She's also under the impression that Henry will leave Celeste, but he needs time."

"And she's willing to wait for him?" Sam asked.

"Yes. She understands, and she respects him for it," Jenni spoke.

"Bro, this is your fault." Stefan looked at Sebastian.

"Why? Because they met at one of my restaurants, douchebag? Like I can control that. They could have met anywhere."

"It's no one's fault but Dad's. I'm convinced something is seriously and mentally wrong with him," Simon said. "Maybe one good punch in the head will set his brain straight."

"I'm beginning to side with Simon," Stefan said.

"So, what are we going to do about this?" Sam calmly asked.

"You know what I say?" Simon sat there shaking his head.

"What?" I asked.

"I say fuck him. All of us need to wash our hands of it. He's a grown man and if he wants to ruin his life, let him. Like Stefan said before, we have our own lives to lead and worry about."

"What about when we have to see him? He does live next to us," Stefan said. "It's not like we never see him. We see him all the damn time."

"Stefan's right, bro. How can we just go on like everything's okay? If one of us were cheating and he found out, he'd make it his business."

"Maybe we should confront him and let him explain," Sebastian said.

"He'll just lie," Simon said. "And that'll piss me off even more. Shaun? What do you think?"

"I honestly don't know."

"I have an idea," Jenni said.

"What, babe?" I asked.

"How about we catch him in the act?"

"That's a good idea, sis," Julia spoke.

"I love catching people in the act." Grace grinned.

"How do you propose we do that?" Sam asked.

"Simon and Grace have people who can tail him. When one of them gets the word that Henry is with Sonya, we'll be right there to catch him."

"Better yet. I say we go to his suite at the Four Seasons and wait for him," Sebastian said.

"How will we know when he's going there?" Sam asked.

"I'll put a tail on Sonya," Grace spoke.

"Enough. Do you all hear yourselves?" Simon spoke. "We need to let it go and distance ourselves from him. It might be hard, but we can do it. We're far too busy to deal with this bullshit. As I said, he's a grown man, and he's made his bed. Whatever happens with him and Celeste is not our problem."

"What about your birthday party?" I asked.

"What about it? We'll be too busy having the time of our lives to worry about Henry," Simon said. "I'm done with this."

"Until he pisses you off somehow and you explode on him," Sebastian said.

"He can't piss me off any more than I already am. Thank you for the amazing dinner, bro. Grace and I are heading home."

I let out a sigh and finished off my drink.

"He's right," I spoke up. "Dad's affair isn't our problem."

"Okay, bro." Stefan nodded his head. "Are we all agreeing to let this go and not discuss it anymore?"

"Yeah," Sam and Sebastian replied. "Agreed."

∽

The birthday party went off without a hitch. Everyone had an exceptional time between the drinking, food, and entertainment. I saw Barb standing in front of the table where the cake was displayed and walked over to her.

"It's a beautiful cake, Barb."

"Thank you, Shaun." She took a sip of her wine. "I have to hand it to you. You know how to throw one hell of a party." The corners of her mouth curved upward. "Thank you for making my son's birthday so special."

"You're welcome. Selena?" She stopped and turned to me as she was walking by. "Come over here."

"Yes, boss?"

"Barb, as much as I'd like to take all the credit for this party, my assistant, Selena, is the one who made it all come together, and I couldn't have done it without her."

"You did a wonderful job, Selena."

"Thank you."

"If you'll both excuse me, I need to find my husband." She patted my arm as she walked away.

"Wow." Selena stared at me.

"What?"

"I can't believe you just did that."

"Knock it off. You deserve all the credit. By the way, you'll be getting a nice bonus Monday morning when you come to work."

"Aw, Shaun. You don't have to do that."

"Shut the hell up and go enjoy the party." I smirked.

When I turned around to go and find Jenni, my father walked up to me.

"Son. Great party." He placed his hand on my shoulder.

"Thanks, Dad."

"I was speaking with Jackson on the phone earlier. He said Sterling Cap is going to be a major investor in Kind Medical Group. That's wonderful to hear."

"It's a good investment opportunity."

"It'll be good to have my nephews here in Los Angeles. They're good men and brilliant doctors, just as their father was."

"Shaun, I need your help with something," Simon shouted from a few feet away.

"I'll talk to you later, Dad."

I walked over to Simon and hooked my arm around him.

"Thanks, bro." I sighed.

CHAPTER 17

TWO WEEKS LATER

Sebastian

It was three a.m., and Emilia had been tossing and turning all night. As my arm was wrapped securely around her, she gasped and quickly sat up.

"Babe, what's wrong?"

"Nothing. I just had a bad dream. I'm sorry I woke you."

"Don't be. Come here."

She snuggled against me as my arm wrapped tightly around her. This had been happening for almost two weeks. She was restless, and I knew something was bothering her.

When the alarm went off the next morning, I shut it down and kept my arm securely around her. Her lips pressed against my chest before she sat up.

"Good morning." I smiled.

"Good morning."

"I'll go make some coffee while you get ready for work," I said as my finger trailed down her arm.

"Sounds good. I need it."

She climbed out of bed and went into the bathroom to shower while I headed to the kitchen. After brewing two cups of coffee, I took them upstairs and set her cup down on the bathroom counter. Leaning up against it, I sipped my coffee and waited for her to finish.

"What was your bad dream about last night?" I asked as she dried herself off.

"I don't remember."

"It seems lately you've been having a lot of those. What's going on, babe?"

"Nothing is going on, Sebastian. Honestly, I have no idea why I've been restless at night."

"Does it have something to do with the wedding?"

"No. Of course not." She wrapped her arms around my neck. "I can't wait to marry you." Her lips met mine. "Maybe it's just the stress of my mother. You know how she is. I have to get ready for work."

"Okay." I kissed her forehead and walked out of the bathroom.

Something was going on with her, and it had me worried. I could sense she was keeping something from me, and I needed to find out what it was. After Emilia left for work, I walked over to talk to Alex.

"Hey, Sebastian. Good morning." Alex smiled as I stepped through the sliding door.

"Morning."

"Hi, Uncle Sebastian." Lily walked over and hugged me.

"Morning, your royal highness."

"Stefan left for work already," Alex spoke.

"I know. I came over to talk to you."

"Oh. Okay. Lily, can you take Henry into the living room and play with him while Uncle Sebastian and I talk?"

"Sure, Mom."

"What's up?" Alex asked.

"Is something going on with Emilia?"

"What do you mean?" Her brows furrowed as she handed me a cup of coffee.

"Thanks. She hasn't been sleeping well the past couple of weeks, and she's been having nightmares. I know you girls talk about everything, and I wondered if she mentioned anything to you. I know all about the 'girl code,' but this is important, and I won't tell her you told me."

"Honestly, Sebastian, she hasn't said a word about anything. I swear to you. Have you tried talking to her?"

"Yeah. I have. She says she's fine, and nothing is wrong, but something is. I'm worried about her. She did say that maybe it was the stress of her mother. I know she's been critiquing everything Emilia and I are planning for the wedding."

"You know how her mom is. I'm sure that's it. Try to talk to her again tonight. If you don't get any answers, let me know, and I'll see what I can get out of her."

"Thanks, Alex." I kissed her cheek. "I appreciate it. I better get going. Bye, your royal highness," I shouted as I opened the sliding door.

"Bye, Uncle Sebastian!"

I got home from the restaurant around six-thirty, and when I walked through the door, a burnt smell infiltrated the air. I chuckled to myself because that meant Emilia was trying to cook.

"What's that smell?" I walked into the kitchen and kissed her.

"I burnt the mac n cheese. I followed your recipe, put it in the oven, forgot to set the timer, and fell asleep on the couch. I'm sorry."

"Aw, babe." I wrapped my arms around her, pulling her into me. "It's okay. Shit happens. I'll whip us up something really quick."

"Let's just order Chinese food tonight," she said.

"Okay. That sounds good. You want the usual?"

"Yeah. If you don't mind, I'm going to take a bath."

"Go ahead." I kissed her forehead. "I'll call the order in now."

It wasn't like Emilia to fall asleep like that. She looked tired, and I knew she wasn't sleeping well at night. I was going to get to the bottom of this one way or another.

After I placed the order for the food, I went upstairs and walked into the bathroom, where Emilia was lying in the bubble-filled tub with her eyes closed.

"Feeling better?"

She opened her eyes and looked at me.

"I think it's making me more tired." The corners of her mouth curved upward.

"I know you say you're fine, but clearly, you aren't. Talk to me, babe. Tell me what's going on with you."

"Nothing, Sebastian. Maybe it's hormones or something."

"Are you pregnant?" I leaned up against the sink.

"Oh my God, no."

"Is it the situation with my dad? Because you made that remark about if I cheated on you, you'd want to know."

"No. I know you would never cheat on me. And as for your dad, he has unresolved issues. Of course, it's sad what's going on, but I would never let it affect me like that."

"Then what is it?"

"I don't know!" she shouted, and I was taken aback. "Fuck, Sebastian, just drop it. I'm fine."

"The hell you are, Emilia." I raised my voice to her. "You aren't sleeping, you're tossing and turning all night, and you're having nightmares. Something is going on!"

"Am I keeping you up at night? Disturbing your sleep? Is that what this is about?" she yelled.

"No. Of course not! This is about me worrying like hell

THE KIND BROTHERS

about you! I know you, and I can tell you know exactly what's bothering you. You need to tell me right now!"

"Really? Now, you're telling me what to do? Get out and leave me alone!"

"No. I'm not going anywhere until you tell me what's wrong."

The doorbell rang, and it was the delivery guy with our food. Pulling my phone from my pocket, I called Sam.

"Hey, bro."

"Hey, can you run outside and grab my food from the delivery guy?"

"You're not home?"

"Yeah. I am. But Emilia and I are in the middle of a discussion upstairs."

"Your brother is being an asshole right now!" Emilia shouted.

"Uh-oh. I'll grab it. Where do you want me to put it?"

"Just set it on the table. Thanks."

"Good luck, bro."

"Thanks."

I ended the call and set my phone down.

"I can't believe you said that," I spoke.

"Well, it's the truth."

"So let me get this straight. Because I'm worried about you, I'm an asshole."

"There's nothing to be worried about for the millionth time, Sebastian!" she shouted.

"Bullshit, Emilia!" I pointed my finger at her. "I don't want this. I didn't come up here to argue with you. But, if you're hell-bent on not telling me, then fine. Whatever."

I began to walk out of the bathroom and stopped when I heard her yell.

"Fine. Do you want the truth? Do you really want to know why I can't sleep at night, and why I keep having nightmares? It's because I'm scared. I'm fucking scared!" she yelled.

I looked at her as I saw her eyes fill with tears.

"What are you scared about?"

"That you're not going to show up on our wedding day." The tears from her eyes streamed down her face. "I keep having the same nightmare over and over again. I'm standing there waiting for you, and you never show up. Then suddenly, all the guests sitting in the chairs disappear, and I'm standing alone at the altar in my wedding dress, holding my bouquet, staring up the aisle, waiting for you to walk in."

Instantly, my heart started to ache.

"Emilia," I spoke in a soft voice.

I walked over to the bathtub and climbed in behind her, fully clothed.

"What are you doing?"

"Shh," I said as I wrapped my arms tightly around her. "Why are you so worried about that?"

"You know why."

"My God, Emilia. You know I would never do that, ever." I tightened my grip around her as my lips pressed against the top of her head.

"I consciously know you wouldn't, but my subconscious is fucked up."

"I love you so much. You are my entire world and the air I breathe. I couldn't even imagine my life without you in it, and I can't wait to make you my wife."

"I know, and I love you so much, Sebastian. It's killing me that these thoughts are happening."

"I want you to stop worrying. I am going to be the first one at our wedding. I will be there before you. And when you walk down that aisle, I will be standing there, the happiest man in the world, waiting to say I do. Do you understand me?"

"Yes." She turned around in my arms and stared into my eyes. "I'm so sorry. This is why I didn't want to tell you. You're hurt by it." Her finger traced my lips. "The last thing I wanted was to hurt you."

"I'm not, babe. I know it's because of what happened last time, and I understand."

"I love you so much." Her lips met mine.

"I love you too."

"I'm starving, and we need to get you out of these wet clothes. I can't believe you climbed in here fully dressed." She laughed.

"There was no time to get undressed. You needed me."

After we climbed out of the tub, Emilia slipped on her robe and went downstairs to set the table for dinner. Stripping out of my wet clothes, I pulled a pair of sweatpants and a t-shirt from the drawer and headed downstairs for dinner.

CHAPTER 18

*S*ebastian

I was up the entire night thinking about the conversation we had. It broke my heart to know that she was worried about me not showing up for the wedding. It was just another scar her ex left on her. As I was awake and a million thoughts were going through my head, she still tossed and turned. I needed to ease her fears, and I knew precisely how.

After opening the restaurant for the lunch crowd, I pulled my phone from my pocket and sent my brothers a text message in our group chat.

"Shaun, Sam & Stefan, are you at the office?"

"Yes." All three of them responded.

"Simon, where are you?"

"Crime scene. What's up?"

"How long are you going to be?"

"We're just finishing up. What is going on?"

"I need a family meeting right now. It's important. Let's meet in Shaun's office. I can be there in about twenty minutes."

"I have a meeting, but I'll reschedule it for later," Shaun replied. *"Come on over. I'll be waiting."*

"Sam and I will be there," Stefan replied.

"Grace and I will be there as soon as we can."

"Marco, I'm heading out for a while. I'm meeting my brothers." I shoved my phone into my pocket.

"Got it, boss. See you later."

I climbed into my car and drove to the building where Sterling Capital and Kind Design was. Taking the elevator to Sterling Capital, I stepped out and went straight up to Shaun's office, where my three brothers were waiting for me.

"Hey, bro," Shaun said.

"What's going on?" Sam asked with concern.

"Simon isn't here yet?"

"He just texted me and said he'll be here in about five minutes," Shaun spoke. "Let's go sit at the table."

Selena walked in with a pitcher of water and six glasses.

"You're kind of worrying me," Stefan said. "What the hell is so urgent?"

"Yeah, and don't tell me this is about Dad," Simon growled as he and Grace walked in.

"It's not about Dad. It's about Emilia."

"Does this have anything to do with your fight last night?" Sam asked.

"What?" Stefan cocked his head. "You two were fighting?"

"Emilia hasn't been sleeping well, and she's been having nightmares. I finally got it out of her last night what the problem is."

"And?" Simon asked.

"She's scared to death that I'm not going to show up for the wedding."

"Oh my God. That poor girl," Grace said.

"You told her she was being ridiculous, right?" Sam asked.

"Can you blame her after what she went through the last time?" Stefan said.

"Bro, that dude was crazy. I almost had to shoot his ass," Simon said. "Sebastian would not show up to his own wedding. Right?" Simon cocked his head at me.

"Shut the fuck up." I shook my head. "Anyway, we talked, and I made her feel more at ease. But I don't think it's enough."

"What else can you do?" I asked.

"I want us all to go to Vegas for the weekend, and I'm going to marry her there in one of those little chapels."

"What?" Stefan exclaimed. "What about the wedding that's supposed to take place here in a couple of months?"

"We'll still go through with the ceremony and reception here, but I want to marry her now. I don't want to wait two more months and have her worrying. I know she can't help it, and she'll say everything is okay. But in the back of her mind, it will always be there until we're married."

"This weekend?" Simon's brow raised. "As in three days?"

"We'll leave Friday morning, spend the day and night doing up our bachelor and bachelorette parties, and we'll get married on Saturday. Sunday morning, we'll head back here."

"Does she know any of this?" Sam asked with a smirk.

"No. I want it to be a surprise. But no one can ever know what we did. This stays between us. Mom and Dad can never know. So as far as everyone attending the wedding here is concerned, they'll be seeing us get married for the first time."

"I love the idea, and I know Emilia will love it too." Grace grinned.

"Bro, as awesome as that sounds, what about the kids?" Stefan asked. "It's such short notice."

"I got it covered. I told Mom we all decided to take a last-minute trip to Vegas, and she said she and Curtis would watch Lily and Henry."

"And the twins?" Sam's brow raised.

"I already spoke to Julia's mom and dad, and they're thrilled to watch the girls for the weekend. Are you and Grace scheduled to work this weekend?" I asked Simon.

"No. So we're up for it. Right, babe?"

"Definitely! I can't wait." Grace grinned.

"We'll take my private plane," Shaun said as he picked up the phone on his desk. "Selena, come in here, please."

"Yes, boss?"

"I need you to call Bobbie and tell him I need him to fly us to Vegas on Friday, returning Sunday."

"On it." She smiled.

"I think we should call Jenni," Shaun said.

"Call me for what?" Jenni smiled as she walked into the office. "What's going on in here? And why wasn't I invited?" Her lips formed a pout.

"What are you doing here, babe?" Shaun asked.

"I was down the street at the resale shop, and I thought I'd stop by and see my sexy boyfriend." She took a seat on Shaun's lap and wrapped her arms around his neck. "So, what's going on?"

"We're going to Vegas this weekend, and I'm going to marry Emilia while we're there."

"What? Hold up. Does she know about this?"

"No. It's a surprise."

"I got news for you, buddy. There's no way I'm lugging that heavy wedding dress to Vegas."

I chuckled. "You don't have to. We're still getting married here on our original date."

"Huh? I'm confused."

"I'll explain it later, babe," Shaun said.

"Emilia will need a dress for Vegas. Can you help us out?" I asked.

"Yes! I have the perfect dress for her sitting in my office.

This is so exciting, even though I have no idea why you're doing this."

"So, we're all in?" I asked as I held my fist out.

"We're all in," everyone said and placed their fists against mine.

~

After I left Shaun's office, I headed to *Emilia's* for a while to check on the staff and make sure everything was running smoothly. After helping with the prep for the dinner crowd, I left the restaurant so I would be home before Emilia.

When she walked through the door, I handed her a glass of champagne and kissed her lips.

"What's this for?" She smiled.

"We're going to Vegas this weekend. We're leaving Friday morning and coming back on Sunday."

"Have you forgotten that I have patients to see on Friday morning?" Her brow arched.

"It's already taken care of. I spoke with Renee, and she checked the patient schedule, and she said it's all well-checks. She's going to take them for you."

"I don't understand, Sebastian."

"We're going to do our bachelor/bachelorette parties there. I know it's last minute, but we figured we all needed to get away for a weekend with everything going on, especially with my dad."

"I love it, and I can't wait to go." She set her drink down, wrapped her arms around my neck, and softly kissed my lips. "But why didn't you tell me? I would have rearranged my schedule."

I smiled as I ran my finger down her cheek. "I wanted it to be a surprise."

"You're too sweet. Is everyone coming?"
"Just us, my brothers, and the girls."
"I can't wait. I really do need this trip."
"I know, babe. We all do." I brushed my lips against hers.

CHAPTER 19

Sam

"Sam, hurry up. My parents will be here to pick up the girls in a second."

"I'm coming," I said as I held Lena and walked down the stairs. "Is everything packed for them?"

"Yes. I made a list and checked everything off as I packed it."

"Hello, hello." Julia's mom smiled as she walked through the door. "Hi, Sam." She kissed my cheek and took Lena from my arms. "Sam, point the way, and I'll start loading the car," Julia's father spoke.

I helped him get the car loaded, and it was time to say goodbye to the girls. I'd been worried about Julia and how leaving them for a couple of days would affect her because I knew how I felt.

"Come here, my girls." I held each of them in my arms. "You be good for your grandma and grandpa. Daddy loves you so much, and we'll be back in a couple of days," I said as I kissed their heads.

We put the girls in their car seats and carried them to the

car. Julia leaned in and gave each of them a kiss.

"Mommy loves you both so much. Be good for Grandma and Grandpa."

I hooked my arm around Julia as my eyes teared up when her parents pulled out of the driveway, and we gave them a wave goodbye. I prepared myself to comfort Julia because I knew she would start to cry.

"Are you crying?" She turned to me.

"Maybe. We aren't going to see them for a couple of days."

"Sam, we're free!" She grinned. "FREE!"

"Julia?" My brows furrowed. "Aren't you the least upset? We haven't been away from them for more than a few hours since they were born."

"I know!" She beamed with excitement. "They'll be fine. They love my mom and dad."

I couldn't believe it. I felt sad about leaving our children, and Julia was doing a little dance in the driveway. Looking over, I saw my mom and Curtis pull up in Stefan's driveway.

"Hi, Sam. Hi, Julia." My mother waved.

"Hi, Mom."

Stefan and Alex walked out and put Henry in the car. Lily followed behind, gave Julia and me a wave, and climbed in on the other side. The second Curtis pulled out of the driveway, Alex ran over, grabbed Julia's hand, and they started dancing. Stefan walked over and placed his hand on my shoulder.

"You okay, bro?" he asked.

"I'm okay. You?"

"Yeah. I take it Julia is doing better than you are." He chuckled.

"Can you believe it?" I stood there and shook my head.

"You both need this break as much as Alex and I do."

"Okay. Come on, Julia. Let's get our bags. The car will be here in a few minutes."

The ten of us boarded the plane and took a look around, for it was the first time we'd been on it since Shaun bought it.

"Damn, bro. This is amazing," Stefan spoke.

"Thanks." He patted his back. "The bar is fully stocked. Just let Darlene know what you want, and she'll get it for you."

Julia and I were seated across from Alex and Stefan in oversized leather seats with a large table between us. Julia reached over and took hold of my hand while Alex did the same to Stefan.

"There's something we want to discuss with you," Julia said.

"Okay. What is it?" I asked.

Julia and Alex looked at each other and, at the same time, spoke, "You're both going in for vasectomies."

"Excuse me?" I spoke.

"Yeah. Okay." Stefan laughed.

"We're serious," Alex said.

"Julia?" I cocked my head.

"It's not up for discussion, Sam."

"Yeah, Stefan. It's not up for discussion. We all agreed that we don't want any more kids, and we're tired of worrying about it every month."

Stefan and I looked at each other, and the color drained from his face, as did mine.

"You're pregnant, Alex. There's no worrying about it," Stefan said.

"I know. But after the baby is born, I don't want to worry about it. So, it's better to do it now and get it over with."

"Get what over with?" Simon asked as he walked over, eating an apple.

"The vasectomies," Julia replied.

"Ouch. Who's getting a vasectomy? You two?" He wiggled his finger at us and then started to laugh uncontrollably."

"What's so funny?" Sebastian asked when he walked over.

"Our two brothers here are getting vasectomies." Simon laughed.

"Damn. Seriously?" Sebastian chuckled.

"Okay, you two," Grace said as she walked over, grabbed our shoulders, and pushed us away.

"Ouch, Grace, that hurt," Simon spoke.

"Yeah, Grace." Sebastian rubbed his shoulder.

"Then stop being assholes and leave them alone."

I rubbed my forehead and shook my head.

"Can you give us time to think about it?" I asked. "You just can't spring something like that on us and expect us to be happy."

"Yeah, Alex. I can't believe the two of you."

"Don't take too long." Julia reached inside her purse and pulled out a business card. "You both have appointments next week. Sam, your appointment is at 8:00 am."

"And Stefan, your appointment is at 8:45 am," Alex said.

"You already scheduled the appointments without talking to us about it?" Stefan exclaimed.

"We're talking to you about it now," Julia spoke.

"Babe," Stefan turned to Alex, "why don't you just get your tubes tied after the baby is born?"

"Babe." Alex's smile was frightening. "I had one child, and now I'm giving you another. Is it so much to ask that you do something!" she loudly voiced as she slammed her fists down on the table.

"Okay. Okay. You're right. I'll go," Stefan looked at me with wide eyes.

"And you, Sam." Julia turned to me, but I already knew what she would say, so I stopped her.

"I know, and you're right. I'll go."

"Thank you." Julia kissed my cheek.

"Thank you." Alex kissed Stefan's cheek.

"Julia, Alex, come over here and watch this," Jenni called out.

Sebastian and Simon slipped into their seats as soon as they got up.

"Are you really going through with it?" Sebastian asked.

"We don't have a choice," I said.

"You always have a choice." Simon smirked.

"Nah, bro. We don't," Stefan spoke. "Can you believe they made our appointments together?"

"I don't want to talk about it." I sighed. "But if Julia wants me to get this done, then she better be prepared for a wild and sex-filled weekend."

"Yeah. Alex too. Cause God knows how long we have to go without it after getting it done."

"It says here that you can have sex about one to two weeks later, but you need to wrap it up for three months." Simon laughed as he looked at his phone. "Oh, and you have to ejaculate about twenty times."

"What? What the fuck?" Stefan said.

"Jesus." I rubbed the back of my neck.

"There's still some sperm in there, so after about twenty squirts, you should be sperm free." His laughter grew.

"What's so funny?" Shaun smiled as he walked over.

"Where were you, bro?" Sebastian asked.

"On a conference call. What's going on?"

"Sammy and Stefan are going in next week to have their little wee-wees snipped." Simon laughed.

"Damn. Really? Well, it's probably for the best since you both decided not to have any more kids. It'll be okay. Guys can do their part and get a little snip if women can grow babies for nine months and deliver them."

Sebastian and Simon began to laugh.

"Here." Simon handed him his phone. "Read that."

I watched as Shaun read whatever Simon gave him. When he was finished, he handed him his phone back.

"I am so sorry," he spoke to us and then walked away.

"What do you mean?" Stefan shouted. "What the hell did you show him? Show us."

"Nah, bro. It's best you don't know. You'll see for yourselves."

"You're a fucking douchebag," I pointed at Simon. "And so are you for going along with it." I pointed at Sebastian.

"Aw, come on. There will be no get-well flowers for you." Simon laughed. "Okay. Unfortunately, all this fun has to come to an end. We will be there to help you both and get you through it. Won't we, Sebastian?"

"Sure thing. I'll bring home a shitload of frozen peas from the restaurant."

"And we'll bring you out on the patio so you two can watch the three of us surf." Simon grinned. "Cause lord knows you won't be doing that for a while."

"You're such an asshole." Stefan shook his head.

"What?" Simon held out his arms. "I'm giving you brotherly love."

CHAPTER 20

*S*ebastian

We arrived in Las Vegas and climbed into the cars that drove us to the Bellagio. After checking in, we each went up to our suites. I was a nervous wreck that my plan wasn't going to work. What if she didn't want to get married tomorrow? What if she only wanted to have the one wedding back in Los Angeles? I was so caught up in wanting to ease her fears that I didn't take a moment to think about how she'd feel. Shit.

When I opened the door to our suite, I watched how her eyes lit up as we stepped inside.

"This is beautiful." She smiled.

"Yeah. It is." I sighed as I set the keycard down on the table.

"What's wrong?" she asked.

"Come here." I took hold of her hand and led her to the couch. "I lied to you, Emilia."

"About what?" Her brows furrowed.

"About this and why we came here."

"I don't understand, Sebastian. What do you mean?"

"The real reason I brought you to Vegas is to marry you."

"What?" She laughed.

"I'm serious, babe." I held both her hands in mine. "I can't stand to see you so anxious and full of fear over our wedding. It shouldn't be like this. This is supposed to be the happiest time of your life, and instead, you're worrying yourself sick with fear that I won't show up."

"Sebastian—"

"Let me finish. I want to marry you now. I want to make you my wife now."

"What about all of our wedding plans?"

"That wedding is still happening." I smiled. "And we'll be married as planned before our family and friends. Everything for the wedding here is planned and just waiting for us at the Bliss Wedding Chapel tomorrow afternoon at four p.m. Nobody ever has to know about this—just us, my brothers, and the girls."

"Do they know?"

"Yes. Jenni has a dress for you to wear, and I brought our wedding bands. Everything is taken care of. The only thing I need is your thoughts on it. I was so caught up in wanting to erase your fears about the wedding that I didn't stop to think about how you'd feel about this."

Tears filled her eyes as she listened to me.

"I can't believe you did all this. You are the most generous and loving man I have ever had the privilege of knowing. I have no words for what you've done except one—yes. Yes, Sebastian. I would be honored to become Mrs. Sebastian Kind, your wife, tomorrow at the Bliss Wedding Chapel at four p.m."

I cupped her face in my hands and wiped away the tears from her eyes.

"Yes?" I smiled.

"Yes." A soft laugh escaped her as she nodded her head.

I kissed her lips and pulled her into me, holding her tight.

"I love you so much, Emilia."

"I love you too, Sebastian. Which anniversary day will we celebrate?" she asked as she broke our embrace.

"Both." I smiled.

Emilia

"I can't believe we're doing this," I said as I stood in the center of the room while Jenni fixed my dress.

"Believe it, sister, because it's happening." She grinned. "Okay. All set. What do you think?" She turned me around, so I faced the full-length mirror.

I stared at myself in the white satin, A-line strapless dress where the front sat right above my knee and the back barely touched the ground.

"I love it. It's perfect, Jenni. Thank you."

"Simple, yet elegant. It's the perfect dress for this occasion."

"Great job, Jen," Grace walked over.

"Thanks. I designed it as part of the wedding collection I'll be revealing in the fall. When Sebastian told me his plan, this dress instantly came to mind."

"Thank you." Emilia hugged me.

When we heard a knock on the hotel door, Alex walked over and answered it.

"You have a delivery." She smiled as she handed me a royal blue velvet square box.

As the girls gathered around, I slowly lifted the lid and gasped at the beautiful pendant inside—a heart-shaped diamond suspended on a delicate chain. Inside the box was a note that read:

A beautiful diamond for a beautiful woman.
You will forever have my heart.
I can't wait to marry you.
Love your future husband,
Sebastian

"Damn, that's gorgeous. It's at least two carats," Julia spoke.

"Way to go, Sebastian." Jenni grinned. "Let me put it on you."

I could feel the tears stinging my eyes as Jenni placed the stunning necklace around my neck.

"I can't believe he did this." I fanned my eyes.

"I can." Alex smiled.

"Shaun just texted me and said the limo is waiting for us downstairs. Let's go get you married." Jenni grinned.

The five of us climbed into the limo and headed to the Bliss Wedding Chapel, where the guys were waiting for us.

~

Sebastian

"Calm down, bro." Simon smirked. "You're fidgeting."

"I'm trying."

"It's okay." Sam placed his hand on my shoulder.

My brothers took their seats in the front row, and the girls joined them. The music started to play, and tears filled my eyes when I saw Emilia start walking down the aisle. She was breathtaking, and I was the luckiest man in the world.

A smile crossed my face as she approached me, and I held out my hand to her.

"You look stunning," I softly spoke.

"So do you."

The pastor spoke a few words before we said our vows, exchanged rings, and became Mr. and Mrs. Sebastian Kind. Our family clapped and whistled as we shared our first kiss as a married couple. After the ceremony, we took pictures and headed back to the Bellagio to celebrate with a beautiful dinner at Le Cirque.

"I can't believe we did it." Emilia grinned. "We're married."

"Now, you're stuck with me forever." I smiled as I brushed my lips against hers.

"There's no other man in this world I would rather be stuck with than you. I love you so much."

"I love you, and I'm never letting you go."

"Promise?"

"You have my word, Mrs. Kind."

After dinner, we gathered at the bar off the lobby and celebrated some more. As much fun as I was having, I could only think about taking Emilia up to our suite and making love to her all night.

"How does it feel to be a married man?" Stefan asked.

"Pretty fucking great." I grinned.

After a few drinks, we decided to walk down the strip and take in the Vegas night atmosphere. Simon and Grace were behind us, and I quickly turned around when I heard Grace's loud voice.

"Oh, hell no! Get back here, asshole! He stole my purse!" She kicked off her shoes and chased after him as Simon followed behind us.

"Bro, what the fuck?"

"She's got this." He smiled.

Grace had the man face down on the ground within seconds with his arm twisted behind his back.

"You think it's okay to steal a woman's purse?" she shouted. "Do you?"

"Damn, lady. You're hurting me."

"You think this hurts? Just wait."

Simon knelt in front of the man. "You better apologize to her, or I'll give her the okay to break your arm. She loves to break people's arms. She's crazy like that."

"I'm sorry, ma'am. I'm really sorry. I'll never do it again. I swear."

"Grace, the man apologized. Let him go," Simon said.

"Do I have to?" she whined.

"Yes."

She let go of him, and the man quickly got up and ran away as fast as he could.

"Damn, Grace." Stefan laughed.

"You disappoint me, Simon," she said.

He hooked his arm around her and let out a sigh.

"I know, babe. I know. But you did the right thing."

We all laughed and continued our walk down the strip.

CHAPTER 21

Stefan

I lay in bed with my hands behind my head with no energy to get up. Today was the day. *The day.* Grabbing my phone from the nightstand, I sent Sam a message.

"Are you ready for this?"

"Fuck, no. I'm still in bed."

"So am I. I can't believe we're doing this. Us."

"I know, bro. I feel sick."

"So, do I. I'll see you soon. Alex just walked in."

She walked over, sat on the edge of the bed, and softly kissed my lips.

"You need to get up and get ready, Stefan."

"I know. I'm trying."

"Dad? Why aren't you up yet?" Lily asked as she climbed on the bed. "You're going to be late for your appointment. I know you're scared, but I promise it'll be okay."

I gave Alex a stern look.

"What?"

"You told her?"

"Yeah. She'll see you while you're recovering and packing yourself with ice packs."

"Dad, I'm old enough, and I know how babies are made. I think it's honorable that you're doing this for you and Mom."

"Excuse me?" I cocked my head at her.

"Mom's been taking all the precautions since you've met not to get pregnant. She carried and delivered Henry, and now she's doing it again with another baby. She's done her part, and now, it's time for you to step up and do yours. Remember when I broke my arm, and you told me that I'd be okay, and once it fully heals, my arm would be like it was never broken? The same goes for you. Once you heal, it'll work again."

I sat there speechless and in disbelief while my blood pressure rose.

"Are you done?" I sternly spoke to her.

"Yeah. I'm done. Good luck, Daddy." She wrapped her arms around my neck and kissed my cheek. I love you."

"I love you too, baby girl." I hugged her as I glared at Alex.

"Come on, Lily. I'll walk you and Henry over to Uncle Simon's," Alex spoke. "You better be dressed and ready by the time I get back." She pointed at me.

I quickly showered and slipped on a pair of loose sweatpants and a t-shirt.

"Good boy." Alex smiled when she stepped back into the room.

"I have to say I'm a little angry with you, Alex," I spoke as I grabbed a pair of socks.

"Be angry all you want, Stefan. But don't forget I'm pregnant and hormonal, so my anger trumps yours." Her brow arched. "I did nothing wrong. She overheard Julia and me talking about it and asked what was going on. We don't lie to her. You know that. What would you tell her when you came home and you're sitting around with ice packs down there?"

"Fine. I'm sorry. I don't want to talk about it. I'm nervous enough."

She walked over and wrapped her arms around my neck.

"I know you are, babe. I love you, and I will be taking good care of you."

"I love you too." I kissed her lips.

Sam

Julia, Stefan, Alex, and I entered the building and took the elevator to the third floor, where Dr. George's office was. I wouldn't lie and say I wasn't nervous because I was. I was scared shitless. The thought of someone cutting into my balls was terrifying.

"Samuel and Stefan Kind."

Stefan and I looked at each other, kissed our wives, and headed through the open door the nurse was holding for us.

"Good morning." She smiled. "Samuel, you're in room three, and Stefan, you can go into room four."

"We got this, bro." I held out my fist to him.

"Yeah. We got this." He fist-bumped me.

While Dr. George did his work, we talked to help ease the anxiety I felt as I lay there. Considering the circumstances, he was a great guy, and we had good conversations.

"Okay, Sam. You're all done. You can stay put until I'm finished with your brother, and I'll have the nurse bring in your wife."

"Thanks, Dr. George."

"You're welcome. Stay off your feet for the next couple of days. I'm going to prescribe you some Tylenol 3's with codeine. Take them if you want. But my suggestion is regular Tylenol, and a few glasses of scotch do the trick just as well." He winked.

After a few moments, the door opened, and Julia stepped inside.

"Hey." She smiled as she walked over and kissed me. "How are you?"

"Uncomfortable, to say the least."

Her lips pouted as she grabbed my hand and held it.

"Thank you for doing this for us," she said.

"I love you, and you know I'll do anything for you and us."

After Stefan's procedure was complete, we walked out of our rooms and looked at each other.

"You okay?" I asked him.

"No. Are you?"

"No." I lightly chuckled as I hooked my arm around him, and we slowly walked out of the office.

A couple of hours after we got home, I went outside to the patio with a bottle of scotch and two glasses. As I sat down on the lounger and reclined it back, I grabbed my phone and texted Stefan.

"Come over. I'm on the patio, and I have a bottle of scotch with our names on it."

"On my way."

I couldn't help but laugh when I saw him *slowly* walking toward the patio with an ice pack in his hand.

"I feel your pain, bro."

"I feel like I've been kicked in the nuts a hundred times over," he said as he carefully sat in the lounger and reclined it back.

Reaching over, I poured him a glass of scotch and handed it to him.

"Thanks, bro."

"Have you taken any Tylenol?" I asked.

"Yeah. You?"

"Hell, yes."

As we were talking, Simon and Shaun walked over.

"Ouch," Simon said as he walked over and saw our ice packs. "Are you two okay?"

"Do we look okay, bro?" Stefan asked.

"Have you forgotten that I was shot? I think I got you beat on that one. I could have Grace come over with her special oil and perform her magic on your balls." He laughed.

"Very funny," I said.

"In a few days, you'll forget all about this," Shaun said.

"Doubt it," Stefan spoke.

As we were talking, our father walked over. We hadn't told him anything because we'd been trying to keep our distance from him.

"Boys, what's going on? Why are the four of you sitting here in the middle of the day? Oh." He looked down and saw the ice packs. "You two went and had vasectomies?" he asked.

"No, Dad. They just like to sit around with ice packs on their balls," Simon spoke.

Our father shot him a look and turned to us.

"We went this morning. We're not having any more kids, so Julia and Alex thought it was the best decision."

"I see."

"Dad, let me ask you this," Simon spoke. "Why didn't you ever have a vasectomy? With all the women you've been with over the years, wouldn't it have been the right thing to do?"

"I never thought about it, son. Besides, if I had had it done, you wouldn't have your sister, would you? What is going on with you boys? I've barely seen you."

"We've been busy," Shaun spoke.

"Too busy for your old man?"

"You've been quite busy yourself, Dad," Simon said.

"What's that supposed to mean?"

"OUCH!" Stefan yelled out as he gripped the arms of the lounger. "Oh my God, the pain. The pain!"

"You two need to rest up. I'll talk to you boys later."

THE KIND BROTHERS

"What the fuck, bro?" I stared at Stefan.

"Someone had to stop that conversation from going any further." He shot Simon a dirty look.

Simon busted out into laughter. "Bro, you're good." He pointed at him. "I actually thought you were in a lot of pain."

"What's going on over here?" Sebastian walked over, holding a large brown bag.

"Dude, tell me that's food," Stefan said.

"It is." He smiled. "I told you I'd take care of you. How are you two feeling?"

"Sore as hell," I said. "But this scotch is numbing the pain." I smiled. "Agree, bro?" I glanced over at Stefan.

"One hundred percent." He grinned.

CHAPTER 22

TWO WEEKS LATER

Stefan

Alex, Lily, Henry, and I sat in the room waiting for Dr. Kota to perform Alex's ultrasound. Today was the day we would find out the sex of our baby.

"I think it's a boy." Alex smiled as she lay on the bed.

"Don't say that, Mom. I really want it to be a girl," Lily whined.

"Are you saying you'll love the baby any less if it's a boy?" I arched my brow at her.

"No." She looked down.

"And what do you think, Henry? Boy or girl?" I smiled as I held him, and he slapped me in the face with both of his hands.

"He wants another sister. He told me."

"Did he now?"

The door opened, and Dr. Kota stepped inside.

"Good day, Kind family. Are you ready to see your baby?"

"We are, Dr. Kota." Alex grinned.

After squirting Alex's belly with some gel, he placed the transducer and pressed down. A happy grin crossed my face when I saw my baby on the screen. Giving Alex's hand a gentle squeeze, she turned and smiled.

"Your baby is growing right on schedule and developing nicely."

"Boy or girl, Dr. Kota?" Lily asked.

He let out a chuckle as he moved the transducer across Alex's belly.

"Let's see if we can tell. What are you hoping for, Lily?"

"A girl. I want a sister."

"Well, it seems like this baby is a girl!" He smiled at her.

"YES!" she exclaimed.

"A girl, Stefan." Tears filled Alex's eyes.

"I'm so happy." I leaned down and kissed her lips.

"Thank you, Dad." She wrapped her arms around me. "I knew you could do it."

"Um, you're welcome." I lightly patted her back.

After we climbed into the car to head home, I looked at Lily.

"Now, remember not to tell anyone before tonight."

"I won't, Dad. I am so excited!" She beamed. "What are we going to name her?"

"I don't know yet, sweetie. Dad and I haven't discussed names yet."

"I have some names in mind. I'll write them down and give them to you. Then you can discuss it."

"Okay." Alex laughed.

Jenni tried her hardest to try and throw us a gender reveal party, but Alex had other plans. This time around, she wanted to be the one to surprise everybody. On the way home from the doctor, we stopped at Party City and picked up enough confetti cannons for everyone in our family.

"Babe, I'm going to run to the restaurant and pick up the subs and salad from Sebastian."

"Okay. I'll finish getting everything else ready." Alex kissed my lips.

When I pulled out of the driveway, I saw Mr. Hawkins, who lived next to my father, outside and a For Sale sign on his lawn.

"Hey, Mark," I shouted as I pulled up and put down the passenger side window.

"Stefan." He smiled as he walked over.

"What's with the For Sale sign?"

"Greta and I have decided to retire in Arizona, where our daughter and son-in-law are."

"Nice. We'll miss you. When are you planning on leaving?"

"Next month. We have an open house tomorrow. Did you hear that Meg and Leon are getting divorced?"

"No. I can't say I'm surprised, though."

"Me either. And things are getting nasty with them. They have no choice but to sell the house."

"Why?" I furrowed my brows.

"Bankruptcy. Leon blames Meg. Meg blames Leon. It's a mess." He waved his hand."

"That's too bad."

"Yeah. It is. Anyway, I need to finish up here before heading to dinner. It was good talking with you, Stefan."

"You too, Mark. I'll talk to you later."

I walked into Four Kinds and went straight to the kitchen.

"Hey, bro."

"Hey. I thought you would have been here sooner," Sebastian spoke.

"I was talking to Mark. He put his house up for sale."

"Really?" Where are he and Greta moving to?"

"They're retiring to Arizona to be closer to Katie and Louis."

"Good for them. I knew how hard it was on them when Katie moved."

"And get this. Meg and Leon are getting divorced."

"Shocker." He chuckled. "We all saw that coming."

"Yeah. Their house will be going up for sale as well. Mark said they had to file bankruptcy."

"Are you thinking what I'm thinking?" Sebastian asked.

"Already thought it when Mark told me." I grinned.

"How did the ultrasound go?"

"Good. She's perfect."

"She?"

"Ah, shit. Bro, act surprised." I shook my head.

"Congratulations. Lily got her wish." He hugged me.

"Thanks. Yeah, she did. She told us she's making a list of names for us to go over."

"Sounds like her royal highness." He laughed.

I grabbed the food and headed home.

It was six o'clock when everyone started arriving. After we ate, Alex handed everyone a confetti cannon, and then I called everyone down to the beach.

"Okay. Is everyone ready? Hold up your cannons and make sure it's pointing up at the sky. Do not point your cannon at someone. Simon, I'm talking to you."

"Bro, you're no fun."

"When I count to three, twist the bottom, and you'll know the gender of our baby. One..Two..Three!"

An explosion of pink confetti showered the air as happiness could be heard across the beach.

"A little girl. Congrats, bro." Shaun hugged me.

"Thanks. We're really excited." I grinned.

"Way to go, Stefan." Sam smiled as he hugged me.

"I guess it's up to me to keep the family name going." Simon smirked as he hugged me. "Congratulations."

"Thanks, bro."

"Wow. What a surprise!" Sebastian smiled. "I'm happy for you and Alex."

"Another little girl in the family." Our dad walked over. "Congratulations, son. At this rate, the girls will be taking over." He extended his hand.

"Thanks, Dad." I shook his hand.

"There's something I want to talk to the five of you about. After everyone leaves, we'll meet over at Shaun's house."

CHAPTER 23

*S*haun

"What the hell does he want to talk to us about?" Simon scowled.

"I don't know. I guess we'll find out later," I said. "And why my house?"

"Who the hell knows," Sam said.

Stefan proceeded to tell us about Mark and Leon's houses for sale.

"They'd be great houses for the cousins," Stefan said.

"There's only two for sale. They need three," Sam spoke.

"Two of them can live together until another one become available. They can make someone move out like Shaun did." Stefan grinned.

"The houses around here go fast. Did you call them?" I asked.

"No. I haven't had a chance. Mark was cleaning up the front for the open house tomorrow."

"Hmm." I pulled out my phone and dialed Bella."

"Hey, Shaun. Grant and I were just talking about you."

"Hi, Bella. There are two houses I want to purchase: cash

offers and a ten-day close. Occupants can stay rent-free for sixty days if need be."

"What are the addresses?"

After Stefan rattled them off to me, I repeated them to Bella."

"Excellent. I'll get on that right now. Grant and I are on a plane to L.A. as we speak. I was going to call you and see if you wanted to meet up for drinks tomorrow night."

"I'd love to."

"Great. I'll text you tomorrow. Make sure to bring your girlfriend. We're excited to meet her."

"Thanks, Bella. I will. Tell Grant I said hi."

"Will do. See you tomorrow, Shaun."

"You're seriously buying the houses?" Simon's brow arched.

"Yeah. If our cousins are interested, they can buy it from me for what I paid."

"And if they're not?" Sam asked.

"I'll sell them. No big deal." I smiled.

"Boys, Curtis and I are leaving now." Barb walked over. "Stefan, I'm so happy to have another granddaughter. Congratulations, sweetheart." She hugged him.

"Thanks, Mom."

She hugged Simon, Sam, and Sebastian goodbye. She shocked us all when she hugged me as well.

"Goodnight, Shaun."

"Goodnight, Barb."

"Whoa. What the hell was that?" Simon laughed.

"What did you do?" Sebastian asked.

"I let her get the cake for your birthday party."

"Damn. A simple cake was all it took to get on her good side?" Stefan chuckled.

After everyone had left, we walked to my house so our father could tell us whatever it was he had to.

"Okay. We're all here. What did you want to talk about?" I asked.

"You all know, don't you?"

"Know what?" Sebastian asked.

"If you're referring to that Sonya woman, you've been fucking. Yeah, we know all about it," Simon spoke sternly.

"I knew it. The way the five of you have been acting over the past few weeks led me to believe you knew something. Which one of you found out first?"

"Does it matter?" Simon shouted.

"I did," I spoke up. "I was at the Four Seasons having a business lunch, and when I was walking to the restaurant, I saw the two of you."

"How did you know her name?"

"Have you forgotten that Grace and I are detectives? We can find out anything."

"And yet you never confronted me?"

"Because we don't give a shit, Dad!" Simon yelled. "We could care less if you want to fuck up your life."

"Simon, calm down," Sam said.

"It's over between us. I broke it off last week."

"Yeah, right." Sebastian breathed out a laugh.

"Why did you do it in the first place?" Stefan asked. "You love Celeste."

"You're right, son. I do love her, and I made a mistake. I realized it one night when I was rocking Nora to sleep. She was staring up at me with those beautiful eyes, and all I could see in them was Celeste and our future." Tears sprang to his eyes. "I've made a terrible mistake."

"Does she know?" I asked.

"No, and I want to keep it that way. There's no sense in hurting her and risking our relationship."

"Don't you think you've already done that when you fucked that other woman!" Simon shouted.

I placed my hand on Simon's shoulder to try and calm him down.

"I regret what I did, and I swear it won't happen again."

"My ass, it won't," Sebastian spoke. "It's who you are. It's who you've always been."

"Not anymore. I swear on your sister's life. Celeste means the world to me, and I fell off track. The last thing I want is for my sons being disappointed in me. So, I'm asking for your forgiveness."

"It's not our forgiveness you need, Dad. It's Celeste's," Sam said.

"As I said, Celeste doesn't know anything about this, and she never will. She's a good woman, and she doesn't deserve to have her heart broken. I will make amends. You have my word. I'm also seeing a therapist."

The five of us stood there and stared at him. His face was pained, and I believed he was genuinely sorry.

"That's the first step," I spoke.

"Oh, come on, Shaun," Simon said. "You haven't known him long enough. We've been dealing with this shit our entire lives. I'm done talking about this." He turned and walked out of the house.

"I'm sorry, boys. I truly am. But I will prove to you that I'm changing my ways."

"Okay, Dad," Sam said. "Keep seeing the therapist and strengthen your relationship with Celeste. It's all you can do."

"Thank you, Sam. I better head home and spend the rest of the evening with my beautiful wife."

After he left, we went to Simon's house. When we stepped through the sliding door, he and Grace were sitting at the table.

"Don't." He pointed at us. "Don't you dare try to defend him."

"We're not," Sam said.

"He's only saying that shit because he found out we knew. I bet he didn't even break it off with Sonya."

"There's one way to find out," I spoke. "I'll see if Jenni will make another appointment with Sonya."

"We can always put a tail on him and see where he goes," Grace said.

"Let's do it. It's the only way we'll know if he's telling the truth," Simon spoke.

CHAPTER 24

TWO WEEKS LATER

*S*imon
Jackson, Conner, and Nathan were back in town for a couple of days to finalize the sale of the building for their medical center and to check out the houses Shaun had purchased. The eight of us were sitting on Sebastian's patio, talking and kicking back a few beers, when we heard Celeste scream. Jumping up from our seats, we ran over, and nothing prepared us for what we saw when we stepped through the sliding door. Our father was lying on the ground, and Celeste was hovering over him, sobbing and screaming his name.

"What happened?" Jackson, Conner, and Nathan ran over to him.

"There's no pulse," Jackson said as he started CPR. "Did you call 911?" He looked at Celeste.

"Yes!" She cried.

Nora was screaming upstairs, so Sam ran up to get her.

"What the hell—oh my, God!" Emilia placed her hand over her mouth as the girls and Lily ran inside.

"Come on, Uncle Henry. You are not dying today!"

Jackson said as he continued CPR, and Conner breathed into our father's mouth.

"Please, Henry!" Celeste shouted, and I grabbed her and held her tight.

"Grandpa!" Lily screamed, and Stefan held her back.

We could hear the ambulance's sirens from down the street, and within seconds they ran in and took over.

"How long has he been down?" one of the paramedics asked.

"About ten minutes," Jackson replied.

The paramedics grabbed their defibrillator and charged it.

"Clear," the paramedic said as he placed it on our father's chest.

They worked on him for over twenty minutes. The reality of what happened set in when they looked at us and said, "I'm sorry. We did everything we could."

Tears filled my eyes as Celeste's grip on me tightened, and she sobbed in my arms.

∼

Sebastian

I gripped Emilia and hugged her tight as I stood there and watched the paramedics put my father on the stretcher and covered him from head to toe. Everyone in the room had tears streaming down their faces. I'd felt like I was trapped in a nightmare that I couldn't wake up from. Our father was gone, and there was nothing we could do about it.

"Celeste, did he grip his chest before he went down?" Conner asked her.

"Yes. That's when I dialed 911."

Simon walked Celeste over to the couch, and Emilia went and sat on the other side of her.

"What happened?" Simon asked.

"I told your father I was leaving him."

"What?" I furrowed my brows.

"He was having an affair."

The five of us looked at each other.

"I can't talk about this right now. I'm sorry." Her body shook from head to toe.

Jackson walked over and knelt in front of her.

"Celeste, I can give you something that will help you calm down."

"Yes, Jackson. Please."

"Okay. I'll be right back."

Emilia got up from the couch and walked over to me.

"I'm going to stay with Celeste tonight. She shouldn't be alone."

"We'll both stay." I kissed her lips and pulled her into me. "Can one of you take Ruby?" I asked my brothers.

"Yeah," Simon spoke. "We'll take her."

Stefan

I picked Lily up and hugged her tightly as she uncontrollably sobbed. My heart broke not only because of my father's death but also because my daughter witnessed it. That sight would be one that would be forever etched in our minds.

"Someone needs to call Mom," I said.

"I'll call her," Shaun said.

"This isn't real, Dad." Lily cried.

"I'm so sorry, baby girl." I held her head against me as tears flowed down my face. "We should go home." I looked at Alex, who was holding our son.

We said goodbye to Celeste, and we headed back to our homes.

"As soon as I get Lily settled, we all need to talk."

~

*S*haun

"I'm so sorry," Jenni said as she laid her head on my shoulder.

"I can't believe he's gone. I think we need to tell Barb in person. It shouldn't be done over the phone."

"I agree."

Jenni and I climbed in the car and headed over to Barb's house. We noticed several cars parked in the driveway and along the street when we pulled up. We could hear talking and laughter coming from the back, so we walked around to the patio and saw she was hosting a get-together.

"Shaun? Jenni? What are you doing here?" Barb asked.

"Barb, we need to speak to you in private."

"What happened?" Panic struck her voice. "Are my sons okay?" she asked as we walked into the house.

"They're fine," Jenni spoke.

I opened my mouth, and the words wouldn't come out as tears filled my eyes.

"Shaun? What happened?"

"Henry passed away."

"What? How?"

"Heart attack. We heard Celeste scream and ran over there. He was already—"

"Did anyone try to save him?"

"Jackson and Conner performed CPR until the paramedics got there. They did everything they could, but—" I shook my head.

She placed her hand on the kitchen table and used it as leverage to sit down.

"I can't believe this. I'm sure Celeste is a wreck."

"Jackson was giving her something to calm down."

"I'm so sorry for your loss. Tell the boys I'll be over first thing in the morning. I can't believe he's gone. Did Celeste say what he was doing when this happened?"

I couldn't tell her the truth.

"They were talking."

"Thank you for coming over here and letting me know."

"We're sorry to ruin your get-together," Jenni spoke.

"Don't be. I'm grateful that you two took the time to come and tell me in person."

After we arrived home, we saw everyone except Sebastian and Emilia sitting on the patio at Stefan's house, so we walked over.

"How's my mother?" Sam asked.

"Shocked and upset. She told me to tell you she'll be over first thing in the morning."

"How do you think Celeste found out about his affair?" Simon asked.

"I don't know," Stefan spoke. "But now isn't the time to ask her."

CHAPTER 25

Sam

My brothers and I spent the week organizing our father's funeral with Celeste. We still couldn't believe he was gone, and it hit all of us very hard.

"Goddamn it!" I yelled.

"Let me," Julia walked over and tied my tie. "We'll get through this, Sam."

"I know, babe. I just can't believe he's gone."

"I know. None of us can."

When she finished with my tie, she kissed my lips.

"We need to leave in about ten minutes," she softly spoke.

"You look beautiful." I ran the back of my hand down her cheek. "I just want to get through this day."

"We will. I've packed the diaper bag. Can you grab a kid?"

I couldn't help but smile. "Of course."

We rented limousines to take us to the cemetery, where the service was held outside. Julia and I were in one, Stefan's family was in another, Celeste and Nora were riding with Emilia & Sebastian, and Simon and Grace were tagging along with Shaun and Jenni.

When we reached the area where our father was being laid to rest, we climbed out and walked to where several white chairs for our immediate family sat in front of his casket. It was an emotional service, and many tears were uncontrollably shed. Stefan held onto Lily as she cried her eyes out. Seeing how distraught she was, made all of our tears intensify.

~

Jenni
I was sitting on the end next to Shaun when something caught my attention out of the corner of my eye. With a slight turn of my head, I saw Sonya approaching.

"Oh, shit."

"What's wrong?" Shaun whispered.

"Sonya is here."

"What?" His grip on my hand tightened. "Stay put."

"I can't!"

"You have no choice. We'll deal with her after."

"We need to get her out of here before Celeste sees her."

"We will."

The service ended after each family member was given a rose to place on Henry's casket. I was the last in line, and after setting it down, I walked over to where Sonya stood a few feet away.

"Jenni?" Her brows furrowed. "What are—"

"No. What are you doing here?" I grabbed her arm and led her behind a large oak tree.

"How do you know Henry?"

"He's my boyfriend's father."

"I thought you and your boyfriend broke up."

"Does it matter? I lied. I found out you were the woman he was seeing, so I made an appointment to get information out of you. You cannot be here, Sonya. You don't belong here."

"I can be here. We shared three months, and I came to pay my respects."

"You mean to rub it in the face of his widow?" I narrowed my eye.

"No. Of course not. She doesn't know who I am."

"Listen to me carefully. See those five men over there. They are Henry's sons, and if they see you here, they will use any force necessary to get you out of here. Let's go."

She jerked out of my grip.

"Keep your hands off me."

"Oh, great," I spoke as I saw Simon approaching.

"What?"

"Now you're really in for it. If I were you, I'd run."

"You think I'm scared of him. You all better leave me alone."

"No can do, sweetheart. It's time for you to go," Simon spoke as he approached us.

"Lay one finger on me, and I will file an assault charge. All I want to do is pay my respects to the man I was in love with."

"A married man you should never have gotten involved with," Simon spoke through gritted teeth. "Please, just leave our family to grieve in peace."

"Oh shit." I turned and saw Celeste walking toward us. "Hug me."

"What?" Sonya frowned.

"Hug me." I pulled her into a hug. "It was so nice of you to come."

"Jenni. Simon. Who's this?"

"Celeste, this is my good friend, Jane. We worked together back when I modeled. She's a makeup artist."

"It's nice to meet you. Thank you for coming." Celeste extended her hand, and Simon stood there slowly, shaking his head.

"I'm so sorry for your loss, Mrs. Kind."

"Thank you. It was very kind of you to come to the funeral. It's time to head to the luncheon," Celeste said.

"Okay. We're right behind you," I said.

I let out a deep breath when she turned and headed toward the limousine.

"Once we all leave and the last limousine pulls away, you can go pay your respects," I spoke to Sonya.

"Thank you."

"Come on, Simon." I hooked my arm in his.

"Jesus Christ. Good job coming up with that story so quick."

"Thanks." I smiled. "I've had a lot of practice growing up. Don't tell my parents I said that." I pointed at him.

~

Shaun

The luncheon was held at Four Kinds, where about a hundred people attended. While my brothers were scattered around talking to our father's friends, Jackson and I were having a conversation.

"After we leave here today, we need to get back to San Francisco," Jackson said. "But we'll be back in a couple of weeks permanently."

"That's great." I smiled as I placed my hand on his back. "It'll be good to have the three of you here. Did Stefan say how long for the remodel on the medical center?"

"At least three months. His crew is starting tomorrow. And thanks to you, all the equipment we need is on order."

"Bella called me yesterday and told me there's a house not too far from us for sale. She thinks you should check it out. I'll text you her number, and you can get in touch with her."

"Or you can buy my house," Celeste walked over and placed her hand on Jackson's shoulder.

I glanced at her with furrowed brows.

"What are you talking about, Celeste?"

"You're selling?" Jackson asked.

"I am. Shaun, this isn't the place to discuss this now, but I would appreciate it if you could round up your brothers and come over to the house later."

"Yeah. Sure. We'll be there."

"Anyway, Jackson, the house is yours if you're interested. I've already had it appraised, and I'll sell it to you at market value."

"Are you sure, Celeste?"

"Yes. I'm very sure. We can go over the details later." She walked away.

"Damn. Talk about a house just falling into your lap," Jackson said.

"I wonder why she's selling. I need to find my brothers. I'll talk to you later."

I rounded up my brothers, and we went into Sebastian's office.

"What's going on?" Sebastian asked.

"Celeste needs us to come over after the luncheon. She just offered Jackson her house."

"What?" Sam's brows furrowed.

"That's crazy. Where is she going?" Stefan asked.

"I don't know. I guess that's what she wants to talk to us about."

"Wait a second," Simon said. "She's selling the beach house and moving away with our sister?"

"Let's not get worked up until we know all the details," I said.

"I'll tell you one thing right now. She is not taking our sister away from us," Simon scowled.

CHAPTER 26

*S*imon

It was an emotional and exhausting day. A day I never dreamed would come so quickly. It was the day that changed our family's lives forever. I glanced over at Grace from across the restaurant as she sat and talked with Julia and Jenni. A strong and beautiful woman whom I was proud and honored to call my girlfriend. The same woman I, without a doubt, wanted to spend the rest of my life with. I'd been waiting for the perfect time to propose to her. At least that's what I told myself. It was an excuse. Perhaps I was nervous, frightened, or thought it didn't matter because our bond was already strong. But life was too short, and my father's death opened my eyes. There would be no perfect time because every moment spent with her was perfect.

"Earth to Simon," Sam spoke as he placed his hand on my shoulder.

"Hey." I turned and glanced at him.

"You were zoned out. What's going on?"

"Nothing."

"You're lying." A smirk crossed his lips.

"I've been waiting for the perfect moment to ask Grace to marry me, but the truth is every moment with her is perfect. So, there will never be that one 'perfect' moment."

"Can I give you some brotherly advice? The perfect moment will be when you buy her a ring. So, when do you want to go look?"

"Soon."

"Okay. Let's get through the rest of today, and we'll round up the others and set a day and time." He smiled as he gripped my shoulder.

"Thanks, bro." I turned and gave him a bro hug.

After we left the restaurant, we headed home until the five of us were ready to go and see Celeste.

"I can't believe she's selling the house," Grace said as she set her purse down.

"I can't either."

"Maybe she doesn't feel comfortable staying there because of what happened to Henry in that house."

"Maybe. As soon as I find out, I'll let you know."

My phone dinged, and a message from Sam came through in our group chat telling us it was time to go and see Celeste.

"We're heading over there now, babe." I kissed her lips.

"Okay. I'm going to do some meditating for a while."

Shaun and I stepped onto our patios at the same time and walked over to my father's house.

"Good. You're all here now," Celeste said as Shaun and I took a seat in the living room where our three other brothers were. "I'm sure Shaun has told you that I offered the house to Jackson."

"What's the rush, Celeste?" Stefan asked.

"And where are you planning on living?" I asked.

"You can't take our sister from us," Sam spoke.

She put her hands up. "I am not, nor would I ever take Nora away from her family. I'm moving to Malibu, where my sister is. Nora and I will be staying with her and her husband until I find a home. That was my plan before your father passed away. When he asked me to marry him, I made it very clear that if he ever cheated on me, there would be no second chances."

"How did you know he was having an affair?" Shaun asked.

"There were signs here and there, and when I'd had enough, I went through his phone one morning while he was in the shower. There were several text messages from a woman named Sonya—inappropriate messages. I confronted your father the next day after I had collected my thoughts. He swore to me that he had made a mistake, and it was over. We talked, we cried, and I told him I needed time to think about things. He begged me to forgive him, and he begged me not to leave. But I was so hurt that he could do that to Nora and me, and I knew it would ultimately happen again. I wasn't about to live in a state of mistrust for the rest of my life, so I decided that I would leave him for my mental health and Nora's. Look what his affairs had done to you boys. The day he passed away, he went out and played golf with his friend, Raul. He came home earlier than I expected and found me in the bedroom packing my suitcases. We began to argue and took it downstairs because Nora was napping. That's when he had his heart attack." Tears filled her eyes.

"I'm sorry, Celeste," Sam spoke.

"I hope you boys don't blame me, but I feel responsible."

"No, Celeste." I walked over and hooked my arm around her. "It's not your fault. You had every right to want to leave. His heart attack would have happened at some point, with or without the argument you two had. We do not blame you at all. Am I right?" I looked at my brothers.

"No. Of course not. It wasn't your fault," Shaun spoke.

"Absolutely not." Sebastian shook his head.

"Don't blame yourself, Celeste," Stefan spoke.

"It's hard not to when he died in the middle of arguing with me." Tears streamed down her face. "I hope you understand why I can't live here."

"Of course, we do." I tightened my grip around her. "Besides, Malibu is only about forty minutes away."

"It's important to me that Nora is close to her father's family. You boys are amazing men, and she needs all of you in her life. You can see her whenever you want. You can take her for the weekend, holidays, anything you want. I promise that I will not keep her from you."

"We appreciate that, Celeste," Sam spoke. "We all love her. She's our sister, and we want to watch her grow up."

"What can we do to help you around here?" I asked.

"I need you to go through your father's things and take whatever you want. Everything else will be donated. The moving company will be here to pack up the house in three days. Jackson sent me a text message after he left the luncheon and told me that he would buy the house from me, which I am grateful for. The sooner I can put all this behind me, the sooner I can move on with my life."

"We'll go through all of his things tomorrow," Simon said.

"Thank you. I appreciate it. Now, if you'll excuse me, I'm going to lie down while Nora is still sleeping."

As we were walking back to our houses, I had an idea.

"How about hitting some waves?"

"Bro, what a great idea. I sure could use some surfing right now," Stefan said.

"Me too. Let me check on Julia first and see if she needs help with the girls," Sam spoke.

"I'll meet you down at the beach," Sebastian said.

"Me too," Shaun said.

I stepped onto the patio and saw Grace sitting on her meditation pillow, meditating. I knew better than to disturb her when she was in deep meditation, so I carefully opened the sliding door and went inside. Running up the stairs to our bedroom, I changed into a pair of boardshorts.

"Hey." Grace smiled when she walked into the room. "How did it go?"

"She's moving to Malibu."

"That's a short drive. Are you going surfing?" she asked as she wrapped her arms around my neck.

"I am."

"Good." She kissed my lips. "I think the five of you need to be together, alone, for a while. Why don't you guys go up to the cabin this weekend?"

"That's an excellent idea. I don't know if Sam and Stefan will be able to."

"Why? Emilia, Jenni, and I are here to help Alex and Julia."

"I'll run it past the guys. I love you." I smiled as I brushed my lips against hers.

"I love you too. Now go hit some waves." She slapped my ass.

"You're going to get it when I get back." I pointed at her.

"I hope so, detective."

I grabbed my board and ran down to the beach.

"Everything okay with Julia?" I asked Sam.

"Yeah. The girls are sleeping."

We put our boards in the water and paddled out.

"Grace had an idea," I spoke.

"Oh yeah? What?" Shaun asked.

"She said the five of us should go up to the cabin this weekend."

"Just us?" Stefan asked.

"Yeah. Just us. No women and no children."

"Count me in, bro." Sebastian high-fived me.

"Me too." Shaun smiled.

"I can't leave Julia alone with the girls."

"I can leave Alex alone with Lily and Henry." Stefan grinned. "She'd want me to go."

"Grace said that she, Emilia, and Jenni would help Julia and Alex out. If you and Shaun aren't home, Jenni would probably stay at your house."

"You're right. I'll talk to Julia about it." Sam grinned.

We spent over an hour on the water, talking and surfing as many waves as possible. I was looking forward to spending the weekend with just my brothers sitting by the lake all day, relaxing, drinking, and talking.

CHAPTER 27

Sam

I picked up Lorelei and hugged her tight.

"Daddy is going to miss you so much." I pressed my lips against her head.

Setting her down, I took Lena from Julia's arms and held her tight.

"Daddy is going to miss you so much." I kissed her head and set her on the floor next to her sister. "And you," I wrapped my arms around Julia and pulled her into me, "I will miss you more."

"I'll miss you too, Sam, but you need this time with your brothers." She broke our embrace and ran her fingers through my hair.

"I know, but I still get to miss my girls."

The sliding door opened, and Stefan walked in.

"Bro, come on. We want to hit the road."

"I'm coming. I love you, Julia."

"I love you too. Go have fun and don't worry about us. We'll be fine."

Our lips locked for a few moments before I grabbed my bag and headed out.

~

On our way to the cabin, we stopped at the grocery store and stocked up on food and alcohol for the weekend. As we stepped inside the house, we set our bags down and unloaded the car.

"Man, it's great to be back here," Stefan said.

"The last time I was here was when I proposed to Emilia."

"It's been a while," Simon said.

"There's only four bedrooms and five of us. Who's going to share a room?" I asked.

"Shaun can bunk with me since the room I usually stay in has two double beds," Simon spoke.

We took our bags to our rooms and then helped Sebastian put the groceries away. Walking over to the hook that sat on the wall by the sliding door, I picked up the fishing hat my father always wore.

"Dad always loved this hat." A sadness washed over me as I stared at it.

"Just like he always loved this place," Stefan spoke.

"He called it his peaceful place," Sebastian said.

"Let's grab some beers and sit by the lake," Simon said.

There were three chairs already in place by the lake, so we grabbed two more from the deck and took them down.

As I sat there in the lounger with a cold beer in my hand, the sun shined brightly as the air was warm with a slight breeze that fell upon our faces. I took in the beauty around me—especially the peacefulness and the tranquility of the lake.

"Remember when we were fourteen, and Dad brought us here?" I asked.

"Are you referring to when we stole his bottle of scotch and got totally wasted in the woods?" Simon laughed.

"Shit. Dad was so mad when he found us." Sebastian chuckled.

"What did he do?" Shaun asked.

"He yelled. Not because we were drunk, but because we drank his two-thousand-dollar bottle of scotch." I laughed.

"He didn't punish you?" Shaun asked.

"He said that our punishment would be the next morning."

"Yeah. Shit." Simon shook his head. "We were so sick and hungover."

"I can't believe he's gone," Stefan spoke in a pained voice.

"I know." Sebastian looked down at his beer bottle. "I feel awful that I never told him Emilia and I got married in Vegas."

I reached over and placed my hand on his shoulder.

"Don't, bro. Nobody knows that. It's the way you and Emilia wanted it. Don't feel guilty at all."

"Speaking of marriage, your wedding is in a couple of weeks. Are you and Emilia ready to fake it?" Simon asked as he chuckled.

"We're more than ready. We want to skip the ceremony and get right to the reception." The corners of Sebastian's mouth curved upward.

"I bet." I laughed.

I pulled my phone from my pocket and looked at it.

"What are you doing?" Stefan asked.

"Just checking to see if Julia texted me. As much as I love being here with you douchebags, I still feel bad for leaving her."

"Okay. I'll give you one pass," Simon spoke.

"What are you talking about?"

"You can Facetime her this one time, and you can see she and the babies are just fine without you."

"It's getting late, Sam," Shaun spoke. "I'm sure the twins are sleeping."

"We'll find out."

I pulled up Julia's number and hit the Facetime button. When the call was answered, Jenni's face appeared on the screen.

"Hello, Sammy."

"Is that Jenni?" Shaun's brows furrowed.

"Damn. It sounds like there's a party going on there." Simon laughed.

"Jenni, where's Julia?" I asked as I could hear music blasting in the background.

She turned the camera around and focused on Julia and Grace standing at the island doing shots.

"What the hell is going on?"

"You're having your bro time, and we're having a sleepover."

"Ha! That's my girl." Simon grinned as he watched Grace slam a shot.

"Knock it off, bro. Put Julia on right now!"

"Where's Alex and my children?" Stefan leaned over and asked Jenni.

"She ran back to your house to get another bottle of booze."

"Hey, babe." Shaun waved.

"Hello there, you sexy man." She kissed the screen.

"She's totally wasted," Shaun said.

"Julia, your husband wants to speak with you!" Jenni shouted and handed Julia the phone.

"Oh, hey."

"What is going on over there?"

"We're having a sleepover."

"Where are the twins?" I asked.

"My mom and dad took them for the night."

"Where are Lily and Henry?" Stefan asked.

"Your mom and Curtis took them for the night. Alex, Stefan is on the phone."

"Oh. Hey, babe." She grinned. "Are you having fun?"

"Apparently, not as much fun as you're all having," he said.

Sebastian pulled out his phone, got up, and went and Facetimed Emilia.

"Gotta go, Sam. I love you."

"Julia, wait."

She ended the call, and I slowly shook my head.

"Did you see the kitchen?"

"Breathe, bro. Breathe." Stefan placed his hand on my shoulder.

Sebastian came back and sat down.

"Emilia is wasted. I can guarantee she won't remember our phone conversation tomorrow."

"They all were." Simon chuckled.

"Not my wife." Stefan grinned.

CHAPTER 28

Simon

We spent the following day taking the jet skis out on the lake and acting like fools, talking about our father, barbecuing, and enjoying our last night at the cabin. When night hit, we lit the fire pit, roasted some hot dogs, and played our guitars.

"We need to expand this place."

"I was thinking the same thing," Sam spoke.

"Our families are growing, and there isn't enough room for all of us to come up at the same time," I said.

"Who owns the property on each side?" Shaun asked.

"Dad," Sam spoke. "He bought it before he had the cabin built. He wanted it to be the only house in the area for privacy."

"He never wanted to expand?" Shaun asked.

"After Julia and I got married, I threw the idea out to him, and he told me the cabin was perfect the way it was, and we'd have to make do if we all wanted to come up at the same time."

"I think it's time we do it," Sebastian said.

"I agree," Stefan said.

"I'll get to work on the design." Sam smiled.

~

A few days after we came back from the cabin, I'd arranged for my brothers to meet me at Cartier for my one o'clock appointment that I'd set.

"How did you manage to ditch Grace?" Stefan asked as we all walked into the store.

"I told her Shaun called an emergency family meeting."

"And what are you going to tell her the meeting was about when she asks?" Shaun's brow arched.

"I'm leaving you to come up with something." I grinned as I patted his back.

"Good afternoon, gentleman. It's good to see you again. Follow me."

We followed him into the back and sat down at the same table as the last three times we were here.

"There were always four of you. May I ask who this is?"

"This is Shaun. He's our brother from another mother." A smirk formed on my lips.

"I see. Welcome, Shaun. I've already taken the liberty of picking out some rings for you to view. A few of them are from our new collection that we haven't displayed yet," he spoke as he removed the black velvet cloth from the display of rings.

I stared at them as my heart beat out of my chest. Picking up the only one that caught my attention, I knew it was perfect for Grace.

"This is the one. What do you guys think?"

"It's perfect." Sam smiled as he placed his hand on my shoulder.

"Grace is going to love it," Stefan said.

"Excellent choice, bro." Sebastian smiled.

"Shaun?" I glanced over at him.

"It's beautiful. Can I see that one on the end?" He pointed.

The corners of my mouth curved upward as I picked up the ring and handed it to him. My brothers and I looked at each other.

"I'll take this one." Shaun held up the ring.

"Seriously?" Stefan asked.

"Yeah. I'm going to ask Jenni to marry me at some point. So, I might as well already have the ring whenever I decide to do it."

"And I'll take this one," I spoke.

It was our usual Saturday get-together, and tonight was the night I was going to propose to Grace in front of my family. As much as I wanted to do something fancy and over the top romantic, Grace's instincts would kick in, and she'd know what I was planning to do. I wanted to catch her completely off guard with the proposal, and I didn't want her to see it coming. It worked out perfectly because we were going to Sebastian's house for a barbecue.

"What are you making?" I asked Grace when I walked into the kitchen.

"A pasta salad to take to Emilia and Sebastian's."

"Sounds good." I kissed her cheek. "I'm running over to Shaun's for a few. I'll be right back."

"Okay." A smile crossed her beautiful lips.

I stepped onto Shaun's patio and opened the sliding door.

"Bro," I shouted. "Where are you at?"

Within seconds, he came running down the stairs in shorts and no shirt.

"Did I interrupt something?" I arched my brow.

"If you would have been one minute earlier, you would have." A smile crossed his face.

"Do the two of you ever not have sex?"

"No." He grinned.

I followed him into his office, where he unlocked his safe, pulled out the ring box, and handed it to me.

"Thanks for keeping this here. I know Grace would have found it if I'd kept it at the house."

"No problem, bro."

I glanced in his safe and saw the ring he'd bought Jenni wasn't in there.

"Where's Jenni's ring?"

"I'm keeping it locked in the safe at my office. I go in this one a lot, and she'd probably see it one day when I opened the safe."

"Ah." I gave him a nod. "Good idea. I better get home. I'll see you over at Sebastian's."

When I stepped back inside the house, I could hear the shower running upstairs. I knew if I walked into the bathroom, I wouldn't be able to control myself, and I'd have Grace bent over the bathroom sink the second she finished her shower. As fierce as the temptation was, I opted to go out on the patio and stay clear of her until she got dressed. The reason being was that I wanted tonight, when we got home from Sebastian's, and after she accepted my proposal, to be extra special. And I didn't want to risk something happening now to where we wouldn't be able to have sex tonight.

I was sitting in the lounger when Lily walked over with Ruby.

"Hey, Uncle Simon."

"Hey, Lils. Hey, Ruby." I ran my hand down her back when she ran over to me. "What's wrong, my beautiful niece?"

She slumped down in the lounger next to me and folded her hands.

"I miss Grandpa."

Shit. I wasn't very good with these kinds of talks.

"I know you do." I extended my hand to her.

She reached over and placed her hand in mine.

"I miss him too. You know, kid, it's complicated and hard to understand. I don't understand it myself."

"You don't?"

"No. But it happens, and there isn't anything we can do about it except live the rest of our lives the best way we know how. You remember the story about my friend, Drew, right?"

"Yeah."

"His death was the first death I ever experienced, and it took me a long time to get over it."

"Were you angry?" she asked.

"I was furious, and I stayed that way until one day, I met a girl who stole my wave while I was surfing. After she apologized for stealing my wave, we spent the day together and talked."

"About what?"

"She had mentioned that her parents died in a house fire, so I told her about Drew. Now, I never talked about Drew's death, not even with your dad or your uncles. It was too painful. But with this girl, something was comforting about her, and I felt comfortable opening up to her."

"Wow. She must have been pretty special."

"Yeah." I grinned. "She said something to me that I would never forget."

"What?" Lily's eyes widened.

"A broken mirror cannot shine."

"That's weird." Lily's brows furrowed.

I chuckled. "I thought the same thing until she explained

it to me. I was the mirror, broken because of my best friend's death. And as long as I stayed that way by being angry and sad all the time, I would never shine. She told me that I needed to make peace with his death, and once I did, my mind would be calm, and the road of my journey would be paved with clarity. And you know what?"

"What?"

"She was right. Once I accepted that Drew was gone and there wasn't anything I could do about it, my mind calmed, and everything else became clear. I know it sucks that grandpa is gone, and he won't be around to do the things with you that he used to, but you have so many wonderful memories of him, and that's what you need to hold onto. It's okay to be sad from time to time, but don't let it consume you so much that you get lost in that sadness and no longer shine."

"Thanks, Uncle Simon." She got up from the lounger and wrapped her arms around my neck. "I feel better."

"Good. So do I, kid. So do I."

"I like that." She smiled.

"Like what?"

"A broken mirror cannot shine. It sounds like something Grace would say."

The corners of my mouth curved upward. "It actually was Grace who said that to me all those years ago."

"Huh?" Her brows furrowed.

"That's a story for another time."

"Okay. I'm going home. I'll see you at Uncle Sebastian's. Come on, Ruby."

The sliding door opened after she walked away, and I felt two beautiful arms wrap themselves around my neck from behind.

"I heard every beautiful word you said to her," Grace whispered in my ear.

"You did?" I turned my head, and my lips met hers.

"Yes." She took a seat on my lap. "I am incredibly turned on right now. How about we have some fun before we head over to Sebastian's?"

She was killing me.

"As nice as that sounds, we need to leave now."

"What?" Her brows furrowed. "We don't have to be there for another forty-five minutes."

"Shit. I forgot to tell you that Sebastian asked if we could come early. He needs my help with something."

"With what?" She cocked her head.

"I don't know. He didn't say. He asked, and I said sure."

"So, you're declining sex with me to help your brother out?"

"As much as it pains me, yes." I scooted her off my lap. "Come on. Grab the pasta salad, and let's go."

I stepped inside the house, and Grace followed behind. I knew this discussion was far from over.

"So that you know, there will be no sex tonight. I'll be too tired from all the wine I'll be drinking. I'm just putting it out there now, so you don't expect anything."

With my back turned, I rolled my eyes as I picked up my guitar case.

"We'll see."

Grace breathed a laugh. "No, detective. I'm serious."

CHAPTER 29

Simon

"Hey, bro." I smiled as I walked over and hugged him. "Follow my lead," I whispered. "What did you want help with?"

"I have to replace a part in the barbecue. Let's go outside."

We stepped out the sliding door and onto the patio.

"A part for the barbecue?" I cocked my head. "How are we going to fake that?"

"We're not. But I do need to replace a part so I can get the steaks going. I was just getting ready to do it before you came so early. What is going on?"

We walked over to the grill.

"Get down here with me while I'm replacing it, so it looks like you're helping."

"I can help," I said.

"Bro, it's a simple fix. It'll take me a minute."

"Well, stretch it out for a few extra minutes."

"What is all this about?" Sebastian asked.

"Grace wanted to have sex before we came here."

"And?" His brows furrowed.

"I want to wait until tonight. So, I made up a story that you asked us to come early because you needed help."

"Ah. I gotcha. Here. Hold this screwdriver and make yourself useful." He smirked. "What if I didn't have to replace this part? Then what? You were just going to put me on the spot like that?"

"Stop being dramatic. And yes, I was. You're quick to think up some lies."

"You're such a douchebag." He laughed as he grabbed the screwdriver from my hand. "There, it's fixed."

"That literally took less than two minutes. We have to make it longer, or she'll suspect something is up. You know her, bro."

"What are the two of you doing down here?" Shaun whispered as he knelt beside us.

"Simon lied to Grace and used me as a cover."

"Ah. About what?"

"She wanted sex before we came over," I said.

"And you lied so you didn't have to do it?" His brows furrowed.

"I want to wait until tonight."

"And? You can't get it up more than once a day?"

Sebastian fell back and started laughing.

"You're a fucking douchebag." I pointed at Shaun. "I want it to be extra special tonight."

"Oh. Okay. Sorry, bro." He grinned as he stood up.

Stefan and Alex walked over with the kids. Alex and Lily went inside, and I took Henry from my brother.

"Come to Uncle Simon, little man."

"Hey. Lily told me about the talk she had with you earlier. Thanks, bro."

"Nah. I was just doing my duty as an uncle."

"Well, you did good. You're going to make a great father one day." He hooked his arm around me.

Once Sam arrived, Sebastian threw the steaks on the grill.

"Have you talked to our cousins?" Sam asked as Shaun handed him a beer.

"I spoke with Nathan today. They'll be here next week."

"Good. I finished the design for the cabin. We can get together at my house tomorrow and go over it."

"Sounds like a plan, bro." I smiled.

After we ate, we helped the girls clean up, and it was almost time to put my plan in motion. A couple of weeks ago, my brothers and I put in a new fire pit on the beach in front of Sebastian's house and placed beach chairs around it. Our family was growing larger than our patios, so we had to do something, especially with our cousins moving next to us.

I grabbed my guitar, took Grace by the hand, and led her to the chairs on the beach. The rest of the family followed and took their seats.

"Dad, can I go home and watch TV?"

"How about you stay with us for a while," Stefan said.

"Dad," she whined.

"Stefan, if she wants to go, let her," Alex said.

"No. She can go after Simon plays us a tune. Deal?" he asked Lily.

"Fine."

"What are you playing for us tonight, detective?" Grace smiled.

"You'll see." I winked at her.

Taking in a deep breath, I started strumming the song *What Would I Do Without You* and sang the lyrics as I stared at Grace, and the smile never left her face. After strumming the last chord, I handed my guitar to Sam and held Grace's hand.

"I honestly don't know what I would do without you,

babe. I never thought in a million years I would fall in love with someone like I have with you."

"Simon, stop it." Tears filled her eyes.

"You have given me a life I never thought I would have. You are the light of my life and the air I breathe every day. Because of you, I'm a better man, and I want to spend the rest of my life thanking you."

I stood from my chair, pulled the ring box from my pocket, and got down on one knee as I held her hand in mine.

"I'm so proud to call you my girlfriend, and I'd be even prouder to call you my wife. Grace, will marry me?" I flipped the top of the box.

She brought her hand up to her mouth as the tears that filled her eyes fell down her face.

"Yes, Simon! Yes! There's nothing I want more than to marry you."

I pulled the ring from the box and slipped it on her finger. My family shouted and clapped as I pulled her from her seat, stood up, and spun her around as I held her tight.

"I love you so much," I kissed her lips.

"I love you more." She grinned.

Lily ran over and hugged us. "I'm so happy for you. I guess this is why my dad wanted me to stay."

I picked her up and kissed her cheek. "Aren't you happy you did?"

"Yeah. Yay! Another wedding."

"It's time to celebrate!" Sebastian shouted as he held up a bottle of champagne.

After pouring us each a glass, he made a toast.

"I never thought I'd see the day when my brother decided he wanted to get married. I'm proud of you, bro, for joining us on the other side." He grinned. "Grace, you're an amazing woman, and there isn't anyone in this world that we'd want our brother to marry. We love you both very much, and we wish you all the happiness in the world. Cheers."

"Cheers!" Everyone shouted.

"Grandpa would be so happy," Lily said.

"He sure would, Lily." I winked at her.

"He's up in heaven watching us right now, isn't he?"

"Yeah. He is." I hugged her.

∽

I thrust in and out of her as several moans echoed through the bedroom. Our bodies were covered in sweat as we couldn't get enough of each other. Her body shook with pleasure as she orgasmed for the second time, making it hard for me to hold back.

"Sorry, baby. I can't hold it anymore," I moaned as I slowed my thrust and buried myself deep inside her while I exploded.

Dropping my body on hers, I buried my face into the side of her neck.

"I love you so much," I whispered as I tried to catch my breath.

"I love you, and I will love you forever." Her arms tightened around me.

I rolled off her and held out my arm as she snuggled against me and held her hand up while she stared at her ring.

"This ring is absolutely gorgeous. You have excellent taste, detective.

"I knew the minute I saw it and held it in my hand that it was meant for you. Can I let you in on a little secret? You can't tell anyone."

"You know all secrets are safe with me."

"Shaun also bought a ring for Jenni."

"What?" She lifted her head. "When is he going to propose to her?"

"I don't know. He doesn't even know. He said he wanted to have the ring for when he decided to. But honestly, I don't think he's in any hurry."

"I'm sure it'll be sooner than we all think." She smiled.

CHAPTER 30

Shaun

"Selena!" I shouted as she walked past my office.

"What's up, boss?"

"I need you to cancel my meeting with the Richter Group this afternoon."

"Okay? What do you want me to tell them?"

"I'm no longer interested in their company."

"You do realize I'm going to get yelled at, right?" She cocked her head.

"I know. You can handle it." I smirked.

She rolled her eyes and walked out of my office.

"Wait! Come back here."

She turned around and stood in the doorway with an irritated look.

"Are you having a bad day or something?" I asked.

"If you want to know the truth, I'm not feeling well."

"Oh. Sorry to hear that. Anyway—you know what? Forget it. I'll do it myself. Make the call to Richter and then take the rest of the day off. Go get some rest."

"Thanks, Shaun. I appreciate it."

"No problem. I hope you feel better."

I grabbed my suit coat and went up to see Stefan and Sam.

"Hey, bro." Sam smiled when I walked into his office.

"Hey. Did you and Stefan pick up your tuxedos yet for the wedding?"

"No. I was going to send Josh to pick them up."

"I'm heading there now, so I can pick them up for you."

"That would be great. Thanks. I'll let Stefan know."

"You're welcome. I'm out of here for the day. I'll drop the tuxes off with Julia and Alex."

"Great." He looked at his watch. "Jackson, Conner, and Nathan should be at their houses in about an hour. I still can't believe they're moving in next to us. It's going to be great seeing them all the time."

"Yeah." I smiled. "I'll talk to you later."

I stopped by the tuxedo shop and picked up our tuxes. As I was walking out, Simon and Grace walked in.

"Hey, bro." Simon smiled. "Did you pick up my tux for me?" He pointed to the four garment bags I had over my shoulder.

"I did. I was going to text you when I got in the car."

"Thanks. Grace and I are on our way to lunch. Why don't you join us?"

I glanced at my watch.

"Okay. I have some time. Where are you going?"

"Excellent." Simon patted my shoulder. "Blue Ribbon Bar & Grill down the street. We can walk after we put the tuxes in our cars."

We reached the Blue Ribbon Bar & Grill and followed the hostess to our table. Stopping dead in my tracks, I stared at Selena sitting in a booth.

"Feeling better, I see," I spoke when I approached.

"Shaun. Hey. Ah, what are you doing here?"

"Having lunch with my brother and his fiancée. What are you doing here? You don't feel well, remember?" I arched my brow.

"I'm meeting Nick for lunch. I texted him to tell him you gave me the rest of the day off and asked him to meet me here."

"Why didn't you just ask for the day off? Why lie to me?"

"I didn't lie. I'm not feeling well at all. But I'm not sick. I'm pregnant."

"Oh. Congratulations." I smiled. "Why didn't you tell me?"

"I just found out a couple of days ago. That's the reason I'm meeting Nick. He doesn't know I'm pregnant yet."

"Wouldn't it be better to tell him in private?"

"No, because I'm not sure how he will react. He doesn't want kids. So, telling him in a public setting is safer."

"Safer how? Does he—"

"No. God, no. He would never. We've talked about it before, and we agreed we didn't want kids. But now that I'm pregnant, I'm really happy."

"Okay. I'll be right over there if you need me." I placed my hand on her shoulder.

"Hey, Shaun." Nick walked over with a smile and shook my hand. "Are you joining us?"

"No. I'm here with my brother. I just wanted to say hello to Selena before I sat down. You two enjoy your lunch." I gave her a sympathetic look before walking away.

"I ordered you a scotch," Simon said as I slid into the seat across from him and Grace.

"Thanks. You're not drinking?"

"No. We're still on the clock," Grace spoke.

We placed our lunch order, and I kept looking over at Selena.

"Bro, why do you keep staring at your assistant?" Simon's brow arched.

"I'm keeping an eye on her and Nick."

"Why?" Grace asked.

"Because Selena just found out she's pregnant, and Nick doesn't want kids. She said it's safer to tell him in a public setting."

"Oh! Good thing we're here then." Grace smiled. "I'm more than ready to intervene if necessary."

"Do you have any plans for tonight?" Simon asked.

"My friends Asher and Everly Remington are flying in and staying with us for the night. I'm taking them to Four Kinds for dinner."

"Wow. I didn't know you had friends." He smirked, and Grace smacked his arm.

"Very funny, douchebag. They're my friends from New York. Asher is in the same line of business I am, so we're meeting about a potential business we want to take over."

"I'd love to meet them before or after dinner."

"Sure. We'll probably be out on the patio later, so come by. But there is something I feel I should tell you about his wife, Everly. Just in case."

"Like?" Simon's brows furrowed.

"She's special."

"Special how?"

"She sees things."

"Bro, I'm lost." Simon's brows furrowed.

"Is she a psychic or something?" Grace asked.

"Yeah. Something like that."

"You can't be serious." Simon chuckled.

"That is so cool. I cannot wait to meet her!" Grace beamed.

I glanced over at Selena and saw things were going well. Nick was gripping her hands from across the table, and it looked like he had tears in his eyes. After we finished lunch, Simon and Grace went back to the station, and I headed home to make sure everything was clean for when Asher and Everly arrived. I'd left the house this morning before Jenni did, and her version and my version of clean were totally different.

Before I stepped into the house, I ran the tuxedos over to Julia and Alex. When I walked into Julia's house, I saw Lucas picking up the toys in the living room.

"Hi, Shaun." He smiled.

"Uh, hi. Is Julia here?"

"No. She's at the coffee shop."

"With the girls?"

"No." He laughed. "I'm babysitting."

"Oh." My brows furrowed.

"I guess she didn't tell you. We're doing a trial run. She needs a nanny, and I could use a part-time job while I work on my paintings."

"Well, that's great. What are your qualifications with children?"

He cocked his head as a smirk crossed his face.

"Sorry. They're my nieces, and I'm an overprotective uncle."

"No worries. I practically raised my seven brothers and sisters, and I worked at a daycare center for the last five years."

"Good enough for me." I smiled. "Speaking of my nieces, where are they?"

"I just put them down for their afternoon nap. A regular schedule is key. I was just cleaning up in here before I started cleaning the kitchen."

"You clean too?"

"Yeah. I'm a little bit of a clean freak. I like the environment I'm in to be clean and organized."

"Does Sam know this?"

"I don't know." He shrugged.

"You know. If things don't work out for you here, I have a job for you at my house."

"Thanks." He laughed. "I'll keep that in mind. Can I take that from you?" He pointed to the garment bag.

"Yes. It's Sam's tuxedo for the wedding."

"I'll go put it up in their bedroom." He took the garment bag from me.

"Thanks, Lucas. I have to run. I'll catch you later."

"Bye, Shaun."

Damn. I liked him. Pulling out my phone, I called Sam.

"Talk to me, bro," he answered.

"You didn't tell me you were doing a trial run with Lucas. I just ran into him at your house."

"Oh shit. I forgot he was coming today. Julia sprung the news on me last night. Was it chaos at the house?"

"Are you kidding? He had just put the girls down for a nap, and he was getting ready to start cleaning. He said he likes the environment he's in to be clean and organized."

"Damn. The trial run is over as far as I'm concerned. I'm hiring him permanently when I get home."

"I told him if things don't work out with you, I have a job for him at my place."

"Bro, you keep your distance from my nanny."

"Yeah. Yeah. I'll let you go. I just got home."

"Okay. Talk to you later," Sam said as he ended the call.

I went upstairs to the guestroom, ran the dust cloth over the dresser and nightstands, and ensured the guest bathroom was spotless. It already was since no one ever used it, but I did a quick clean anyway. Jenni had walked in by the time I was done washing the wood floors.

"It smells like lemons in here," she spoke as she walked over to where I stood and kissed me. "Did you rewash the floors?"

"For your information, floors should be washed once a week."

"It's only been three days, Shaun."

"And we have company coming to stay with us."

She placed her hand on my chest. "You have issues, but I love you anyway." She turned away and walked up the stairs.

"Gee, thanks, babe. Love you too." I shouted.

CHAPTER 31

Shaun

As I glanced at my watch, the doorbell rang. Walking over to the door, I opened it and greeted my friends from New York.

"Asher, it's good to see you." I smiled as I hugged him.

"Good to see you too, Shaun. It's been way too long."

"Everly, you look just as beautiful as ever." I hugged her.

"And you look very happy. California suits you." She grinned.

"Come in." I took their suitcases.

"What a gorgeous home, Shaun," Everly spoke as she looked around.

"Thanks, Everly. I'm very happy here."

Jenni walked down the stairs, and I introduced her.

"Jenni, this is Asher Remington and his wife, Everly. This is my girlfriend, Jenni."

"It's a pleasure to meet you, Jenni." Asher extended his hand.

"It's so great to meet you. Thank you for inviting us into your home." Everly smiled as they shook hands.

"We're happy to have you," Jenni spoke.

I poured Asher and myself a glass of scotch while Jenni poured herself and Everly a glass of wine. Taking our drinks out to the patio, we sat down in the loungers.

"So, Shaun told me you can "see" things," Jenni said.

"Jenni!" I cocked my head at her.

"What? I didn't know it was a secret."

"It's okay, Shaun." Everly laughed. "It's not a secret, and yes, I do have a gift."

"That is so cool," Jenni spoke.

"It can be, but it can also be annoying."

"Is your dad still hanging around?" I asked Asher.

"Every once in a while."

"Oh. Your dad lives with the two of you?" Jenni asked.

"Not exactly. He refuses to move on," Everly said.

"Move on?" Jenni furrowed her brows. "Wait. Is he—"

"Yes," Asher spoke. "Very much so."

"Wow." Jenni chugged her wine.

It was time to head to Four Kinds for dinner. When we walked in, we were immediately seated at an outside table that Sebastian reserved for us.

"What a great restaurant." Everly smiled.

Sebastian walked over with a smile on his face and an expensive bottle of wine.

"Welcome to Four Kinds," he spoke to Everly and Asher.

"This is my brother and fine owner of this place, Sebastian. Sebastian, this is Asher and Everly."

"It's good to meet you." He shook Asher's hand. And it's a pleasure to meet you, Everly." He extended his hand to her.

"Congratulations on your marriage." Everly smiled.

"Thanks. I can't believe the wedding is next weekend." The corners of his mouth curved upward.

She cocked her head at him. "Weren't you recently married in Vegas."

Sebastian glanced over at me, and I put my hands up.

"I didn't say a word. I swear."

Everly laughed. "It's okay. I promise not to tell." She gave him a wink.

We talked, laughed, and had great conversations as we enjoyed our dinner. Jenni and Everly hit it off immediately like I knew they would. We left the restaurant and headed back to my house. After lighting the fire pit, I grabbed the four of us some beer, and we sat down on the beach.

While we talked, Everly kept staring down at either Sebastian's or Jackson's house.

"Is everything okay?" Asher asked her.

"I'm not sure." She stood up from her chair and started walking down the beach.

"Asher?" I asked him.

"I'm assuming there's something she has to do."

Asher, Jenni, and I all stood up and followed her down to Jackson's house. When we stepped through the sliding door, Jackson, Conner, and Nathan were standing in the empty kitchen talking with my brothers.

"Hey, bro." Simon grinned. "We were just going to come out and join you."

"Everyone, these are my friends from New York, Asher and Everly Remington."

Everly began walking up the stairs, and Jackson glanced over at me. I gave him a shrug, and we followed her to the primary bedroom and over to the large walk-in closet.

"Is there something wrong?" Jackson asked her.

"He has unfinished business here," she spoke as she knelt down inside the closet.

"Who?" Jackson asked.

"Your uncle."

Jackson whipped his head around and looked at me. Jenni grabbed my arm and squeezed it.

"Is he here?" Jenni asked.

"Yes, he is."

She moved to the very back of the closet, where one of the floor planks was loose. The corner popped up after pushing on it, and she lifted the board. She pulled out a small wooden box and handed it to me.

"Your father wants you to have this."

I looked at Jenni and my brothers as I slowly lifted the lid. Inside were photos of my mother and me when I was younger. They were photographs of different stages in my life.

"What the fuck," Simon spoke as he stood over my shoulder.

I stared at the photos as my heart beat out of my chest.

"He knew the whole time," I softly spoke. "He knew I was his son."

"This is crazy." Sam rubbed the back of his neck.

"This—this was his unfinished business?" I angrily asked Everly.

"Yes. He had kept tabs on you and your mother since you were born."

"Just another lie." Simon shook his head. "If he weren't already dead, I would have killed him myself."

"He says he's sorry, and he should have told you the truth, but he was afraid you would never have forgiven him if he had."

"Way to go, Dad!" Stefan shouted.

"So, I guess the story about his "friend" seeing Shaun's mother and Shaun was also a lie," Sam spoke.

"He wants me to tell you boys that he loves you very much, and if he could go back and change things, he would. He wanted you to have the pictures of your mother, Shaun."

I put the pictures back in the box and closed the lid.

"We could have had more time together if he'd only acknowledged me from the start."

"Trust me, bro. You were better off." Simon squeezed my shoulder.

"I'm sorry, Shaun. I had no choice. He wouldn't stop until I gave you the box."

"Sounds like him." Sebastian shook his head.

"How did he find out my mother was pregnant? Is he still here?"

"Yes. He's here," Everly spoke. "Six months after he moved to California, he flew back to New York for a business meeting. He was having lunch outside at a restaurant and saw her walk by. He says he had to use every bit of strength not to go after her. So, he hired a private investigator in New York to find out what he could after you were born. Once it was confirmed that you were his son, he kept tabs on you. Even though he never reached out to you, he still loved you very much."

"What's going on in here?" I heard Lily's voice in the doorway.

We all turned around and looked at her.

"We're just checking out the room, baby girl," Stefan said.

"Lily, come here." Everly held out her hand.

Stefan took a step forward to stop her, and I grabbed hold of his arm.

"Who are you?" Lily asked as she took Everly's hand.

"My name is Everly, and I'm a friend of your Uncle Shaun's. I have a message for you from your grandfather."

"Okay."

"He wants you to know that he's okay, and he doesn't want you to be sad. He loves you so much, and he will always be watching over you."

"I see him in my dreams sometimes," Lily spoke.

"Remember those dreams and always carry them with you." Everly smiled.

"I need a fu—drink," Simon said.

"Me too, bro." Sam hooked his arm around him, and they walked out of the room.

"Come on, Lily." Stefan held out his hand to her.

"Umm, is he gone?" Jackson asked. "Because I really don't need Uncle Henry hanging around my house."

"Yeah. No shit. That's weird," Conner spoke.

"He's gone," Everly said.

"For good?" Shaun asked.

"He moved on." She placed her hand on my arm before walking out of the room.

"Are you okay, Cous?" Nathan asked.

"I don't know. The past is the past, and it's better left there."

We all left the room and headed downstairs. Over by the sliding door was Jackson's guitar.

"Do you mind?" I asked Jackson.

"Not at all."

I grabbed his guitar and took it down to the beach, where we all sat down in front of the fire. Giving the guitar a strum to ensure it was in tune, I strummed the chords and sang *Nobody Knows*.

I wasn't sure how I felt. A part of me was angry, and the other part was numb. As I looked around at my family, I felt nothing but love and support. They were the reason why I was here and chose to stay in California, especially the beautiful woman sitting next to me. What my father did in his life, he had his reasons—reasons none of us would ever understand. The secrets and the lies were ones he'd have to spend eternity with, not us.

CHAPTER 32

ONE WEEK LATER

*S*ebastian

"Are you ready to do this again?" Sam smirked as he patted my arm.

"As ready as I'll ever be." I patted his back.

The five of us left the suite and took our places next to the floral archway in the Crystal Gardens at the Beverly Hills Hotel. I didn't know why I was so nervous. We were already married. I looked at my cousins, who were sitting in the front row. Conner gave me a thumbs up and a smile. I'd told them about our Vegas wedding when we got back. We told them everything because they were more like brothers to us than cousins.

The music started, and the bridesmaids began to walk down the aisle one by one. When Alex started to walk down, I whispered to Stefan.

"Alex looks stunning but huge in that dress."

"Don't tell her that. I made that mistake this morning, and she started bawling her eyes out. It took me over fifteen minutes to apologize and convince her that I wasn't suggesting she was fat."

Lily made her entrance as a junior bridesmaid and looked like the royal highness she was. The wedding march began, and the moment I saw my wife walking down the aisle on her father's arm, tears filled my eyes. As she approached, her father shook my hand and placed his daughter's hand in mine. We smiled at each other as we took our place under the archway, and I lifted her veil.

"You are the most beautiful woman I've ever seen." I grinned.

"More beautiful than the first time?" she whispered and gave me a wink and a smile.

The minister spoke a few words. We exchanged our wedding vows, exchanged rings for the second time, and we were once again Mr. and Mrs. Sebastian Kind.

"I present to you Mr. and Mrs. Sebastian Kind. You may kiss your bride," the minister spoke.

Everyone stood from their seats, shouted, and clapped as our lips met.

"I'm so happy we finally get to wear our wedding bands." Emilia smiled.

"Me too. It's been hard, babe. Really freaking hard." I kissed her lips again. "I love you, my beautiful wife."

"I love you, my handsome husband."

We walked up the aisle hand in hand and climbed into the limo, where the driver was taking us to a different spot to have wedding photos taken.

"Jenni, you outdid yourself with Emilia's dress." I smiled as I kissed her cheek.

"Thank you, Sebastian."

"Alex, you look gorgeous." I kissed her cheek.

"Thank you, but I look like a beached whale." She shot Stefan a look.

"Babe, that is not what I said."

"I'm siding with Alex," Grace spoke. "She told us how you said it."

"I—"

Simon placed his hand on Stefan's shoulder. "Don't, bro. It's not worth it. Just accept that you were in the wrong and move on."

After pictures were taken, we headed back to the Beverly Hills Hotel and into the Crystal Ballroom, where our reception took place.

"How is Lucas working out?" I asked Sam as we stood and stared at him with the twins.

"He's incredible. Julia is less stressed, which makes me less stressed. The girls have slept through the entire night all week. We couldn't believe it. I can't remember the last time I slept so much. And the house is spotless. It's like a breath of fresh air when I walk through the door."

"That's awesome." I chuckled.

Simon walked over and placed his hand on my back.

"Great reception, bro."

"You and Grace are getting married here, right? It's a family tradition now."

"Probably. Grace seems to really like it here. Are Alex and Stefan looking after Ruby while you're on your honeymoon?"

"Yeah. She loves playing with Lily and Henry."

⁓

We'd spent our wedding night in a suite at the hotel, had a great breakfast with our family, and headed home to finish packing for our honeymoon in the Maldives.

"Hey. There are the newlyweds." Jackson smiled as he walked through the sliding door.

"Hey, cous." I hugged him.

"I hope I'm not interrupting, but I wanted to speak to Emilia before you two left for your honeymoon."

"Of course, Jackson." Emilia smiled. "Can I get you a cup of coffee?"

"No. Thanks. I've had enough already trying to get rid of this hangover."

"Come sit down. What did you want to talk about?" Emilia asked.

"Conner, Nathan, and I would like you to move your pediatric practice to our medical center."

"Really?"

"Yeah. It's only a mile from where you're at now. You'll have a bigger space, and your new patient growth will be astronomical. Our mission is to be an all-in-one medical center. We want to hire various specialties under one roof, so patients have all their options in one building instead of driving from one place to another every time they have to see a doctor. For example, we'll have a position open for an OB/GYN. That doctor will refer their patients to you as a pediatrician for their child."

"I really like that idea," she spoke.

"I think it sounds awesome," I said.

"Anyway, take a look at my proposal." Jackson handed Emilia a legal-sized envelope. "Give it some thought and let me know."

"I definitely will. Thank you, Jackson."

"You're welcome, Emilia." He stood up from his seat. "You two have a wonderful honeymoon, and I'll see you when you return." He gave us each a hug.

I ran upstairs, grabbed our luggage, and brought them downstairs just as the car service pulled up to drive us to the hanger where Shaun's plane was waiting for us.

"Are you ready to go honeymooning, Mrs. Kind?" I asked with a smile.

"I'm more than ready, Mr. Kind. Should we say goodbye to Ruby one last time before we go?"

"Nah. We said goodbye earlier when we dropped her off at Stefan's. She is in her happy place."

CHAPTER 33

TWO MONTHS LATER

Stefan

I was sitting in Sam's office talking about the renovations for the cabin when Jackson walked in.

"Hey, cous." I smiled.

"Hey, Jackson. What brings you by?"

"I was just downstairs in a meeting with Shaun, and I thought I'd come up and see how my douchebag cousins were doing." His lips formed a smirk.

"Where's Conner and Nathan?" I asked.

"They're at the medical center. More of the equipment is coming today."

"By the way, who was the girl leaving your house so early this morning?" I smiled.

"Just some chick I picked up at the bar last night."

"I remember those days." Sam grinned as he leaned back in his chair.

"You do not." I laughed. "You only slept with your assistants."

"Shut the fuck up." He picked up a paper clip and threw it at me.

"Is there a party going on here?" Alex smiled when she stepped into Sam's office.

"Hey, babe. I didn't realize what time it was." I got up from my seat and kissed her. "Are you okay?" I asked because she didn't look too well.

"I'm fine. I've been having Braxton hicks all morning."

"Are you sure you want to go to lunch? I can take you home."

"Stop worrying. I'm fine. The baby isn't due for another three weeks. It's just Braxton hicks. I had them with Henry."

"Okay. Wait. Where's Lily and Henry?"

"They're over at Sam's. When I went to tell Lily it was time to leave, she said she wanted to stay, and Lucas told me to leave Henry. Who was I to turn him down? It's not very often I get to have lunch with my handsome husband alone."

"True. Very true." I hooked my arm around her. "How lucky am I to have lunch with a beautiful woman?" A grin crossed my face. "See ya, bro. See ya, Jackson."

"I'll head out with you. I need to get back to the medical center. See ya, Sam."

"Bye, guys."

We walked to the elevator, pushed the button, and waited for it to come up.

"What is taking so long?" Alex asked.

"It's been doing this all day. It'll be up in a second. Don't forget, Jackson. We're surfing tomorrow morning."

"I haven't forgotten. We'll be there."

The doors opened, and we stepped inside. Jackson pushed the button to the lobby, and the elevator started to go down. Suddenly, it jerked, and I grabbed onto Alex.

"Shit!"

"Don't tell me it's stuck." Jackson let out a sigh.

"It's not stuck." I frantically began pushing all the buttons.

I pushed the emergency call button, and Howard came over the speaker.

"We're aware the elevator is stuck between floors. How many people are in the elevator?"

"Howard, it's Stefan."

"Hey, Stefan. Who's in there with you?"

"My very pregnant wife and my cousin Jackson. What the hell is going on?"

"We're not sure. It's been having issues all day."

"Then why didn't you shut it down?"

"It was just slow. Nothing major."

"Well, now it's major."

"Hold on. Let me get the maintenance crew. I'll be back in a few."

"Damnit." I rubbed the back of my neck. I turned and looked at Alex, who was gripping her belly. "Are you okay, babe?"

"I'm not sure. These are some pretty strong Braxton hicks."

"How long have you had them?" Jackson asked.

"Since I woke up this morning, but they're getting stronger."

"You could be in labor, Alex," he spoke.

"No. I've been through this before. It's Braxton hicks. I'm just going to sit down on the floor."

"Okay, babe." I took her hand and helped her down.

I turned and looked at Jackson. "Sorry about this."

"Nah. It's not your fault. We'll be out of here soon enough."

"Stefan," Howard spoke. "Umm. Bad news."

"Don't say that, Howard."

"Our guys don't know the problem, so we had to call the elevator company. They'll be here in about an hour."

"An hour!" I shouted.

"I'm sorry. There's nothing else I can do. Just sit tight."

"Sit tight, he says. How does one sit tight stuck in an elevator?" I asked Jackson.

"Might as well make ourselves comfortable," Jackson spoke. "It's not the first time I've been stuck in an elevator. At least I have you two. The last elevator I was stuck in was with some claustrophobic guy who cried the entire time while having panic attacks."

"If he was claustrophobic, why was he in the elevator?"

"He had a broken foot and had no choice. It was the worst thirty minutes of my life." He laughed. "I had to keep doing visualization techniques with him."

I couldn't help but laugh.

"Stefan!" I heard Alex's panicked voice.

I turned around and saw her looking down. Instantly, my eyes caught sight of the puddle underneath her.

"Is that what I think it is?"

"My water broke."

"Oh boy," Jackson said.

I ran to the panel and pushed the emergency call button.

"Howard!" I yelled.

"Nothing yet, Stefan."

"I need you to listen to me. My wife's water just broke, and she's having contractions. You need to get this damn elevator working so we can get to the hospital."

"I'll call the elevator company again and find out how much longer."

"Oh, God!" Alex yelled.

"Babe, I'm here." I grabbed hold of her hand as I looked up at Jackson.

He glanced at his watch. "We have to time her contractions. If they start coming closer together and we're still stuck in here, we're going to have to deliver your baby."

"I am not having my baby in an elevator!" she yelled through gritted teeth.

"No. You're not, babe. We're going to get out of here, and you're going to have our little girl at the hospital as we planned."

She let out another yell and threw her head back.

"Stefan, take off your suit coat and place it under Alex's head. Alex, you need to lie down."

I took off my suit coat and placed it under Alex's head as I helped her lay on her back with her knees up.

"Oh, God!" she yelled again.

"Stefan, the company is twenty minutes out," Howard spoke over the speaker.

"Howard, I'm Dr. Jackson Kind. I need you to call 911 and tell them to send a mother and child ambulance service. Tell the operator that there's a pregnant woman in labor who is about to give birth."

"Okay. I'll do it now."

"I am not having my baby in an elevator!" Alex yelled. "Oh, God! It hurts, Stefan."

"I know, babe." I brought her hand up to my lips.

"The contractions are too close. Alex, I need to check you and see how far you're dilated."

"Really?" I furrowed my brows at him. "Have you ever delivered a baby before?"

"I'm a doctor, Stefan."

"You're a brain surgeon."

"I've delivered many babies. Alex, I'm going to check now, okay?"

She nodded her head and squeezed my hand.

"You've already dilated to six and ninety percent effaced."

"No. I can't be. Stefan, do something. I can't have our baby here." Tears filled her eyes.

"Listen to me. You're safe, and our baby is safe. Jackson is here with us, and he knows what he's doing."

"Really? Because just two seconds ago, you doubted my ability to deliver your baby."

"Yeah. Well, I'm panicking here."

"Ow!" Alex screamed.

"Breathe, babe. Breathe. I love you so much." I kissed her forehead.

"Stefan, the elevator company just arrived. Hang on," Howard spoke.

"Is the ambulance here yet?" Jackson asked.

"Yes. They're here and ready."

"Stefan." I heard Sam's voice over the speaker. "How's Alex?"

"She's hanging in there, bro."

"No, I'm not!" she yelled as another contraction hit.

"Try to relax, sweetheart. They're fixing the elevator now. It'll all be over with soon."

"No. She's coming now. Jackson, I have to push. I have to push."

"Don't push yet, Alex. Damn. You're dilated to ten. This baby is coming right now. Stefan, get behind her and hold her."

I scooted behind and positioned her, so she was between my legs with her back pressed against me.

"You got this, babe."

CHAPTER 34

Stefan

"When the next contraction hits, I want you to bear down and push," Jackson said.

Alex let out a scream as she started pushing.

"That's it, baby. You're doing great."

"That was good, Alex. Try to relax."

"I can't. It hurts so fucking bad!"

"I know it does." I lowered my head and pressed my lips against her forehead. "Remember how much pain I was in after the vasectomy."

"Bad choice of words, cous." Jackson shook his head.

"Are you seriously comparing your little ass vasectomy to my pushing out a human being?!" she yelled.

"No. No. I'm not."

Alex let out another scream as she pushed.

"Alex, stop pushing," Jackson said.

"I can't. I have to. I need this kid out of me!"

"Alex, the baby is in a breech position."

"What?" I furrowed my brows. "Oh my, God."

"No!" Alex cried.

Jackson leaned closer to her and wiped the tears from her eyes.

"Listen to me," he spoke in a calm voice. "I need to turn the baby around, but I need you calm and relaxed. So, I want you to take slow deep breaths. That's it. That's it. Good."

"Have you ever turned a baby before?" I asked with fear.

"Now is not the time to ask me that. Okay, Alex, I'm going to try and turn her."

I was filled with fear. Even though I trusted my cousin with my life, I was still scared as hell. Alex let out several screams as Jackson tried to turn our daughter.

"Come on, baby girl. You can do it. Just a little more," Jackson spoke.

I watched as he let out a sigh of relief.

"Her head is down and exactly where it's supposed to be. You know what to do, Alex."

She screamed as she pushed as hard as she could.

"That's it, Alex. I see her head." Jackson smiled as Alex fell back into me. "A couple more pushes, and you'll be able to meet your daughter."

"I can't. I'm so tired, and I don't have any strength left in me," Alex spoke in a weary voice.

"You can do it, babe. You're strong, and I love you and our little girl so much. It's time to meet her."

The screaming started as beads of sweat poured from her forehead.

"That's it, Alex. One huge push. She's almost here."

Tears filled my eyes as I saw my daughter's head, and within seconds, she was out.

"Congratulations." Jackson smiled as our baby took her first breath and started crying.

"Look at her, Alex. She's beautiful." Tears ran down my face. "You did it. I'm so proud of you." I pressed my lips against her as Jackson placed our daughter on Alex.

Suddenly, the elevator started moving, and as soon as the doors opened, the paramedics were standing there with a stretcher and blankets. They quickly ran in, placed Alex and the baby on the stretcher, and covered them with a blanket.

As soon as Jackson and I stepped out of the elevator, I hugged him.

"Thank you. I don't know how I can ever repay you for this. Thank God you were in that elevator with us. Alex and the baby could have—"

"Stop. Alex and the baby are perfectly healthy. And you don't ever need to repay me. I'm happy I was in that elevator too. It's been a long time since I delivered a baby." He smiled.

Sam and Shaun ran over to us.

"How's Alex?" Shaun asked.

"She and the baby are fine."

"Congratulations, Dad." Sam hugged me.

"Congrats, bro." Shaun hugged me. "Nice job, Dr. Kind."

"All in a day's work." Jackson smiled.

"Sir, we're ready to take your wife and your daughter to the hospital," the paramedic said.

"I'll catch you guys later!" I grinned as I hopped in the back of the ambulance.

I sat there and stared at my daughter.

"Hi, Aurora Nicole. I'm your daddy. Your mom and I have waited a long time to meet you." I softly stroked her head. "You are beautiful, just like your mommy." I looked at Alex. "I love you so much. Thank you. Thank you for giving me this precious gift."

"I love you too, Stefan. I can't believe I had her in an elevator." She began to laugh.

"Mom, Dad!" Lily ran into the hospital room and hugged me.

"Hey, bab—Lily." I smiled.

She turned to Alex, who was holding Aurora.

"Hi, Rori. I'm your sister, Lily. We are calling her Rori, right?"

"Yes, sweetheart." Alex smiled.

My mother walked in holding Henry and handed him to me.

"Congratulations." She smiled as she kissed my cheek. "You're a star, Alex," she spoke as she placed her hand on Alex's arm. "Who needs a conventional birth in a hospital, right?"

"Right." The corner of Alex's mouth curved upward.

"Thank goodness Jackson was there. I'm not sure how Stefan would have handled the situation alone," my mother spoke.

"Gee. Thanks, Mom. I would have delivered my daughter if I had to."

"Of course, dear." She smirked as she patted my cheek.

My brothers and the girls walked in, and the room was filled with family who came to welcome Aurora.

"Damn." Simon grinned as he hugged me. "Good thing Jackson was in that elevator with you."

"Why does everyone keep saying that? I could have done it."

"Keep telling yourself that, bro." He smirked. "Anyway, she's gorgeous. Good thing she's the spitting image of Alex."

"Shut the hell up." I punched his arm, and he laughed.

"Congrats, bro." Sebastian walked over, and we hugged."

"Don't say it," I spoke.

"I wasn't going to. But now that you brought it up, it's a good thing Jackson was there."

CHAPTER 35

Shaun

"What a great movie." Jenni smiled as her arm was wrapped around me.

"Mhm, it was okay."

"Oh, come on." She laughed as we walked down the street. "It was so romantic."

"I saw zero chemistry between the main characters. You and I have more chemistry times a billion than they did."

Jenni let out a laugh. "True." She laid her head on my shoulder. "I have a craving."

"Oh yeah? We'll be home soon." I kissed her head.

"Not for that." She laughed. "I want ice cream. A double scoop of chocolate chip cookie dough in a waffle cone. There's an ice cream shop by where we parked."

"Ice cream it is."

"I'll thank you later." She grinned as she lifted her head from my shoulder.

"I know you will." I winked at her.

We walked to the ice cream shop, ordered our cones, and sat outside. It was ten p.m., and we were on our way home.

As I took exit 21 to get on I-10, I saw bright headlights approaching us at a high speed.

"Shaun!" Jenni screamed.

My arm flew out and pressed up against her as I gasped, and I tried to swerve and slam on the brakes, but it didn't matter. The deafening sound, the deployment of the airbags, and the shattered glass falling on us as the car flipped over. Everything went black. Slowing opening my eyes, I could hear the sirens approaching. Looking over at Jenni, she was unconscious, and suddenly I'd felt as if all the air had been sucked out of me.

"Jenni." I placed my hand on her shoulder and shook it. "Baby, wake up!" I screamed.

She quietly moaned as she slowly opened her eyes. Blood dripped down her face from the large gash on her forehead and the one on her cheek.

"Shaun."

"Don't move, baby."

"My arm. I can't move it. It hurts so bad."

"Shh. It'll be okay. I promise. Help is coming."

I was so worried about her that I didn't notice I was also bleeding. The sirens grew closer, and suddenly, I heard voices.

"Don't move. We're going to get you out," I heard someone say.

After prying the doors open, they carefully removed Jenni and me from the vehicle.

Jenni was crying my name, and it killed me not to be able to help her.

"It looks like her arm is broken." I heard the paramedic attending to her yell.

One of the police officers was by my side in an instant.

"Shaun? Oh my God."

"I need you to call Simon right now."

"Of course."

~

Simon

My brothers, cousins, and I were sitting in front of the fire pit at my house when my phone rang.

"Who the hell is calling me this late?" I said as I picked up my phone from the side table.

"Probably another murder," Stefan said as he brought the beer bottle up to his lips.

"Detective Kind," I answered.

"Detective, it's Lawrence."

"What's up, Lawrence?"

"I'm at the scene of an accident. It's your brother Shaun and Jenni."

"What?" I yelled as I abruptly stood up from my seat. "Are they okay?"

"They're banged up pretty badly, and I heard the paramedic say that Jenni's arm was broken. The car was flipped over when we got here."

"And the other car?"

"They're loading the driver into the ambulance now."

"I'll be honest with you, Simon. It's a miracle your brother and Jenni are alive. The paramedics are taking them to Cedars-Sinai right now."

"We're on our way. Thanks, Lawrence."

"What the fuck happened?" Sam asked.

"Shaun and Jenni were in a car accident. All I know is they're banged up pretty bad, and Jenni's arm is broken."

"Broken arms are my specialty," Conner said as he and everyone else jumped up.

"I'll meet you guys there," I said as I ran into the house. "Grace!" I ran up the stairs and into our bedroom.

"Simon, what's wrong?"

"Shaun and Jenni were in a bad car accident."

She jumped up from the bed, threw on a pair of jeans and a top, and we flew out the door.

Jenni

The pain in my arm was nothing to the severe abdominal cramping I had. Tears streamed from my eyes, and I wanted Shaun.

"My stomach. I'm having severe abdominal cramping," I said to the paramedic.

He pulled back the blanket and looked at his partner, who was on the other side of me. I could feel myself drifting in and out of consciousness. I wanted to escape all the pain, so I closed my eyes.

The paramedics rushed me into the ER while they rattled off my stats as they took me into a room.

"Jenni? Jenni?" I heard a woman's voice say.

"Are you pregnant?"

"No."

"I want a blood panel drawn, stat," she said.

Suddenly, Conner and Jackson ran into the room.

"Hey, you." Conner gave me a sympathetic smile as he leaned over me. "I hear you have a broken arm. I'm going to take care of it for you. I want x-rays stats!" he told the nurse.

"Jenni, follow the light," Jackson said as he shined his penlight in my eyes, and I immediately closed them.

"Did the light hurt your eyes?" he asked.

"I can't stay awake. I have to go to sleep."

Jackson

"I want a CT scan with contrast now!" I yelled.

"As soon as I'm done with this ultrasound," Dr. Smithfield said.

I stared at the monitor and then looked at Conner as he looked down at Jenni.

"Call OB down here," Dr. Smithfield said.

I tore off my gown and threw it in the trash as I walked out of the room and down to where Nathan was stitching up Shaun.

"How is she, Jackson?" Shaun asked with worry.

"Her arm is broken, and she has a concussion. I've ordered a CT scan to ensure there's nothing else going on."

"Do you think I give two shits whether I'm allowed back there or not!" I heard Simon yelling from the hallway.

Stepping out of Shaun's room, I hooked my arm around Simon.

"It's okay. He can come back here," I told the nurse.

"You can see Shaun, but not Jenni right now."

"Why?"

"She's going into CT. Nathan is stitching up Shaun."

After taking Simon to where Shaun was, I took a seat next to Conner in the control room. As the images of her brain started appearing on the screen, I stared at them.

"Okay. Everything looks good on my end."

"Now, let's look at her arm," Conner said. "Shit." He sighed. "I'm going to have to go in."

"Yeah. I'd say you do."

CHAPTER 36

Simon

"What the hell happened," I spoke as I walked in and placed my hand on Shaun's shoulder.

"I was on 21, and suddenly, this car was coming straight at us. There was nowhere to go, Stefan. She could have been killed." Tears filled my eyes.

"She wasn't, and neither were you. As much as I hate to say this, I think Dad was watching over you two."

"Her arm is broken, and she has a concussion. That's all they'll tell me. I need to see her." He went to get up.

"Whoa. Don't move," Nathan said. "Do you want me to wreck this pretty face of yours?"

"Calm down," My grip on his shoulder tightened. "You'll see her soon. I promise. I'll be right back."

I walked over to Lawrence, standing at the nurses' station.

"How is the driver of the other car?" I asked.

"They just took him up to surgery for a ruptured spleen."

"Who is he?"

"His name is Mitch Caldwell, and he's forty-six years old.

He's beyond drunk and positive for meth. We'll have to wait to question him in the morning."

"I want to be there when you do."

I walked out to the waiting room where my family was.

"Simon, what's happening?" Julia ran over to me.

"Shaun has some bruises and a broken rib. Nathan is stitching up his cuts. As far as I know, Jenni has a broken arm and a concussion. She's in CT right now with Conner and Jackson."

"Did you get the info on the other driver?" Grace asked.

"Yeah. We're questioning him in the morning. He's in surgery right now for a ruptured spleen. Not only was he drunk, but he was also high on meth."

"Oh my, God," Grace wrapped her arms around me.

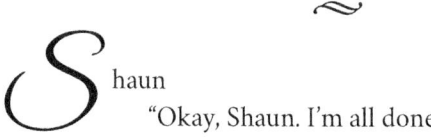

Shaun

"Okay, Shaun. I'm all done."

"Thanks, Nathan."

Conner and Jackson walked into the room, and I could tell by the looks on their faces that something was wrong.

"How's Jenni?"

"She's going to be okay, Shaun," Conner said as he walked over to the bed. "I'm going to have to do surgery on her arm. It's bad, and I need to put in a plate and some screws so the bone will heal properly."

"Okay. And her CT scan?" I looked at Jackson.

"No injuries except a concussion."

"Thank God." I blew out a breath.

"Shaun, there's something else, and we told the attending doctor that we would tell you ourselves."

"What?" My brows furrowed.

"Jenni had a miscarriage."

"What?" Tears filled my eyes. "She was pregnant?"

"Yeah. But she didn't know she was. The doctor said she was about seven weeks."

I placed my hand over my mouth as the tears streamed down my face. Jackson grabbed my hand and gave it a gentle squeeze.

"I'm so sorry."

"Does she know?" I asked.

"They just told her," Conner spoke.

"I have to see her!"

"Okay. Let me get a wheelchair, and I'll take you to her," Jackson said.

"When are you doing the surgery?" I asked Conner.

"As soon as possible. I don't want to risk any more injury to it. So, go see her while they're getting her prepped."

Jackson grabbed a wheelchair from the hallway, helped me into it, and wheeled me down to where Jenni was. When I entered the room, she was sobbing. Jackson wheeled me to her bedside, and I grabbed her hand.

"I'm here, baby. I'm here." I laid my head on her arm.

"It hurts so bad, Shaun. My heart is so broken. Our baby," she screamed.

"I know." I cried.

"I didn't know. I swear I didn't know," she sobbed.

"I know you didn't. It's not your fault." Tears streamed down my face as I ran my thumb across her forehead. "We'll get through this, Jen. I promise you. I promise we'll get through this."

"Jenni, we're giving you something to relax you before we take you up to the O.R.," the nurse said as she placed a needle in Jenni's IV.

"I love you so much." I cried.

"I love you too. Don't leave me, Shaun."

"I'm not going anywhere, baby."

"I'm sorry, Mr. Kind, but we have to take her upstairs now. Dr. Kind is waiting for her."

"Okay." I brought her hand up to my lips. "Conner is going to fix your arm, and I'll be there when you wake up."

They wheeled Jenni out and I looked at Jackson.

"And I'm taking you up to your room," Jackson said.

"You're admitting me?" I furrowed my brows.

"Damn right, I am. I want you monitored tonight. I got you a semi-private room with two beds. They'll bring Jenni in when she's out of surgery."

"Thank you, Jackson."

"As soon as you're settled, I'll send the family up."

I felt helpless, and there was nothing I could do about it. The emotions running through me at that moment were ones I'd never felt before. She needed me as much as I needed her. Conner would fix her arm, but other pieces inside her were shattered, and I needed to be stronger than I ever had been to piece her back together again.

"Hey, bro," Sam said as he and my brothers walked in.

"How are you?" Sebastian asked.

That's all it took for the tears to come back.

"Hey, we're here." Stefan walked over and grabbed my hand.

"And we're not leaving either," Simon spoke.

"Conner said her arm will be good as new when he gets done with it," Sebastian said.

I couldn't stop the emotions I'd felt and started full-blown crying, which worsened the pain from my broken rib.

"Bro, she's going to be okay." Stefan gave my hand a gentle squeeze.

"Physically, she will, but emotionally she won't. She was seven weeks pregnant."

"What?" Simon shouted.

"We had no idea." I cried.

Sam walked over and placed his hand on my shoulder. "I'm so sorry."

"I need to be with her."

"You will be," Sebastian said. "Jackson said they're bringing her in after surgery."

The rage in Simon's eyes wasn't unexpected, for he and Jenni had a special bond.

"Oh. Wow. I didn't realize there were so many people in here," the nurse spoke as she walked into the room. "Visiting hours are—"

"I don't care if visiting hours are over. We're not leaving," Simon scowled.

"Okay. Well, I'm just here to give you something for your pain, Mr. Kind."

"No. I want nothing. I need to be awake when my girlfriend is brought up."

"It'll help you relax."

"I said no!"

"Okay. You need to keep this ice pack on you for at least twenty minutes. I'll bring you more in a while. If you change your mind about the medication, push this button right here."

"You guys, as much as I appreciate you staying, you don't have to."

"Yeah. We do," Simon spoke.

"Sam, what about Julia and the girls?"

"Grace took Julia home, and her mom is on her way over to spend the night. She's coming up first thing in the morning."

"Stefan? You have three kids and a wife to get back to."

"My mom is over there."

"This is what we do, bro," Sebastian said. "When one of our own is suffering, we don't leave."

"That's right," Sam said. "Why don't you close your eyes and get some rest. We'll wake you when Jenni comes in."

"I can't." I tried to reposition myself and couldn't.

"Grace can take care of that rib for you." Simon smiled.

"No thanks. I think I'd rather suffer for a while."

CHAPTER 37

Shaun

"One of you can have the bed. I need you to help me to that recliner by Jenni's bed."

"Bro, I don't think that's a good idea," Sebastian spoke. "It might be too uncomfortable for you."

"I don't care. I need to be by her."

"Yeah. We all get that," Sam said.

Simon and Stefan helped me from the bed as I held the ice pack against me.

"One of you can take that bed. I'll be damned if I'm ever getting on one of those again," Simon spoke.

"We need a couple more chairs," Sebastian said.

"I don't think anyone is in the room next door. Check in there," Stefan said as he tried to make himself comfortable on the bed.

Just as Sam and Sebastian left the room, they wheeled Jenni in.

"Shaun."

"I'm here, babe. I'm right here." I grabbed hold of her hand.

"Hey, guys." Conner walked into the room. "The surgery was successful, Shaun. I put in a plate and a few screws to help heal the bone properly. She will need to wear that splint for at least four to six weeks to keep her arm stabilized. The perks of having an orthopedic surgeon living next door is that I can check in on her every day." He smiled.

"Thank you, Conner."

"You bet. Any questions?" He looked at Jenni.

She slowly shook her head as she stared straight ahead at the wall.

"Okay. I'm going to head home. You'll be here for a couple of days, and I'll be back tomorrow to check on that arm."

After Conner left, Simon walked over and pressed his lips against Jenni's forehead.

"You're going to be okay," he whispered. "I will make sure the guy who hit you is put away for life. You have my word."

Tears streamed down her face as she closed her eyes. Simon gave me a sympathetic look.

"We'll give you some privacy," he spoke as he placed his hand on the curtain that separated the beds. "If you need anything, we're right here."

"I sat in the chair next to the bed and stared at Jenni as I held her hand and softly stroked it. I was exhausted and in pain but refused to sleep in case she needed something. How could such a beautiful night turn into such a nightmare?

She opened her eyes and looked at me.

"Try and get some rest, babe. We'll talk tomorrow."

$\sim$

*S*imon

"Damn. That bed was so uncomfortable," Stefan said as we headed down to the lobby.

"No shit." I chuckled as I patted his back.

We stopped at the coffee bar and grabbed a cup of coffee. None of us really slept all night, and my brothers were heading home.

"Is Grace on her way here?" Sam asked.

"Yeah. She should be here in a few minutes."

"Okay. We're going to head out. We'll be back later. You really should go home and get some rest, bro," he said.

"I'm fine. I'll head home to shower and change clothes after I have a chat with the asshole who hit Shaun and Jenni."

I bought two coffees. One for myself and one for Grace. When she walked into the lobby, I kissed her and handed her the cup.

"Thanks. How are Shaun and Jen?" she asked.

"They were both sleeping when we left the room. Did you pull his record?"

"I did. He's the president of Caldwell Tech Group. He's divorced and has two children, ages fifteen and twelve, and he was arrested two years ago for a DUI."

"Let's go have a chat with Mr. Caldwell."

We took the elevator up to the floor his room was on. When Grace and I stepped in, he was awake.

"Who are you?" he asked.

"Did you hear that, Grace? He asked who we were. I didn't like the tone in which he asked that question." I smiled.

"I didn't like it either."

I reached in my pocket, pulled out my badge, and flashed it.

"I'm Detective Simon Kind with the LAPD, and this is my partner Detective Grace Adams. We're here to question you about the events of last night."

"I don't remember anything." He looked away from us. "I'm exhausted, so you need to leave."

"Did you hear that, Grace? He wants us to leave."

"It's a shame that we don't care," she said.

Grace walked over to the other side of the bed while I stood on the other.

"Let me refresh your memory, asshole," I said as I set my cup down and leaned over him. "You were drunk, high on meth, and going the wrong way on an exit ramp, hitting a vehicle head-on."

"And yet you lie here with only a few bruises and a ruptured spleen," Grace said.

"The car you hit was my brother's, which could have been avoided since you weren't supposed to be driving in the first place."

"The nurse told me they were okay," he said.

"They're far from okay," I spoke through gritted teeth as my hands grabbed his gown.

He went to push the call button, and Grace ripped it from his hand.

"My brother has a broken rib and stitches on his face. The woman he was with happens to be one of my best friends. She's lying in a bed with a broken arm and a concussion. Because of you, she suffered a miscarriage. Do you know what that means?" My grip on his gown tightened. "That means I'm going to make sure you go to prison for murder."

"Where did you get the meth?" Grace asked.

He laid there and didn't say a word.

"My partner asked you a question, asshole," I spoke through gritted teeth. "Who's your dealer?"

"Some guy."

"What's his name?" Grace asked.

"He goes by Bongo."

Grace and I looked at each other as I released my grip on him.

"How long have you been doing meth?" I asked.

"About six months."

"I hope it was worth ruining your life over," Grace spoke.

"Because that's exactly what you did. How will you explain to your children that their father is a drug addict and a murderer?"

"I didn't murder anyone."

I went to grab him, and Grace grabbed my arm from across the bed and shook her head.

"Yeah. Yeah. You probably have some fancy lawyer who's going to try and get you off on a technicality or some shit like that, but I can promise you this, you're going to prison. Driving under the influence of alcohol and drugs, drug possession, and vehicular homicide, you can kiss your company goodbye while sitting in a prison cell and reflecting on how much your life sucks. Come on, Simon, let's get out of here before I kill him myself."

I glanced over at Grace while we left the room.

"I think we need to pay Vinnie a visit." I smiled.

"I was just thinking the same thing."

"Did you grab my gun?" I asked.

"It's in my car."

I hooked my arm around her as we walked out of the hospital.

We stepped inside Vinnie's new business venture—a vape bar and lounge on Ventura Ave.

"Detectives. Good to see you again." Vinnie smiled. "What do you think?" He lifted his arms.

"Nice place, Vinnie. I hope it's legit," I said.

"Of course, it's legit. You know I'm out of the drug business. You're looking lovely as ever, Grace." He smiled.

"Thank you, Vinnie."

"What can I do for you fine detectives today?"

"Do you know a guy who goes by the name of Bongo?" I asked.

"I've heard of him. I think he runs with the Francisco Cartel. Why? You work DEA now?"

"No. It's personal," I said. "Find out what you can for me."

"I'm not your CI anymore, Kind."

"Did you really just mean to say that?" Grace stepped closer to him, and Vinnie put his hands up.

"What I meant was, I'll find out everything I can."

"That's what I thought," Grace spoke.

"Thanks, Vinnie. You have my number," I said as Grace and I turned and walked out.

CHAPTER 38

TWO WEEKS LATER

Shaun

Jenni refused to get out of bed since we'd been home, and all she did was sleep. I knew she was depressed, which was understandable considering the trauma we'd been through, but it was also because she couldn't do much since her right arm was in a splint.

"How are you, buddy?" Paul asked as I handed him a cup of coffee.

"Trying to hang in there," I spoke as we took our coffees and stepped onto the patio.

"I'm sorry. It'll get better in time."

"I want you to pull all the financials on a company called Caldwell Tech Group."

"Okay. Why?"

"Because we're taking it over," I said as I brought the cup up to my lips.

"Any particular reason you're targeting Caldwell Tech Group?"

"Mitch Caldwell is the person who hit us. He's responsible for the death of my unborn child. He took something from me, and now I'm taking something from him."

"Shit. I'm sorry, Shaun. I'll get right on it."

"I want you to make it your only priority."

"I will. How's Jenni doing?"

"Not good. I feel like she's sinking more and more every day."

~

Jenni

Being awake was emotionally painful. My broken arm I could handle. The miscarriage, I couldn't. I hadn't a clue I was pregnant. I'd only forgotten to take my pill once during our relationship and doubled up the next day. I guess that's all it took.

"Hey, sis." Julia opened the door and stuck her head in. "Can I come in?"

"Yeah." I managed a tiny smile as I sat up.

She climbed next to me, opposite my broken arm, and hooked her arm around me.

"How are my girls?" I asked her.

"They're amazing. I was going to bring them over, but they fell asleep. How are you?"

"You know how I am."

"I know." She kissed the side of my head.

"I'm so lost, and I don't know how to find my way back," I cried.

"I know, Jen. I'm your twin, and I can feel it, remember? Besides, I've been where you are when Justin was killed. I know exactly what you're going through."

"I lost a baby, Julia. My and Shaun's baby. I think what I'm going through is a little bit worse."

"Are you saying that me losing Justin doesn't compare?"

"Yeah. That's exactly what I'm saying. I lost a child. You didn't. You have two perfectly healthy babies at home."

Julia

I needed to leave the room before I said something I regretted. I knew she was in severe pain and torn apart, but for her to say what she just did, hurt.

"You're right. I better get home. I just wanted to come over and see how you were." I bit my tongue so the next words wouldn't come out.

She didn't say a word and scooted herself, so she was once again lying down. I walked out of the room and down the stairs, where I saw Shaun sitting out on the patio alone. Opening the sliding door, I stepped out.

"What happened?" he asked as I sat down next to him. "You weren't up there very long."

"All I can say is I love my sister very much, and if anything were to happen to her, I wouldn't know what to do. But my god, how the hell can you stand it?"

Shaun inhaled a breath and blew it out.

"She's in pain, both physically and emotionally. You should know better than anyone else because you lost your boyfriend in a car accident."

"You're right, and I do. But your girlfriend just told me that Justin's death didn't matter because it wasn't the same as losing a child."

"She said that to you?" His brows furrowed.

"Yep. That's when I left the room before I said something I would regret."

"Smart. I'm sorry, Julia. You know she's not thinking clearly right now. If you can't get through to her, and I can't get through to her, what do we do?"

"Has Simon tried?" I asked.

"He's been up there, but I think it was more to comfort her. I think he's afraid he will say the wrong thing."

"I know. But the longer this goes on, the harder it will be to get through to her. Trust me, I know. It's okay to grieve and be angry, but she can't stay in bed all day and keep replaying what happened. She can grieve and be angry walking around, taking care of herself, and being with her family and friends."

"I agree with you. I just can't get her up. I've tried."

"When was the last time she took a bath?"

"She hasn't since the accident. I keep trying to get her to, and she won't get out of bed. The only time she gets up is to use the bathroom, and then it's right back in bed. I've been giving her sponge baths."

"And her hair?"

"She's been using dry shampoo."

"You're her person, Shaun, and she'll listen to you. You need to be strict with her."

He let out a chuckle. "You do know your sister does whatever she wants, right?"

"I do, but this is different. She's falling down the rabbit hole, and when she hits bottom, it will take twice as long to pull her out."

"I know." He sighed.

"If you can't do it, we'll have to figure something else out. Maybe I'll give Dr. Strong a call. I talked to my parents, and they're really worried about her."

"I'll do everything I can," Shaun spoke.

CHAPTER 39

Shaun

I went upstairs, and when I walked into the bedroom, Jenni was lying in the same spot and the same position she had been in the last two weeks.

"Hey." I smiled as I sat on the edge of the bed and ran the back of my hand down her cheek. "How about we order some Thai food for dinner?"

"I'm not hungry."

"Jen, you've barely eaten in two weeks."

"I don't have much of an appetite. Plus, Thai food is too heavy."

"Okay. What do you want then?"

"I don't know. I just want to sleep."

"That's all you've been doing. I miss you, babe. How about I start the water for a bubble bath? Then I can wash your hair for you. Jackson gave me a waterproof cover for your arm, so your splint doesn't get wet. You can't keep using a dry shampoo like you've been."

"Maybe tomorrow," she spoke. "Can you get me a couple of bottles of water?"

THE KIND BROTHERS

My patience was wearing thin, and I could feel the anger that had been locked up inside me trying to escape.

"Sure." I carefully leaned over as the pain in my rib pierced me and pressed my lips against her forehead.

I stood up from the bed, and I stopped when I reached the doorway.

"No. If you want water, you'll have to get it yourself. You will have to climb out of bed, walk down the stairs, and get it."

"Are you being serious right now?"

"Yeah, Jen. I am."

"Whatever, Shaun. You're a real asshole."

That was it. I snapped.

"I'm an asshole? After everything I've done for you these past two weeks, I'm the asshole?" I shouted.

"Stop it, Shaun. Just leave me alone." She turned her head to the side.

"NO!" I yelled. "Enough is enough. You have every right to grieve and to be angry. Every right, Jenni. But I will not allow you to lay in the goddamn bed all day and all night feeling sorry for yourself."

"Get out of here!" she yelled as she grabbed a pillow and threw it at me.

"You're not the only one who's grieving and angry at the world! I am too, but I'm not going to stop living! I hate the fact that we were in that accident." I picked up the lamp off my nightstand and threw it against the wall. "I hate that we lost our child." I picked up the picture frame with our picture and threw it.

"Shaun, stop it. You have a broken rib!"

"I hate the fact that I have a broken rib, and I hate that you have a broken arm!" I walked over to her side, grabbed the lamp, and threw it. "I hate the fact that you're so lost, and I can't find you!" In one sweep, I took my arm and knocked everything on the dresser onto the floor."

"Shaun, stop," she cried. "You're scaring me."

The pain from my broken rib intensified as I placed my hand over it.

"I'm scaring you? You're scaring me. I've been strong for you, but I can't do it anymore. This is me falling apart! You deal with it your way, and I will deal with it my way."

I placed my hand on the back of my head and paced around the room. While she lay in bed and sobbed, it broke my heart. I couldn't listen to her cry anymore, so I left the bedroom, went downstairs, and poured myself a scotch. I threw the golden liquid down my throat and poured another one. I took it into my office and sat down, bringing my hands to my face.

Simon

I was sitting on the patio with Grace and Jackson when we heard the yelling coming from Shaun's house.

"Damn. What is going on over there?" Jackson asked.

"I don't know, but I sure as hell will find out." I stood up from my seat.

Grace got up and blocked me.

"No, you're not." She put her arms out to the side.

"Grace." I cocked my head. "Please, step out of the way. I will not sit here and let him yell at Jenni like that, especially in the condition she's in."

"You're not going over there. He's finally letting out his hurt and anger over the accident. He's been nothing but strong and a rock for her. This is what they need right now."

"How can you say that?" I furrowed my brows. "What if he hurts her?"

"Do you honestly believe your brother is capable of that?"

"No, but—"

"Then sit down."

"Better do as she says, cous." Jackson chuckled.

"If Shaun or Jenni need you, they'll let you know," Grace spoke.

"Yeah, well, I'm not waiting."

"You really want to try and get past me?" Her brow raised.

"Are we really going to do this?" I asked.

"You're not going over there."

Suddenly, all was quiet next door. The yelling stopped, and so did the sounds of things being thrown. I turned around, grabbed my beer, and sat down.

"I can't believe you were actually going to fight me." I smirked as I looked at Grace.

"You were giving me no choice. We can resume later tonight." She grinned.

"I look forward to it."

"You two are killing me." Jackson smiled.

"You need to find a woman like this one." I pointed at Grace.

"Nah, I'm good." He brought the bottle up to his lips.

∼

*S*haun

I was sitting behind my desk with my face buried in my hands when I felt a soft touch on my back. Looking up, Jenni was standing next to me, her eyes red and swollen from the tears she shed. Holding out my arms, she sat down on my lap, being careful of my rib.

"I'm so sorry," she whispered as she laid her head on my shoulder and buried her face in my neck.

"No. I'm the one who's sorry. I shouldn't—"

She lifted her head and placed her finger on my lips.

"You had every right. I've been so consumed with how I felt that I couldn't see you were hurting. I mean, I knew you were, but you've been so strong."

"I had to be for you."

"I appreciate that, and I love you even more for it." She smiled as she pressed her lips against mine. "We're going to get through this—one day at a time. How's your rib?"

"It hurts like a bitch." The corners of my mouth curved upward.

"Do you need a pain pill?"

"Yeah. I think I do."

She climbed off my lap and held out her hand.

"Let's go get you one, and then I'm going to take a shower."

"Nope. You're going to lie down and rest," I told her.

After I took a pain pill, we slowly walked up the stairs and stopped as we entered the bedroom.

"Shit." I shook my head as I looked around at the mess. "I'm sorry."

"Don't be. I feel bad for you." She snickered.

"Why?" I glanced at her.

"Because I know you can't stand this mess, and it's eating you up inside."

"You're right." I tried to bend over to pick up one of the lamps. "I have to get this cleaned up."

"Stop, babe. You're in too much pain."

"I am not allowing you to clean up my mess. Besides, you only have the use of one arm."

A wide grin crossed her face. A beautiful grin I hadn't seen since before the accident.

"That's what brothers are for."

"Ah." I smiled. "I'll text them now."

"Can you put the cover on my arm first?"

"Of course." I ran my hand through her hair. "Wait. I have an idea."

"What?"

"Wait to take a shower after my brothers get this room cleaned up. I'll take one with you and wash your hair for you."

"I like that idea." The corners of her mouth curved upward as she brought her lips to mine. "I want to sue the guy who hit us, and I'm serious. I won't let him get away with what he did to us and our baby."

"We're not suing him, Jen. I have other plans in motion."

"Like what? Are you going to kill him?"

I let out a chuckle. "Do you want me to go to jail for the rest of my life? I'm going to take over his company, and once I'm done, he will have nothing."

"God, I love you." She smashed her mouth into mine.

CHAPTER 40

Sam

Julia and I had just put the girls to bed when a text message from Shaun came through in the group chat.

"Bros, I need your help ASAP!"

"What's wrong?" Julia asked.

"Shaun needs our help." I kissed her lips. "I'll run over and see what he needs. I'll be back soon."

Placing my phone in my pocket, I saw Stefan and Sebastian heading over, so I ran up to them. When we stepped into the house, we went upstairs, and I froze when I walked into the bedroom.

"Damn." Stefan laughed.

"What the hell happened?" I asked Shaun as Jackson was checking his ribs.

"Shaun had a temper tantrum." Jenni grinned.

"Wow," Sebastian spoke as he looked around the room.

"You should have heard them," Simon spoke. "Bro, next time you go on a tangent like this, make sure your bedroom windows are shut. I could have stopped all this, but Grace wouldn't let me come over."

"Yeah. You should have seen her." Jackson chuckled. "She was ready to take him down if he took another step."

"You need us to clean this up for your sorry ass?" Stefan smirked.

"Jenni and I would appreciate it since we're both not capable at the moment," Shaun said.

"Maybe we can leave this for Sam. He loves to do this shit." Sebastian smiled. "Nah, just kidding, bro. We'll have this cleaned up in no time."

"You do realize you broke the lamps?" I raised my brow at Shaun.

"Yeah. My bad."

After we cleaned up, I walked over to the side of the bed Jen was on and took hold of her hand.

"Are you doing okay?"

The corners of her mouth curved upward. "I am, but I'm taking it one day at a time."

"That's all you can do." I smiled at her.

"Tell Julia I'll stop by the coffee shop in the morning. I owe her a big apology."

"I will." I kissed her forehead.

We said goodbye to Shaun and Jenni and headed home. When I walked through the sliding door, I went into the living room and took a seat on the couch next to Julia. Hooking my arm around her, I pulled her into me.

"What did Shaun need help with?"

"The mess in their bedroom."

"What do you mean?" She cocked her head.

"According to Jenni, Shaun had a temper tantrum."

"Oh my God. Are they okay?"

"They're fine. Jenni wanted me to tell you she's stopping by the coffee shop in the morning to apologize to you."

"Really?" She beamed. "That means Shaun got through to her. I knew he could."

"It seems like it. But did he have to be so messy about it?" I smirked.

"What kind of mess?"

"Broken lamps, everything from the dresser was on the floor, broken picture frames."

"Oh. I bet Shaun was flipping out at the mess." She laughed.

"I was flipping out at the mess."

She brushed her lips against mine. "But you loved cleaning it up, didn't you?"

"Only because it was for my brother."

"Okay, baby. Keep telling yourself that." She patted my chest.

∼

Stefan

When I walked into the house, Lily was in the family room watching TV.

"Hi, Dad."

"Hello, sweet daughter of mine. Where's your mom?"

"Upstairs folding laundry."

"And your brother and sister?"

"Henry is sleeping, and Rori is laying on your bed."

"Okay."

"How's Aunt Jenni and Uncle Shaun?"

"They're good, baby girl."

"Dad! You promised me that you wouldn't call me that anymore once Rori was born. A promise is a promise, remember?"

"I slipped. I'm sorry. I've been calling you that since you were born. It'll take me time to adjust to not calling you that anymore." I walked over and kissed the top of her head. "I'm going upstairs to talk to Mom."

I started to walk out of the family room and turned around when Lily called my name.

"Dad?"

"Yeah?"

"I love you. It's been a while since I told you that."

"I love you too, bab—Lily. See, I caught myself." I smiled.

"Good job, Dad."

I went upstairs and wrapped my arms around Alex as she stood at the foot of the bed folding laundry.

"I'm home."

"Welcome back. How did it go over there?"

"It was a total mess, but we got it cleaned up for them." I kissed her cheek.

Picking Rori up, I sat on the bed against the headboard and laid her on my lap.

"What Shaun and Jenni are going through is heartbreaking."

"I know it is, Stefan. But they're a solid couple, and they'll get through it."

"I know they will. I'm not worried. It's just scary how life can change in an instant. I will never take you, our children, or our life together for granted. I hope you know that."

She walked over, sat on the edge of the bed, and placed her hands on each side of my face.

"I know you never will, and neither will I." Her lips kissed mine.

"I'm kind of regretting getting the vasectomy."

"What?" Her brows furrowed. "Why?"

"Maybe one more kid wouldn't have been such a bad idea." I smiled.

"Were you smoking something over at Shaun's?"

I chuckled. "Look at our beautiful daughter. We make beautiful babies."

"We do make beautiful babies, but I'm not sure you could

handle four children when I go back to work at the restaurant."

"What? I thought you weren't going back after Rori."

"Babe, that's what you wanted to believe. I never said that." She smiled as she patted my face and stood up from the bed.

"But, Alex, I need you."

"So does your brother." A smirk crossed her lips.

"Who cares about him. He can find another bartender."

"Are you trying to tell me that I shouldn't work and just stay home all day with three kids and have no life besides cleaning, cooking, laundry, grocery shopping—"

"Okay. You've made your point. I apologize."

"You're never going to win, Stefan." She grinned.

"I know, but a guy can try, right? Did you hear that, Rori? Mommy is abandoning you to go and be with your Uncle Sebastian."

"Stefan!"

She walked over to the bed, scooped Rori up, and set her in her bassinet.

"Hey, I was playing with my kid."

She climbed on top of me, grabbed my wrists, and held my arms above my head.

"You are such an asshole."

"I know, but I'm your asshole, and you love it." I grinned.

"Why is it that I can't stay mad at you every time you flash that sexy smile at me?"

"Because you love me."

"Yeah. I guess I do." She smiled.

I broke out of her grip and rolled her on her back.

"You guess you do? You've given me no choice. I'll just have to remind you why you love me."

"Good idea, but Lily is right downstairs," Alex said.

I climbed off her, walked over to the bedroom door, and shut and locked it.

"She knows what the closed door means." I grinned as I climbed on the bed and slowly took down her shorts.

CHAPTER 41

ONE MONTH LATER

*S*ebastian

It was a Friday afternoon, and I had left the restaurant early. When I got home, Emilia was already there, and she was on the phone. After kissing her cheek, I went upstairs and changed into my boardshorts because I wanted to go surfing.

"Are you going surfing?" she asked when she walked into the room.

"I am, and I'd like my beautiful wife to join me." The corners of my mouth curved upward.

"Sure. It sounds like fun. It was a crazy day today."

"What happened?"

"Nothing happened. We're just packing everything up to move over to the medical center."

"When did Jackson say the building was opening?"

"Next month. Things are running behind schedule."

"You still have some time."

"I don't want to wait until the last minute." She slipped into her bikini.

"I told you I'd help you."

"You're running two restaurants, and you're busy enough."

"I can still help. Just ask, and I'll be there." I kissed her lips.

We grabbed our boards and walked down to the beach. We paddled out, and Emilia sat on her board as her feet dangled in the water.

"Who were you on the phone with when I walked in?" I asked.

"My friend, Georgia."

"The OB/GYN you've known since college?"

"Yeah. Remember, she's the one who couldn't attend our wedding because her flight was canceled due to some bad storms over on the East Coast?"

"That's right. What's she up to?"

"She's thinking about moving back to L.A."

"I didn't know she lived here before."

"Born and raised. Her parents were killed in a small plane crash when she was twelve. She moved to New York to live with her grandmother, and she hasn't been back since."

"Why is she thinking about moving back?"

"As much as she likes New York, she said she needs a change. She recently broke up with her ex-fiancé. So, I'm sure that's a big factor."

"She's a doctor, so finding a job here won't be an issue."

"I know. She's thinking about starting her own practice, and I was going to ask the guys if they're still looking for an OB/GYN for the medical center."

"Good idea. Are you ready to catch some waves?"

"Let's do it." She grinned.

*E*milia and I were sitting out on the patio when Conner and Nathan walked over.

"What's up, cousins?" Conner grinned.

"Why are the two of you so dressed up?" I asked.

"We're going to hit up a couple of bars. We're just waiting on Jackson," Nathan said.

"I'm glad you guys dropped by," Emilia spoke. "Are you still looking for an OB/GYN, or did you already find one?"

"We're still looking," Nathan spoke.

"Why? Do you know of someone?" Conner asked.

"I have a friend in New York whom I think would be perfect for the medical center. She's an OB/GYN specializing in reproductive endocrinology and fertility."

"Ah, a two for one special," Conner grinned. "Give her my name and my email address and have her send over her resume and credentials."

"Great. I will," Emilia spoke.

"You ready to hit the bar?" Jackson smiled as he walked over.

"What the hell," Nathan spoke. "Did you take a bath in your cologne?"

"Shut the fuck up, douchebag."

"Don't forget. Tomorrow morning at six a.m., we're hitting the waves," I said.

"We'll see. We might have some company over." A grin crossed Conner's face.

"You know the rule. Out by five-thirty, waves at six."

CHAPTER 42

Shaun

"I am really impressed with this place," I spoke to Conner as he led us to the x-ray room.

"Thanks. We couldn't have made it what it is without your help."

After Conner x-rayed Jenni's arm, he removed her splint.

"The bone healed nicely. I can guarantee that you'd still be in that splint if any other orthopedic surgeon fixed this." He smiled as he gave her a wink.

"You are the best." Jenni grinned.

"Damn right, I am."

"It feels so good to have my arm back."

"You're going to need physical therapy to regain your motion and strength. We talked about that, remember?"

"Yes. I remember."

"Good. I'll write you a script. Unfortunately, we don't have a physical therapist here in the medical center yet, so you'll have to find one."

"No worries. I already have one hired," I said.

"You do?" Jenni cocked her head.

"I do, and he's one of the best."

"Aw, thank you. I love you, babe."

"I love you too." I gripped her hand. "Only the best for you."

"I have to say, you two are nauseating," Conner spoke.

I laughed as I patted his back.

"One day, you will be this nauseating, my friend."

"No way, bro. Not me."

We left the medical center and climbed into my new car—a brand new Bentley Continental GT with a convertible top in a color called Moonbeam.

"Before we head to lunch, I need to stop by the office and pick up some papers."

"Okay."

"Let me just text Selena to make sure they're ready."

I pulled my phone from my pocket and sent Selena a text message.

"I'm stopping by the office to get Jenni's ring from the safe. She's with me. Do not let her follow me to my office."

"Exciting! I won't let her follow you."

"Thank you. I'll be there in less than ten minutes. By the way, put a legal-size envelope on my desk stuffed with some papers."

"What papers?"

"I don't know—just blank printer paper. I don't care. I told her I was picking up papers."

"Ah. Got it."

"Everything okay?" Jenni asked.

"Yeah. Selena was just giving me grief." I lied.

"About what?"

"Nothing. She does it for pleasure."

I parked inside the parking garage, and Jenni and I took the elevator up to Sterling Capital. Selena was standing by the stairs talking to Miranda when we stepped out.

"Oh hey, Jenni. Wow. You finally got your cast off." She smiled.

"Yes, and it feels so good."

"I'll run up and grab those papers, then we can go to lunch," I said.

"I'll come with you."

"Jenni, I'm in a pickle about what to wear to an event Nick and I are going to. Can I ask your advice?"

"Of course." Jenni smiled.

I ran up to my office, opened my safe, grabbed the ring I'd bought for Jenni, and shoved the box in my pocket. As I was closing the safe, Paul walked in.

"You're here. Good," he spoke.

"No. I just ran in to grab something." I picked up the large envelope off my desk.

"What time is the meeting tomorrow with the board for Caldwell?"

"Nine a.m."

"You're going to want to look at this first." He handed me a file.

"What is it?"

"Caldwell has been embezzling money from his own company. Probably to cover his meth expenses."

"Karma at its finest." The corners of my mouth curved upward. "Thanks, Paul. I'll look this over tonight. Be ready for tomorrow. We're going in with smoking guns." I patted his back.

I left my office and walked down the stairs, where Jenni and Selena looked at her phone.

"Are you ready, babe?"

"Yeah. I would definitely go with the red dress," she said to Selena.

"Thanks, Jenni. I appreciate your help."

We had a late lunch at Emilia's and then headed home. I could tell something was bothering her.

"What's wrong?" I asked.

"Nothing. One day at a time. Right?" Her lips formed a soft smile.

"That's right. One day at a time."

Later that evening, while Jenni was upstairs getting ready for bed, I sat on the patio with a scotch in my hand and flipped the lid on the ring box. As I stared at it, several thoughts flooded my mind. I could have lost her in that accident, and then what? She would never have known that I was planning on proposing to her. I pulled the ring from the box, placed it in my pocket, and went inside.

When I reached the bedroom, she was in the bathroom brushing her hair. I walked in, took the brush from her hand, and brushed her hair.

"What are you doing?" She smiled at me through the mirror.

"Brushing your hair."

"I can finally brush my hair with my right hand, and you're taking that away from me?"

"For now, yes." The corners of my mouth curved upward. "Place your hands on the sink."

"Why?" She smirked. "What dirty thoughts are swirling around in your head."

"You'll see."

I set the brush down, placed my hand in my pocket, and held the ring in my fist, keeping it down at my side while my other hand stroked her left arm. My lips grazed her neck, and a light gasp escaped her.

"I want you to close your eyes," I whispered in her ear.

"Do you now?" A sexy grin crossed her lips as she closed her eyes.

Bringing my hand that held the ring around, I took it and slipped it on her finger.

"What are you—" She gasped as opened her eyes and stared down at the ring.

"Marry me, Jen."

"Stop it. Are you being serious right now?"

I chuckled as I took hold of her hand and stared at her through the mirror.

"I know it's probably not how you imagined it would be—being proposed to in the bathroom. But I couldn't wait for another second to ask you to spend the rest of your life with me."

She turned around and wrapped her arms around my neck.

"You have no idea how much I've missed doing this." Tears filled her eyes. "I would be honored to marry you and become Mrs. Shaun Sterling Kind."

"Is that a yes?"

"Yes, Shaun. Yes!" She beamed with excitement.

I pulled her in and hugged her before smashing my mouth into hers.

"I love you so much, baby."

"I love you too. This ring is gorgeous. Oh my God. I'm so in love with it." She held out her hand.

"I knew you would the moment I saw it."

"When did you sneak out to buy it?"

"I've had it a while."

"Really?" Her brow arched as she cocked her head. "How long?"

"I bought it when Simon bought Grace's ring."

"And you were waiting to ask me, why?"

"I didn't want to ruin Simon's moment. You know. I was afraid he'd kick my ass."

She let out a laugh. "He probably would have."

"You know he would have." I smiled as I pressed my lips against hers.

I swooped down to pick her up.

"I don't think that's—"

"Yeah. Probably not," I moaned as I placed my hand on my ribs.

"Come on, Mr. Broken Rib, let's go down to the beach and scream our engagement." She took hold of my hand.

"Seriously?" I laughed.

"Seriously."

When we stepped outside, we walked down to the beach and faced my brother's and cousin's houses. Sam, Sebastian, and Simon were sitting on Sebastian's patio.

"What the hell are you two doing?" Sebastian shouted.

"You first," Jenni spoke.

"SHE SAID YES!" I yelled as loud as I could.

The three of them stood from their seats.

"What?" Sam shouted.

"We're getting married!" Jenni yelled as she held up her hand.

"It's about fucking time!" Simon shouted as the three of them walked down to us.

Everyone emerged from their houses and ran down to where we stood with excitement and congratulated us. Sebastian ran up to the house, and he and Emilia brought down a bottle of champagne and glasses for each of us. Sam lit the fire pit, and our entire family gathered around.

"Bro, I can't believe you did it without us," Stefan said.

"How did you do it?" Sam asked. "Knowing you, I'm sure it was extravagant."

"I proposed to her in the bathroom. I couldn't wait anymore."

"Bro, the bathroom?" Simon's brows furrowed. "Were you at least in the bathtub together?"

"No. She was brushing her hair."

"Damn." Simon shook his head. "The bathroom? Really? Have we taught you nothing?" He hooked his arm around me, and we all laughed.

CHAPTER 43

Simon

Grace and I sat on the hilltop and stared at the warehouse where Bongo ran his operation through our binoculars. When a truck pulled up, two men climbed out and went inside, while two burly men stood outside guarding the place.

"Are you ready for this?" I glanced at Grace.

"I'm always ready." A smirk crossed her lips.

"I still think I should take the front," I spoke.

"They'll suspect you're a cop. Look at me. I look homeless. You go around the back as planned."

I held out my fist to her. "Let's do this."

"Let's do this." She grinned as she fist-bumped me.

We drove around the block from the warehouse and parked the car.

"Good luck, babe." I kissed her lips before we parted ways.

Grace

I slowly walked up to the front of the warehouse, and immediately, the two men standing guard drew their guns and pointed them at me.

"Hey." I put my hands up. "I ain't looking for no trouble."

I played the part well with disheveled hair and tattered clothing.

"Who are you, and what are you doing here?" the man on the left asked.

"I'm looking to score, and someone told me I could get it here."

"Who the fuck would tell you that?"

"I didn't catch his name when I was blowing him. He gave me this address and told me you could hook me up because he was out. I think he works for you."

"None of our guys would send you here. I think she's a cop." He glanced at the other guy.

"Do I look like a cop, asshole? I'm just looking for some meth. I got the cash." I pulled out a wad of cash and held it up. "As I said, I don't want any trouble. Can't you help a girl in need of a fix out?"

"What did the guy look like?" the man on the left asked.

"I don't know. He was short, had a buzz cut, and was stocky. Oh, and his left arm had a tattoo sleeve with crosses, rosaries, and skulls."

"That's Loco."

"Whatever. I don't care what his name is. Are you going to help me out or not?"

"It will cost you more than just that money you're holding." He grabbed his balls.

"Fine. Whatever. I just need the stuff."

"Let's go." He gestured.

"Be careful, babe," Simon spoke through my earpiece.

I followed him over to the side of the building, where he stood up against the brick, grabbed the money from my hand, and unbuttoned his pants.

"On your knees, bitch."

"I want my drugs first."

"You're in no position to make demands here. I said on your knees."

"How do I know you're going to give me the drugs?"

"You'll get your drugs. And if you're exceptionally good, maybe I'll throw in a little extra for you, sweetheart. Again, get down on your knees and keep your hands behind your back."

"It would be my pleasure." I smirked as I got down on my knees.

Placing my hands behind my back, I grabbed my gun and shoved it into his balls.

"Make one move, and I will blow them off so fast you won't have time to react."

"You stupid bitch!"

"Ah, shit. He shouldn't have called you that," Simon spoke.

I let out a sigh as I stood up and struck him in the face with my elbow, sending him to the ground.

"You're fucking dead, bitch."

Taking my gun, I whacked him in the head, knocking him out.

"Shut up."

"Good job, babe." I heard through my earpiece.

"Thank you, my love."

Walking around the corner, the other guard turned his back while talking on his phone. Carefully walking up to him, I hit the back of his head with my gun, and he fell to the ground.

"I'm going in," I spoke to Simon.

"I'll meet you in there."

THE KIND BROTHERS

Tucking my gun in the back of my pants, I opened the door to the warehouse, and when I stepped inside, four men immediately drew their weapons.

"Who the fuck are you?" one of the men asked.

"Is that any way to talk to a lady?"

The four of them frowned as they looked at each other.

"I'm looking for Bongo."

"This bitch must be trippin' on something."

"I'm Bongo." One of the men stepped forward. "Before I kill you, I'll give you the chance to tell me what you want."

"I have a beef with you."

"Did you hear that, fellas?" He laughed. "This bitch has a beef with me. Okay. Okay. I'll play along." He walked over to where I stood. "What kind of beef you got? Cause it ain't for screwing you and leaving you behind. I'll try to be respectful, but you look like you just climbed out of a dumpster. I got standards. You feel me?"

I saw Simon approaching the other guys from behind.

"Yeah. I feel you." I grabbed his wrist, kicked the gun out of his hand, turned him around, held him in a chokehold, grabbed my gun from my back, and pointed it to the side of his head. "Put your guns down, or I will shoot him."

"Shoot her!" Bongo screamed.

"Do it, and I'll kill every one of you," Simon spoke. "Drop your weapons now."

"Nah, there's two of you and four of us," one of the men spoke as he turned around and fired his gun. Simon dove out of the way, and Bongo broke out of my hold and knocked the gun out of my hand. Shots were fired, and when I reached for my gun, Bongo grabbed me by the hair from behind and started pounding my face into the cement floor. I heard Simon yell my name as he fought off the other three. I needed to get over there and help him, but this big buffoon wouldn't stop. He knelt beside me as his grip on my hair tightened.

"You're gonna pay for this, bitch."

Reaching into my back pocket, I pulled out a switchblade, swung my arm around, and slit his throat. The second he let go of me, I picked up my gun and ran over to help Simon with the two guys that were pounding on him, hitting one of them in the back of the head and pulling the other off him, holding his face down on the ground with my knee as I locked his arm behind his back.

"Are you okay?" I asked Simon.

"Yeah." His brows furrowed. "I think you need stitches."

"I'll be fine. Are you going to call this in?"

"I left my phone in the car."

"You're hurting me!"

"Excuse me?"

"I'd shut up if I were you. You're lucky she hasn't broken your arm yet."

Simon got up, grabbed a roll of duct tape, and wrapped it around his hands and ankles. We threw him in a chair and tied him to it. Grabbing the other two men who were still unconscious, we tied them to a pole.

"Let's go call this in," Simon spoke as he grabbed my hand.

As we walked past Bongo, Simon stopped and looked down at him.

"You weren't supposed to kill him. You really had to slit his throat? You couldn't have just stabbed him in the eye or something."

"Look what he did to my face. I didn't have a choice."

He let out a sigh, and we walked back to his car. He reached inside the glove box and pulled out a cloth.

"Here, put that on your cut while I call Nathan."

"For what?" I asked.

"You need medical attention."

"Simon, I'm fine. We'll butterfly it."

"If you don't believe me, take a look for yourself." He lowered the visor and flipped open the mirror.

"Oh shit. Yeah. I don't think a butterfly is going to do it."

"No, babe. It won't."

CHAPTER 44

*S*imon
    I grabbed my phone and called Nathan.

"Talk to me, Simon Kind," he answered.

"Are you at the medical center?"

"Yeah. The three of us are here putting things away. Why?"

"Grace needs medical attention."

"What? What the hell happened?"

"We got into a scuffle with a drug gang. She needs stitches."

"Bring her to me. I'll be waiting at the door for you two. How far out are you?"

"About twenty minutes or so."

"Are you okay?"

"Yeah. I'm fine."

We pulled up to the medical center, and I helped Grace from the car.

"Jesus Christ," Nathan said as he took us inside and locked the doors.

"I'm fine."

"Your face is telling a different story," Nathan spoke.

"Hey, you—What the hell?" Jackson said. "Come on, Simon. Let me check you out."

"I'm fine, Jackson."

"I don't care. You're still getting checked out."

Nathan took Grace into one exam room while Jackson took me to another.

"Did this have anything to do with Shaun's accident?" Jackson's brow raised.

"Yeah."

"And the guy who sold that Caldwell guy the drugs?"

"Grace slit his throat."

"Shit. Really?"

"Yeah. She just doesn't listen."

He checked me over, and besides a few bruised ribs and a bruised face, I was fine. Walking over to Grace's room, I stepped in and held her hand while Nathan finished stitching her up.

"Okay. You're all set, Grace. You need to ice your face for the rest of the day. Fifteen minutes on and fifteen minutes off. Got it?" Nathan asked.

"Yes, doctor." She smirked.

My phone rang, and it was Captain Burrows.

"Shit." I held up my phone to Grace.

"Let's just get this over with," she said.

"Captain." I put him on speaker.

"KIND, I WANT YOU AND GRACE IN MY OFFICE IN FIVE MINUTES!" he shouted.

"We'll be there in fifteen. It's the soonest we can get there."

"You better not be one minute late."

"Okay, Captain."

I ended the call and looked at Grace.

"Do you think doughnuts will work this time?" I asked her.

"Nope." She shook her head.

~

After we left the station, we headed home. Both Shaun and Jenni were at their house, so we walked over. As I opened the sliding door, they looked at us.

"Oh, my freaking God," Jenni said as she came running over. "What the hell happened to you?"

"Bro, what the fuck?" Shaun asked with worry.

"We got the guy who sold the meth to Caldwell," I said.

"Wow. He'll go to jail for a long time, right?" Jenni asked.

"Not exactly," I said.

"What do you mean?" Shaun asked.

"Grace, would you like to tell them what you did?"

"I killed him."

"She slit his throat."

"Oh," both Shaun and Jenni spoke at the same time. "Thank you for that." Jenni hugged her.

"I can't imagine Captain Burrows is happy about that," Shaun said.

"No, he's not." I sighed. "Grace and I are suspended for two weeks. We have a meeting with Internal Affairs tomorrow morning."

"We stepped on the DEA's toes." Grace rolled her eyes. "But it's fine. We get two weeks off, and I think we should go on vacation."

I couldn't help but laugh as I hooked my arm around her.

"I'm sorry, bro. I—"

"No, Shaun. Don't be. It was all worth it. Besides, maybe if Grace hadn't slit the guy's throat."

"Really, Simon?" she cocked her head. "You saw what he was doing to me. I had no choice."

"You could have gone for his eye."

"Even if I did, I would have had to kill him anyway."

"Keep telling yourself that, babe." I smirked. "Come on, we have to go home, ice, and get our stories straight for tomorrow."

CHAPTER 45

TWO WEEKS LATER

*S*am

Julia and I were in the kitchen prepping for the family barbecue we were having when we heard one of the girls stirring in their crib.

"Sounds like someone is about to wake up from their nap," I said.

"It has been two hours," Julia spoke. "Can I ask you something?"

"Of course, babe." I turned to her.

"Do you regret getting your vasectomy?"

"Uh, no." My brows raised. "Why? Do you regret me getting it done?"

"No. Alex told me that Stefan told her that he kind of regrets it because they make beautiful babies, and maybe one more wouldn't have been so bad."

"Oh shit." I laughed. "What the hell is wrong with him?"

"Maybe he was just having a moment, who knows. But I wanted to make sure you were okay."

I placed my hands on her hips and brought my forehead to hers.

"I am very happy with my two daughters, and I feel like our family is complete the way it is."

"Me too." She smiled.

"I'm going to finish putting the beer in the cooler outside." I kissed her lips.

"Need any help?" Jackson asked as he walked over with Conner and Nathan.

"No. Everything is all set."

"I love the volleyball net," Conner spoke. We'll have to put teams together and play."

"I'm one step ahead of you. Teams are already set."

"You better not have put Grace and Simon on the same team." Nathan smirked.

I let out a chuckle. "I'm not that stupid."

"What time is Shaun's plane taking you to Cabo tomorrow?"

"Flight leaves at eight a.m.," Nathan said.

"I can't wait to get away and relax for a week," Conner spoke.

"I bet. You three have been working your asses off with the medical center. You're opening the doors when you get back, right?"

"Yeah. We'll be back Sunday afternoon, and we open the doors on Monday morning."

"What are you douchebags talking about?" Simon and Grace walked over.

"Their trip to Cabo," I said.

"Your face is healing nicely, Grace." Jackson smirked.

"Thank you, Jackson."

"But I think those stitches are going to leave a scar."

"They will not, douchebag," Nathan said, and we all laughed.

"Hey. Is Celeste coming with Nora?" Conner asked.

"Yeah. They should be here soon. We haven't seen Nora in

a couple of weeks, so it'll be good to see her."

There couldn't have been a more perfect day to get the family together for a barbecue. As I stood on my patio holding Nora, I stared at Julia, Alex, and Celeste, who were down at the beach with Lily and the kids. Shaun and Jenni were playing volleyball with Sebastian and Emilia, Simon and Grace were sitting by the firepit while Simon played his guitar, and Stefan, Jackson, Nathan & Conner were in the water with their surfboards.

"See all those people out there, Nora. That is your family—a family who loves you very much and will protect you for the rest of your life. You will have no worries as long as we're around. We'll help you navigate through life and help you make the best choices possible. You're one of us. You're a Kind, and you're strong."

"What are you doing, bro?" Sebastian walked over and took Nora from me.

"Just telling our sister how much we love her and how we'll always protect her."

"Damn right, we will." He grinned as he held Nora in the air.

Our family had endured a lot in the past year between our father's death, the secret that he kept, Shaun and Jenni's accident, and the loss of their baby. But through it all, we've grown stronger, and the ties that bind us will allow nothing to tear us apart. We are the Kind family.

Thank you for reading book six in the Kind Brothers Series: The Kind Brothers.

I hope you enjoyed it!

You've met the brother's three cousins, Jackson, Conner, and Nathan Kind. Now it's time to get to know them better,

starting with the seventh book in the Kind Brothers Series:
Six of a Kind.

PREORDER HERE

If you're unfamiliar with Asher & Everly, you can read their story in
The Merger

I want to invite you to join my Sandi's Romance Readers Facebook Group, where we talk about books, romance, and more! Come join the fun!

. . .

I'd love for you to join my romance tribe by following me on social media and subscribing to my newsletter to keep up with my new releases, sales, cover reveals, and more!

Newsletter
Website
Facebook
Instagram
Bookbub
Goodreads

Looking for more romance reads about billionaires, second chances, and sports? Check out my other romance novels and escape to another world and from the daily grind of life – one book at a time.

Series:

Forever Series
Forever Black (Forever, Book 1)
Forever You (Forever, Book 2)
Forever Us (Forever, Book 3)
Being Julia (Forever, Book 4)
Collin (Forever, Book 5)
A Forever Family (Forever, Book 6)
A Forever Christmas (Holiday short story)

Wyatt Brothers
Love, Lust & A Millionaire (Wyatt Brothers, Book 1)
Love, Lust & Liam (Wyatt Brothers, Book 2)

A Millionaire's Love
Lie Next to Me (A Millionaire's Love, Book 1)
When I Lie with You (A Millionaire's Love, Book 2)

Happened Series
Then You Happened (Happened Series, Book 1)
Then We Happened (Happened Series, Book 2)

Redemption Series
Carter Grayson (Redemption Series, Book 1)
Chase Calloway (Redemption Series, Book 2)
Jamieson Finn (Redemption Series, Book 3)
Damien Prescott (Redemption Series, Book 4)

Interview Series
The Interview: New York & Los Angeles Part 1
The Interview: New York & Los Angeles Part 2

Love Series:
Love In Between (Love Series, Book 1)
The Upside of Love (Love Series, Book 2)

Wolfe Brothers
Elijah Wolfe (Wolfe Brothers, Book 1)
Nathan Wolfe (Wolfe Brothers, Book 2)
Mason Wolfe (Wolfe Brothers, Book 3)

Kind Brothers
One of a Kind
Two of a Kind
Three of a Kind
Four of a Kind
Five of a Kind
The Kind Brothers
Six of a Kind
Seven of a Kind
Eight of a Kind
Nine of a Kind

Standalone Books
The Billionaire's Christmas Baby
His Proposed Deal
The Secret He Holds
The Seduction of Alex Parker
Something About Lorelei
One Night in London

The Exception
Corporate Assets
A Beautiful Sight
The Negotiation
Defense
The Con Artist
#Delete
Behind His Lies
One Night in Paris
Perfectly You
The Escort
The Ring
The Donor
Rewind
Remembering You
When I'm With You
LOGAN (A Hockey Romance)
The Merger
Baby Drama
Unspoken
The Property Brokers

Printed in Great Britain
by Amazon

HUMOR ALL THE WAY

RENEÉ SERVELLO

EXPLORA BOOKS
700 – 838 West Hastings St. Vancouver, BC V6C 0A6
www.explorabooks.com
Phone: (604) 330 6795

No part of this book may be reproduced, stored in a retrieval system, or transmitted by any means without the written permission of the author.

Because of the dynamic nature of the Internet, any web addresses or links contained in this book may have changed since publication and may no longer be valid. The views expressed in this work are solely those of the author and do not necessarily reflect the views of the publisher, and the publisher hereby disclaims any responsibility for them.

ISBN: 978-1-83430-097-9 (*Paperback*)
978-1-83430-148-8 (*Hardback*)

© 2026 Reneé Servello. All rights reserved.

Other books by Reneé Servello

You're Kidding... I'm a Senior?
Petey the Pug Escapes for 24 Hours
Baby Barney Needs Hugs and Food!
Freckles Finds a Forever Home

"It is rare a book can make me laugh aloud, but *Humor All the Way* by Reneé Servello did. You can tell Reneé is spunky and good-humored in all of her entries."
—*Theresa Kadair*, San Francisco Book Review

***

"A fun and lighthearted read that will brighten anyone's day, *Humor All the Way* incorporates all of the little elements in life and will make its readers chuckle from one page to the next."
—*Kristi Elizabeth*, Portland Book Review

***

"She writes about everything with a wonderful sense of humor, and the result is a refreshing read."
—*Lily Amanda*, Pacific Book Review

***

"Author Reneé Servello has a keen eye for finding the comic in the everyday and the skill to deliver it in concise verse in *Humor All the Way*, an amusing and entertaining compendium of short observations on life."
—*Kent Lane*, IndieReader

***

"This book is clean fun, and the reader will not find any edgy punching down and making fun of people that makes up the bulk of contemporary comedy. This is mainstream humor."
—*David Keenan*, Seattle Book Review

This book is dedicated to my brother and all of
the incredible caretakers. He gave my mom a
very important last year.

To Arne Sorenson, great humanitarian and
our special pen pal.

Contents

DYING	2
PLANT-BASED FOODS	3
FACES	6
LAST CHANCE TO OBTAIN A CONCEALED CARRY CERTIFICATE	7
STORAGE UNIT	8
WHAM	9
T.V.	10
DANGER ZONE/BASEBALL	11
BASEBALL	12
GOLF	13
BRAKES	14
POINTS	16
PASSWORD REQUESTS	18
HEATED DEBALTES	19
OLD TEETH	21
MEDICATION	24
ARE YOU POPULAR?	26
BACKING UP	27
CARDIO CLASS	28
HAIR	29
TRAVELING	30
COFFEE	31
FRIDGE	32
HEARING AIDS	33
THINGS I HAVE LEARNED	34
MULTITASKING UPDATE	37
QUESTION	38
55 PLUS LIVING	39

RECLINERS	40
MONDAY AGAIN … ?	41
DIFFERENT SPOTS	42
HAIR	43
POWER SNEEZES	45
TOP SECRET: JELLO	46
CRUISE	48
CRUISING	49
DOCTOR'S	51
SUNTAN	52
SWIPE AND GO	53
55 PLUS	54
HEARING AIDS	55
CARDIO CLASS	56
PRAYERS	57
TRICKLE DOWN EFFECT	58
ANOTHER QUESTION	59
WHO KNEW?	60
PHONES	61
LADIES	64
GROCERY LISTS	66
MEDICINES	67
VACATIONS	68
MALE RADAR	70
SENIOR LATE?	72
MEMORY	74
REALITY CHECK	77
WORLD IS CHANGING	79
RESTAURANT MENUS	85
GLOBS	86

NEWS FLASH	87
EMPLOYMENT ADS	89
NO HURRY	90
PERCALE SHEETS	91
FOOD	93
PULEEZE	96
MEDITATION	97
FEET/DANGER	102
POINTS OR MILES	106
SUMMER HEAT	107
RUBBER BANDS AND SUPER GLUE	108
THYROID	109
NO SELFIES	110
SENIOR FUN	111
GROCERIES	112
TAN'S	113
OLD TEETH	114
FEMALE SENIOR CLOSETS	116
SPECIAL GIFTS	117
TEETH BRUSHING	118
POP/PAIN	119
WINTER SHOWERS	120
AGING	122
BON VOYAGE	123
RETIREMENT	125
DATING	126
EXPLOSION	129
SPRING	130
MAKE UP	131
UPDATES	132

VIDEOS FOR YOUR HEALTH	134
CIA	135
TECH TEAM	136
ANCESTRY	137
WORK DAYS/RETIREMENT	138
SENIOR SLEEPING	139
PANDEMIC	140
PANDEMIC	141
PANDEMIC	142
PANDEMIC QUARANTINE	143
QUARANTINE	144
QUARANTINE NEWS	145
PANDEMIC LONG DAYS	146
PANDEMIC NEWS	147
PANDEMIC REAL ESTATE HUMOR	148
MORE PANDEMIC REAL ESTATE HUMOR	149
I GERMS	150
WHO?	151
PANDEMIC	152
PANDEMIC/TESTS	153
PANDEMIC CHILDBIRTH	154
SCARY	155
NO EXCUSES/ENCOURAGEMENT	156
WORN OUT AND STILL IN LOVE/ ENCOURAGEMENT	158
ACKNOWLEDGMENTS/ CONTRIBUTORS	160
SPECIAL THANKS AND ACKNOWLEDGMENT TO OUR FAMILY AND FRIENDS WHO ARE VETERANS WITH OUR SINCERE GRATITUDE FOR YOUR SERVICE	161

Humor All the Way

Does anyone realize why you retire? Let me help you. You retire to fill out forms until you DIE! Banking, Real Estate, Power of Attorney, Insurance, Loans, IRS, Utilities, Stocks, Trusts, Annuities, IRAs, Credit Cards, Social Security, Senior Living, Medicare, Medicaid, Burial, Reverse Mortgages.

Kids don't understand how quickly our days pass, but SENIORS sure do!

DYING

If you plan on this, remember that you
CANNOT UNTIL ALL PAPERWORK
is filled out.
Believe me I KNOW THIS!

PLANT-BASED FOODS

Everyone seems to be into eating plant-based
foods for a healthier lifestyle. If cows eat plant-based
hay and gain thousands of pounds are
we sure this is good?

I promise you... none of this is PLANT based!

Humor All the Way

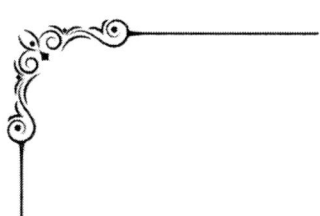

When you hear the words "bonding and veneers" from your dentist… basically your gums are dropping folks!
Just pull out the checkbook!

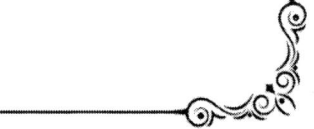

FACES

Guys run out of their homes everyday with their own face. Girls have a choice, the birth face or their applied face. Speaking strictly for myself… if I run out the door with my birth face the STOCK MARKET WILL CRASH!

LAST CHANCE TO OBTAIN A CONCEALED CARRY CERTIFICATE
(This ad is everywhere)

Carry what exactly I ask? If it's groceries I say thanks and come on over!!

Reneé Servello

STORAGE UNIT

Folks just think of yourselves as a STORAGE UNIT.
Your kids and grandkids move in and out, in and out.
Guess where their junk stays??

WHAM

When a man is parking a car and there
is a curb in front it's full speed ahead and
WHAM he hits the curb.
Then he goes forward some more so the
underside of the front of the car is scraped.
Job completed.
When a female parks a car in the identical
circumstances she will stop the car one foot
from the curb. Job completed and the car is
NOT scraped.
Sound familiar?

T.V.

My husband makes fun of some of the things I watch
on T.V.
When he does that, I tell him his programs are far
superior to mine.
One program he loves is football.
This is a group of guys who first get in a circle on the
field, bend over and whisper to each other.
When that finishes, they run and look for someone to
crash into so they can leave after the game with a
concussion.
When this game ends there will be concussions,
broken bones, busted lips…
Far SUPERIOR than MY STUFF!

DANGER ZONE/BASEBALL

CATCHERS are surrounded by danger.
They are tough hombres for sure.
They have bats swung at them nearly
knocking their heads off or knocking
them down.
They are wearing about 500 lbs. of gear.
With this on them they have to squat down to catch
balls and then leap in the air to throw a ball…
someplace.
How I ask is this possible?
Once I squat down, I'm down, period!
P.S. NO team is trying to recruit SENIORS I
can assure you.

BASEBALL

Spit, spit, spit. That's what baseball players do.
Then a hitter comes along, hits a ball and then
they hit a puddle of spit while running.
That folk, is what's known as a SLIDER.
I know these things.

GOLF

One summer in July my husband felt like
it was the perfect time to drag me out on a
course and teach me golf.
This man thinks he reads me like a book.
(He skipped A LOT of chapters).
Off we go, me thinking it will be my last day
on Earth due to the heat, humidity, mosquitoes
and sun!
After barely hitting the ball, I made it to a
clump of trees. I was told to go find the ball.
I did find it in a clump of poison ivy.
I declared that class was over and he was SHOCKED!
"Why do you want to give up so quickly?"
Let me list the ways:
Can't seem to hit the call with this sweat
rolling down my face.
His ball remained the same size, mine shrunk
and became invisible.
My body was now on fire with itching.
My face, not a happy face was RED!
Marriage 101 – Spouses whatever you
THINK you know about your partner, realize
that it is probably the exact opposite!

BRAKES

Have your spouse's driving habits changed?
My husband used to come to slow stops prior
to traffic lights and stop signs.
Now he slams on the brake at the last second
as his dearly beloved is propelled to the front
windshield. Right before I go through it the
seatbelt yanks me back.
Rather than being decapitated I survived with
ONLY whiplash.

Humor All the Way

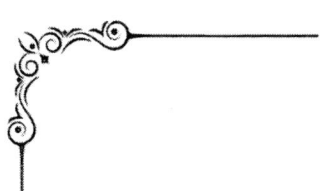

Sometimes I forget to turn my computer OFF
at night.
I'm quite sure that all of the crime families
worldwide are now part of my family.

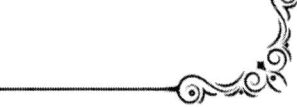

POINTS

We all cherish our:
Airline points
Hotel points
Car rental points
Remember we actually expire like our points!

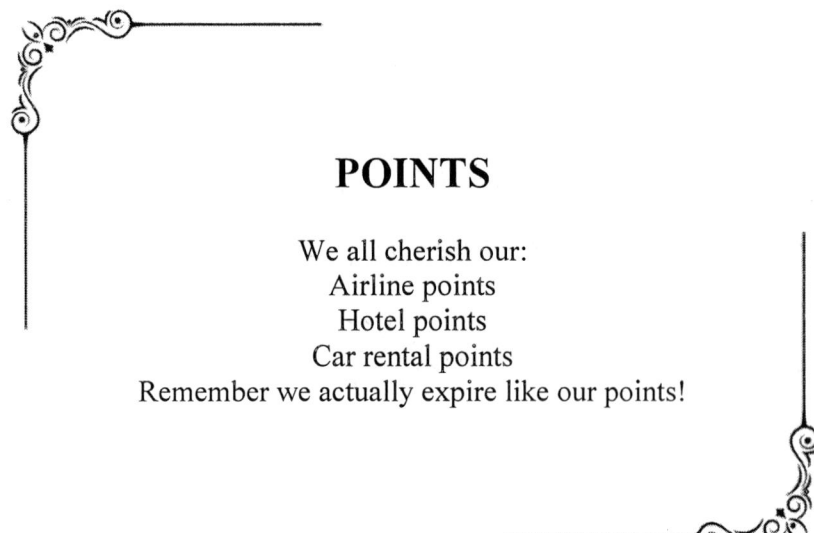

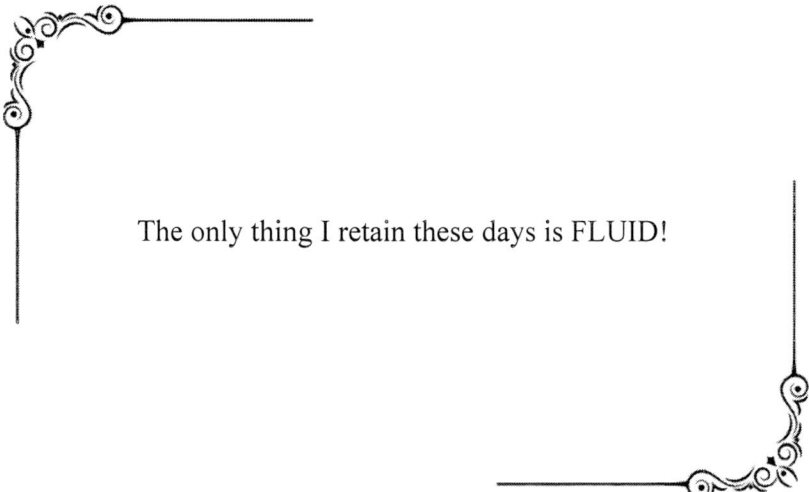

The only thing I retain these days is FLUID!

PASSWORD REQUESTS

Please… no further requests for me to change
ANOTHER one!
I am now password DEPLETED!

HEATED DEBATES

If you want a heated debate with SENIORS
ask one question.
You would be wrong to think it's politics...
Ask them what type of mattress they sleep on.
I can almost GUARANTEE they hate their mattress.
Folks if we are going to have world peace...
WE NEED SLEEP!

Reneé Servello

I know we need to save our planet.
Honestly though I am 100% focused on saving
my hair and teeth at this point!

OLD TEETH

You know you have them. Just try biting some candy and then guess where you will be the next day.
Yep, in a chair getting a tooth IMPLANT OR A CROWN!

Girls, if you want an illusion of more hair book
a ticket to Las Vegas.
That desert air does something, but I'm not
sure what.
In Vegas I have hair volume, it almost looks
like I stuck my finger in an electrical socket.
I return home and the illusion in FINITO!

LOSING HAIR

My husband is convinced that he is losing a lot
of hair.
To that end he now checks the shower drain
after a shower.
We know it will be a good day if there is NO
hair in the drain!

MEDICATION

Dr.'s usually request for you to arrive in their offices with a list of the medications that you are currently taking.
Forget the list, SENIORS just grab a large garbage bag of meds, and throw everything in it and head to their Dr.'s.
Present to your Dr., and they develop a certain LOOK.
Of course, SENIORS are their favorite patients! Right!
-Jeanette Sellier

NOISE

OMG, there is a reason I am deaf.
Most public restrooms have automatic hand
dryers… do I need to say more?
They are so powerful that it sounds like a jet
going down a runway at top speed.
Some of these dryers can literally blow you out
the door.
So far no broken bones, whew! I'm JUST deaf.

ARE YOU POPULAR?

Apparently, I am. I am bombarded daily
with such wonderful offers that are not to be
believed:
Burial plots on sale
Supplements for my belly fat
Supplements for the disappearance of my hair
Pills for overactive bladders
Timeshares off the coast of India
College loans
Vitamins guaranteeing that I'll feel like
mountain climbing
Loans for motorcycles
Self-winding water hoses
So many companies worried about me and to
think we've never even met!

BACKING UP

When backing up your car it may have the navigation system which gives you a red line on the left and one on the right. That system is to help you back out of your garage and prevent hitting things.
My question is where the heck am I in this picture??

CARDIO CLASS

I now consider myself as the WALKING DEAD when this class is over.

HAIR

Has anyone noticed that you may be able to now see the back of your head from the front hairline?
WHERE did that hair go and WHEN did it go?
Think this means that I've been DE-FORESTED!

TRAVELING

We all know what to do prior to traveling.
GO into your safe room two weeks prior to
your trip.
Stay away from germs… (Grandkids)!
Remember, Grandkids, "deliver and you catch"!

COFFEE

Coffee strong enough to curl your toenails…
No, I don't need coffee that strong.
Did I mention my toenails are already curled?
-Dallas Peterson

FRIDGE

Everyone including me, seems to have about 55
jars and bottles residing on the inside door of
the fridge.
Open the door and then DUCK. It sounds
like a ball from a bowling alley is headed right at you!

HEARING AIDS

I just purchased new hearing aids. I can actually hear when people whisper.
Reneé is convinced I've accidentally been hooked up to an NSA satellite.
SENIORS just know where to get the good stuff!
—Judy Campos Scott

THINGS I HAVE LEARNED

Do NOT argue with a SENIOR…
Your lifespan could be INTERRUPTED!

Humor All the Way

My friends and family share their stories of
sideswiping other cars, backing into cars and
hitting curbs while driving.
Whew, I keep all of that at home. I just back
into either the left or right side of our garage.
The garage trim goes with me!

Reneé Servello

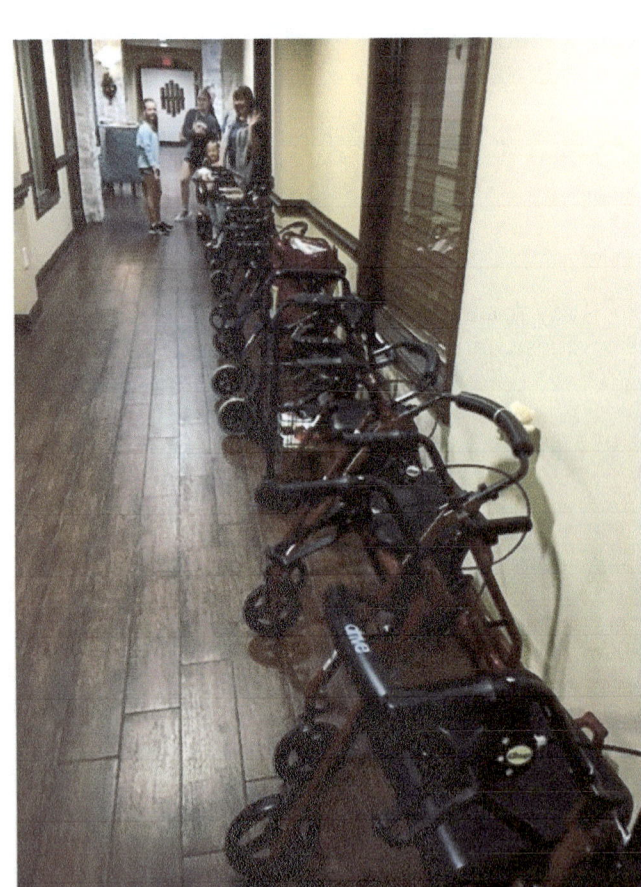

Senior Corvettes

MULTITASKING UPDATE

Today's multitasking simply means you MAY
be able to complete ONE TASK.
Upon awaking write the task you hope to
complete on a sheet of paper.
As your day goes along with activities, phone
calls, etc… well you know where I'm heading.
Your one task was totally forgotten but yes,
keep telling yourself and everyone else that
you are a multitasker! The meaning has
changed.

Reneé Servello

QUESTION

Ask a SENIOR how they are and they'll reply "fine."
Translated: They're still breathing!

55 PLUS LIVING

Listen up newbies: You will quickly learn to NEVER ask anyone how they feel. You may still be listening to the replies from the resident two weeks later. Stick to: What's for dinner?

RECLINERS

I bought a recliner for my senior living home and changed it out four times.
The first two weren't for me, but the third and fourth were memorable.
When number three was delivered it had buttons on the side panel for adjustments.
I did not realize that when you pushed a button it had to line up exactly with the drawing.
Consequently, once when I pushed the button the chair went wild a couple of times and landed on top of me! The facility had to bring in a hoist and lift it off me. On a few occasions I went flying to my wheelchair which was positioned in front of me. A few times I went flying into the arms of my nurse who was ready to catch me if anything went wrong. It did.
Finally, the fourth recliner was delivered. I promptly fell asleep and I didn't leave it for two days as I had been so traumatized from chair number 3! On Day 2 I awoke and had sciatica so bad from barely moving that I screamed with the slightest movement. I am now on heavy drugs.
Who knew recliners could drive you to drugs?
—Lilian Roberts

MONDAY AGAIN…?

Will someone please explain to me how my
Mondays became CUSTOMER SERVICE
DAY?
All weekend alarms come in over the phones
and computer that I have been hacked.
"Change your password and call us Monday"
Then you find out there are charges on various
statements that don't belong to you.
Call on Monday and straighten it out.
I mistakenly thought I was a retired person…

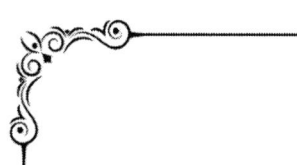

DIFFERENT SPOTS

We already know that many of us have white
spots all over our skin.
Guess what? It gets better! Stay in the sun too
long and then you have little red spots near the
white spots.
No, it's not darling. You will now resemble a
cherry lifesaver.

HAIR

Why is it that when you age your
nose and ear hair grow out faster than the hair on
your head?
—Anthony Servello

ROBO CALLS

If ROBO calls are so important why do they
appear as:
Invalid
Unknown
Unidentified
Not Available?
Gotta be Russia again!

Humor All the Way

POWER SNEEZES

I sneeze in the Spring and fall nonstop and then my back goes out. Can I just stay in bed during those months and pretend that I'm an active guy?
—Ty Servello

TOP SECRET: JELLO

While on a cruise we met a DASHING and DEBONAIRE couple, Dolly and Walter Womack.
They glided into the dining room each evening, tres chic, tres suave.
I made note that each evening thy refused all desserts and instead ordered JELLO!
Well, it's been several months of being on the famous Womack dessert.
I still do not GLIDE, I am not DASHING or DEBONAIRE, I am not TRES anything! I should have started this plan 70 years ago.
I just don't get it, but obviously Dolly and Walter do!

The "KID" always returns home with useful STUFF!

CRUISE

On the same cruise we met another fab couple,
Jean and Ed Reynolds.
By the time we reached the dining room each
evening Jean and Ed had already greeted
each person and found out what everyone was
ordering for drinks and dinner. That's called
SPEED VISITING!
Did I mention that they were from a foreign
country? They had to repeat everything
they said to us at least twice as we just didn't
understand their accent.
They then began to speak in a louder voice
thinking we were both deaf. The foreign
country that they are from in North Carolina!
Every word they spoke was broken down into
eight syllables! No kidding.
We love them for their humor and having such
patience with us by repeating every sentence
spoken… again and again.
I'm sure they were happy to put us in their
rearview mirror!

CRUISING

Cruising to some means a cruise ship.
To my husband and I it means weekly cruising
to Dr.'s and Dentists.
Ok, so one is on the water for bucks and ours
is on land for bigger bucks!
—Dallas Peterson

These are the people on cruises!

Humor All the Way

DOCTOR'S

If you're giving SENIORS instructions or medications… please write them down. Remember the SENIOR MEMORY takes a hike after two seconds.

SUNTAN

I don't know what your suntan looks like but
mine consist of freckles and more freckles.
The freckles then expand to look like brown globs.
Not to worry folks, I have faced this head on. I
realize I have become a GLOB!

Humor All the Way

SWIPE AND GO

That's the program that our food retailers
expect us to go with now.
You, the customer ring up your own items, bag
and then submit payment.
Now let's pretend you have lots of vegetables
and fruits PLUS gift cards.
Do we see a problem yet? Just try it and you
will quickly realize the program is a failure for
some!
We are not SWIPE and GO people.
That ship has sailed and we are still on the
dock.
Shouldn't we get paid for doing all of this
work?

55 PLUS

I just hope that if I move to a 55-plus facility they
can assure me that they have an OPENING
ENGINEER on the premises.
We all know that we cannot open bottles, jars,
creams etc, Nothing, nada!
Really, I don't see the point in pretending that
I'm SUPER WOMAN!

HEARING AIDS

When visiting an attorney for important
matters and you wear hearing aids… I
recommend a SOUND CHECK prior to the appointment.
The appointment can go sideways very quickly.

CARDIO CLASS

You know you can really make it through
this class when instructor Carrie hollers the
magical words; "Shoulder rolls now." That
means we've come to the end of the torture.
Folks I LIVE for those words.
God bless shoulders!

PRAYERS

My sister-in-law prays in English and Spanish.
Hope Jesus is bilingual.
-Tom Peterson

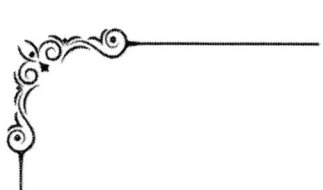

TRICKLE DOWN EFFECT

When I don't sleep my husband is terrified. It can be 2, 3, 4, or 5 a.m. that I awake. I make coffee and take hubby a cup. He never looks at the clock. He may notice that it's been several hours and the sun still hasn't appeared.
Folks this is what is known as the Trickle-Down Effect. If I can't sleep that means he can't either.
Then we go into the daylight hours as complete ZOMBIES!

ANOTHER QUESTION

We all know that guys break out in hives if
they have to ask for directions.
We also know that we now have GPS which is
not always totally accurate.
So, my question is what have you accomplished
by running around in circles for five hours? At
the end of the five hours, you get blamed for
not knowing where we were headed!
Girls, help me out please. This is so wrong!

WHO KNEW?

I'm telling you this now so that you won't be alarmed.
When you become a SENIOR not only does your body wrinkle, but so do your earlobes!
Who else tells you this STUFF?

PHONES

Have you noticed that when kids and grandkids visit that they never turn their phones loose?
They respond to messages INSTANTLY.
Now, you send THEM a message. Spring will turn into summer and possibly then you will receive a response.

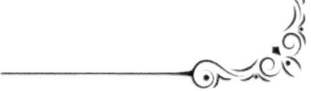

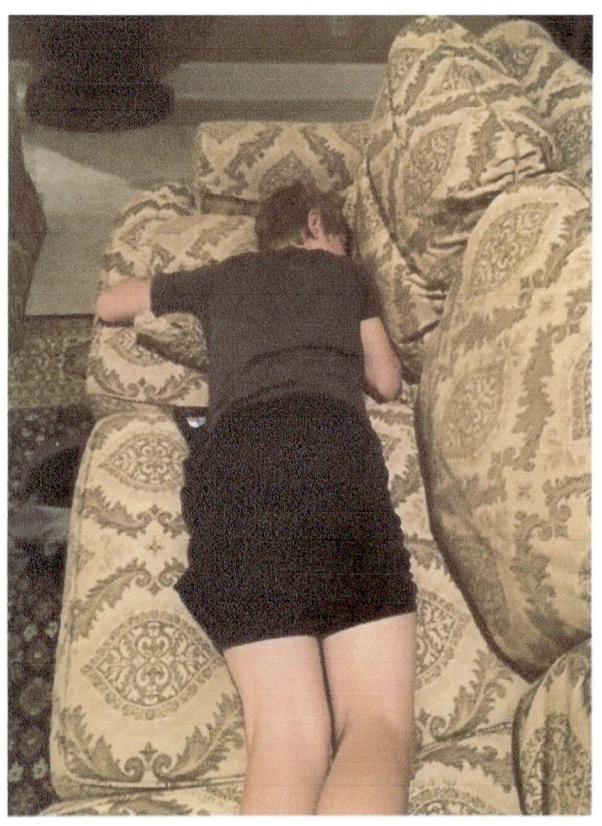

Grandmothers feed the grandkids who then become comatose for the day!

Humor All the Way

Please keep your distance from rattlesnakes!

Reneé Servello

LADIES...

While walking through an airport a salesman
grabbed me and insisted that I sit for 10
minutes and let him apply an eye cream that
will help vanish my eye bags.
Now we all know NOT to do that.
Well, I sat! Ten minutes later I walked away
with one young eye and an old eye.
I guess sometimes it's good to be grabbed!

Yes, I will admit that when I eat salads invariably a lone sprout makes it down into my blouse.
How did that happen? The wind of course.
I am now IN BLOOM year-round!

GROCERY LISTS

I enter a grocery store fully armed and loaded
with a LIST.
Look around you. Note the customers that
have full shopping carts and are NOT reading
a list.
That makes my heart sing. Some folks still
have their memory!

Humor All the Way

MEDICINES

When you pick up your new med's they come
with many disclaimers.
After reading for an hour you suddenly realize
there are more disclaimers than benefits.
If you survive the disclaimers, you might get
lucky and LIVE!
-Jo Fuchs Luscombe
-Anthony Servello

VACATIONS

I'll leave vacation planning and all that it
entails to everyone else.
My only concern is one thing:
EMERGENCY CLINICS in the area and
their rating.
I'm a SENIOR and I take precautions.
-Ron Briggs

The KID at play!

MALE RADAR

Ladies you know it's true.
You hate to turn your car over to your partner.
In my case I love my old car.
However, if I turn over to my car to my husband there
in not a pothole out there that he doesn't end
up in!

Humor All the Way

I went to the hair salon and then out to dinner.
Bananas Foster for dessert. The flame shot
straight up and then it was headed my way.
Toward my hair chemicals?
I feel lucky to have escaped THAT dinner
with ANY hair!
—Brenda Briggs

SENIOR LATE?

Never! If I have an appointment the following
day it means no sleeping the night before.
We may be a little grouchy the next day
so don't push your luck, we can become
aggressive!

Humor All the Way

You visit your Dr. feeling bad.
No matter what the diagnosis is on the way
home you suddenly feel wonderful.
Yes! You are out of there!
—Joanne Cotten

MEMORY

Sometimes my husband may ask me the same
question multiple times in one day.
He hasn't realized that my memory is now on
a timer!

Humor All the Way

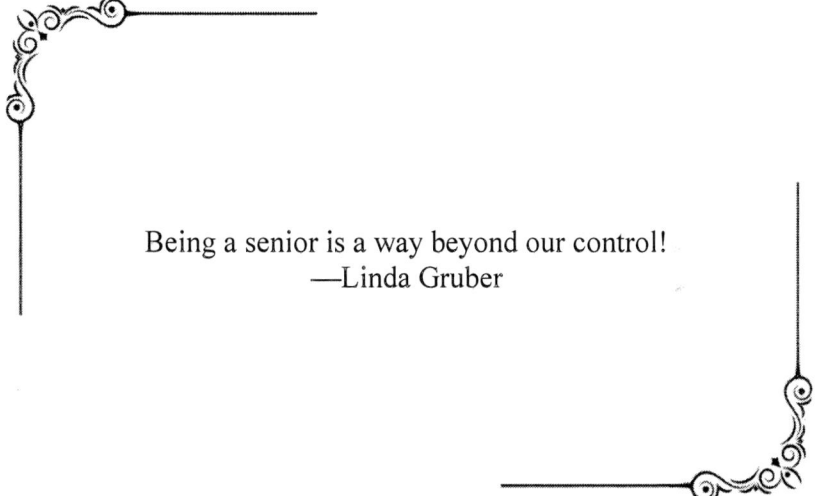

Being a senior is a way beyond our control!
—Linda Gruber

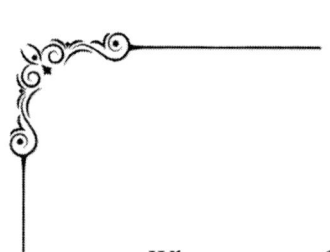

Where are my legs? You know they used to exist.
Why is the distance between my knee and ankle now 12 inches?!

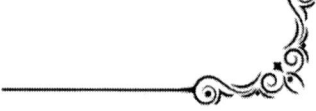

REALITY CHECK

Small hand-held hair dryers can become a hair
eating monster.
Once while drying my long hair, it just sucked
a long strand right up.
I screamed, my husband came running and
unplugged the dryer.
Too late! There was no way he could remove
the hair. I also had an intense headache at that point.
He had to CUT my hair out of that dryer.
As a result, I do not resemble anything
normal. I am a SENIOR with a huge bald spot!

Has anyone realized the difference when you
walk bare-footed?
You have lost the cushion on the bottom of
your feet, it's just bone's folks.
No Zip-a-Dee-Doo-Dah for you!

WORLD IS CHANGING

So many changes:

1. More SUVs vs. sedans, means they are higher.

2. Pickups that extend 20 feet, good luck being able to see anything around them.

3. Beds that have 2 and 3 mattresses piled on top of the frame.

4. There is one thing that has NOT changed, I am still short and UNBOOSTABLE!

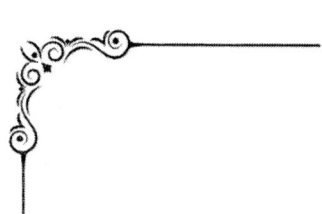

You know you have become a GLOBAL
person by the number of times you have been
asked to change your passwords.
Mi Familia es Su Familia.
China, Russia… who knows?!

Humor All the Way

If I mention any new symptoms to my Doctor,
I know he'll just order another pill for me to take.
Therefore, I mention no new symptoms or
pain and I end up with no new pills.
Works for me!
—Dallas Peterson

O.K. I raised two kids, including burping
them at all hours.
Now I REBOOT T.V.'s and computers.
Burping to rebooting folks!
It's been a long road.

Humor All the Way

Too much caffeine and I prowl all night
looking for fun stuff to do.
Not unusual to have my evening destroyed
during an ALL-NIGHTER.
Next morning my husband greets me with
"how are you?"
My response is "I'm exhausted and I'm going
to bed! Don't ask!"
Believe me he DOESN'T!

Reneé Servello

My husband assures me he is in good shape.
He lifts his chin up 50 times a day to avoid a
turkey neck!
Really? Impressive!
—Anthony Servello

RESTAURANT MENUS

Better carry your own lighting with you if you
care to know what you'll be eating.
Why? Because restaurants have gone from
MOOD LIGHTING to NO LIGHTING.
SENIORS have been left in the DARK!
—John Luscombe

GLOBS

How many of you remind your spouse to
remove articles from their pockets before washing?
Exactly! All of you including me.
Do they listen? Of course not.
Each week I remove GLOBS out of pockets
that have been washed and dried. No one can
identify the globs; however, they smell good.

NEWS FLASH

I would say that the first hour of each day is
NOT humorous.

Reneé Servello

Once I get my HOMEOWNERS INSURANCE POLICY increased, I will consider exercising at home!
—Ron Briggs

Humor All the Way

EMPLOYMENT ADS

Companies advertise:
Flexible Times
Part Time
Full Time
I used to respond to ads that advertised:
FUN!
So, where's the fun nowadays?

Reneé Servello

NO HURRY

Folks, my grandparents lived to be 100.
My mother-in-law lived to 104.
I'd say this group was in no hurry… just stop
looking at clocks and calendars! Relax.

PERCALE SHEETS

Where the heck are they hiding?
When did it become necessary to go to thread count school?
It used to be percale, cotton, flannel, or silk sheets PERIOD!
Now one half of bedding stores are taken up with sheets that are all DIFFERENT thread counts.
My first purchase was for a smaller thread count. After going through the dryer, they were the size of a paper towel.
I'm STILL confused.

My mom received a ticket after a ROLLING
STOP at a STOP sign.
She decided to go to driving school to get the
ticket erased from her record.
Upon arrival at the school each person is
studying each other wondering how bad their
driving sin was.
When my mom noticed them looking at her
she threw her hands in the hair and screamed,
"I'M INNOCENT."
You know what they say about
MEMORABLE SENIOR EXPERIENCES!
P.S. STOP means STOP
—Joanne Cotten

Humor All the Way

FOOD

I've always heard that food prepared with love
is far superior.
SOOO… where does that leave my food?
I'm a KAMIKAZE cook, in and out of the
kitchen in a flash!
Good luck family.

Reneé Servello

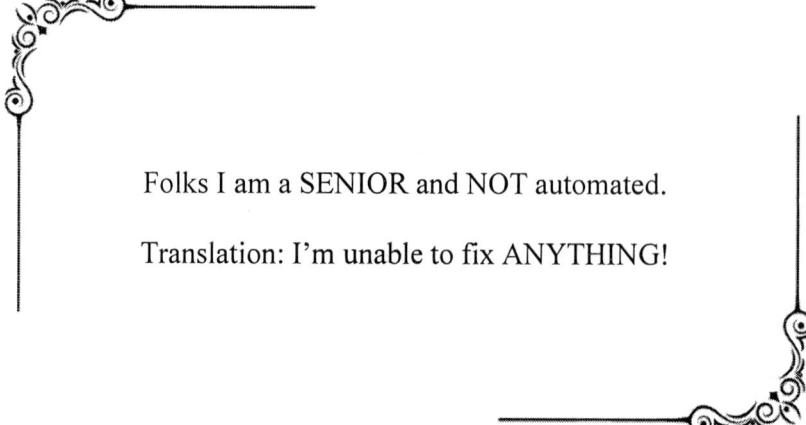

Folks I am a SENIOR and NOT automated.

Translation: I'm unable to fix ANYTHING!

Humor All the Way

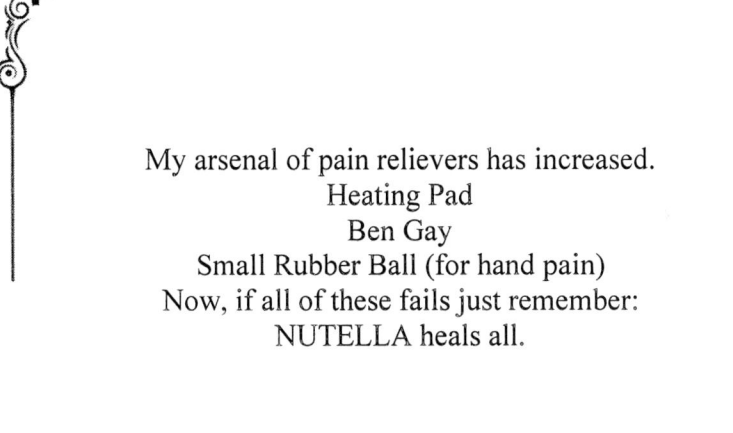

My arsenal of pain relievers has increased.
Heating Pad
Ben Gay
Small Rubber Ball (for hand pain)
Now, if all of these fails just remember:
NUTELLA heals all.

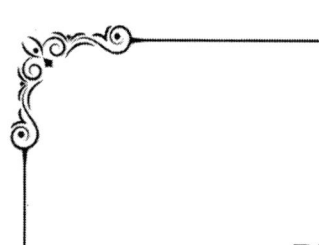

PULEEZE...

Never put me in a hotel, home, or resort on a golf course.
Death by a golf ball is NOT in my plans.

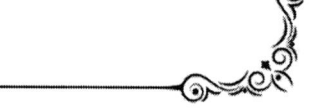

MEDITATION

I have suggested to my sister-in-law that she should meditate to lower her blood pressure.
Went to my Doctor's appointment and decided I would meditate on the way there.
It worked so well for me that I flew by my Doctor's office. It took another half hour to reverse directions on the freeway and get there a SECOND time.
My word of advice… meditate at home!

Reneé Servello

> I'm on plenty of drugs.
> However, not one of them helps me rip through
> a day!
> —Linda Gruber

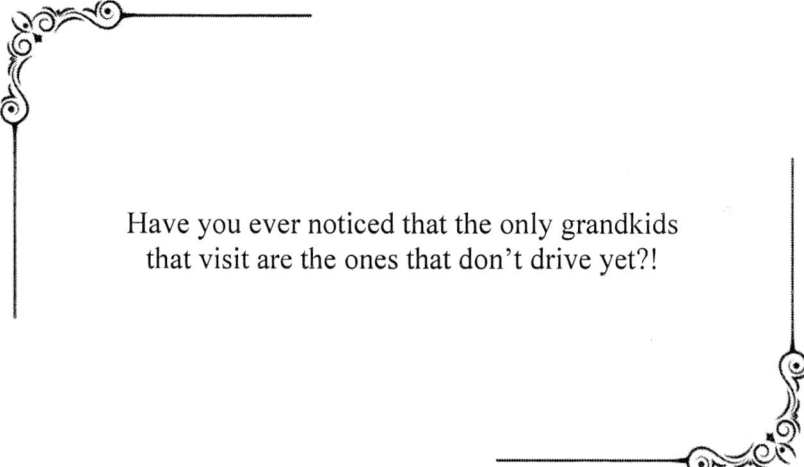

Have you ever noticed that the only grandkids that visit are the ones that don't drive yet?!

Reneé Servello

House cleaning 101… got to get a Statue of
Limitations on this.
After all, some of us are WORN OUT!

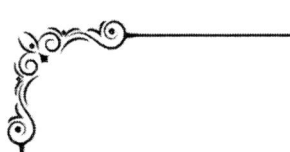

You have a clue you're aging by the amount of
pill bottles on your counter and they increase
annually.
Not necessary to look in the mirror.

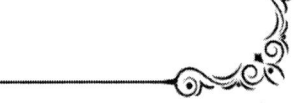

FEET/DANGER

Usually, it's my mouth that gets me in trouble.
What does it mean when it becomes your feet?
Mine can become tangled for no reason other
than just crossing a room.
I become a human rocket and become jet
propelled at 70 miles an hour.

Humor All the Way

Remember when you met new people when you were younger? You remembered their names instantly.
How come it now takes two years to remember a name?

Reneé Servello

> Some days I feel like I just came out of the dishwasher!
> —Carrie Russ Gimmestad

Humor All the Way

You know your cheeks have dropped when
you bend over your plate and something is flapping.
You then discover it is your own cheeks,
UGH!
—Joanne Cotten

POINTS OR MILES

If you have a bank, airline, or cruise credit
card it can be confusing.
The companies have so many titles for their
customers and programs.
Medallion, Gold, Silver, Platinum, Titanium,
Elite, Premium, Ambassador, Chairman's
Club… well it goes on and on.
See where I'm going with this…?
I'm lost when dealing with these companies. I
can't remember WHAT I AM.
I just know WHO I AM and they need to
figure out the rest.

SUMMER HEAT

Temps can go to 90-105 degrees in the summer.
It makes me wonder… if I'm dragging milk
home from the store in a very hot car, well?
Could this possibly mean DEATH BY MILK?

Reneé Servello

RUBBER BANDS AND SUPERGLUE

In cardio class, instructor Carrie sometimes
has us kick our legs.
Am I seriously the only one that doesn't want
to do this?
Everyone knows that SENIORS are held
together by rubber bands and superglue.
SENIORS are FRAGILE folks!

Humor All the Way

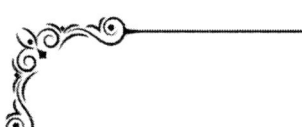

THYROID

Folks if your thyroid is dead don't despair.
I make a beeline to any Marriott Thrive class
that I can find.
You will be amazed what it does for your energy!

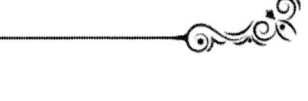

NO SELFIES

If you have short arms this could mean that
you'll be photographing a double or triple chin!
Just saying…

SENIOR FUN

Run around each week and visit your Doctors
and Dentists.
THEN, try and remember what they told you
and record it.
Mucho LUCK!

Reneé Servello

GROCERIES

I go to the store.
I drag groceries home.
I put food in the pantry in the next two days.
Have my priorities changed? This experience
used to take about 15 minutes!

TAN'S

Back from vacation and people comment on
your beautiful tan.
RIGHT!
All it means in my case is that the freckles
expanded… that's IT folks.
I didn't for one second think that I looked tan
and wonderful.

OLD TEETH

Get ready for the OLD TEETH DAY.
It's coming I promise you…
They begin to crack, break, and fall out folks!
Hurry and eat that last ear of corn and peanut
brittle and then retire those teeth.

Humor All the Way

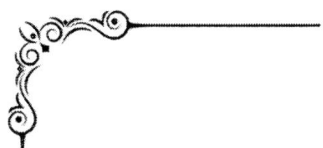
When SENIORS go dancing the question becomes how will we get out of the bed the next day? Double Ibuprofen!
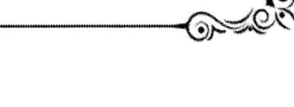

FEMALE SENIOR CLOSETS

If moving into Senior Living THAT decision
isn't the most difficult.
The MAIN decision is your new closet.
Will you continue to haul around four sizes
of clothing? You'll probably only be able to
Accommodate one size.
It all depends on how long you intend to be
sucking that stomach in.

Humor All the Way

SPECIAL GIFTS

One year when my husband and I were
celebrating 40 years of marriage I just KNEW
there was a special gift out there that I wanted
to give him.
I thought about it for nearly a year and then a
lightbulb went off.
YES! Colonoscopies for both of us!
The man is still in shock many years later and
I know will try and get even someday.
He is now suggesting that we no longer need
to celebrate anniversaries… the guy is a big chicken!

TEETH BRUSHING

Who out there besides me gets so deep in
thought while brushing that you return 5
minutes later and brush again?

POP/PAIN

After dragging home from cardio class one
day, I thought it would be quicker to remove
socks and shoes standing up.
Once I put me left leg on top of my right foot
and yanked my sock off… there was a distinct POP.
Just remember two things:
Shortcuts are dangerous.
Where there is a pop, PAIN follows!
One day I'll be walking again.

WINTER SHOWERS

Stepping out of a hot shower in the winter
means pain! Going hot to cold is not good.
We need showers that come equipped with
two buttons:
Hot blow dryer for your body.
A hot espresso or latte upon demand.

When a SENIOR wakes up in the morning it automatically becomes a "STATE OF THE BODY" theme.
Forget politics folks!

AGING

I'm not sure who that lady is in the mirror that
keeps following me around.
I would have been arrested if I could just catch
hold of her.
—Carol Robinson

BON VOYAGE

SENIORS it's your time to travel.
If we were younger, I'd say don't forget the suntan lotion.
Moving right along in years it is now, don't forget the floss, Maalox, Kaopectate, Tylenol, mouthwash, Metamucil, Bengay, meds.
Maybe it's easier to just have a STAYCATION?

The "KID" enjoying a double… hot chocolate!

Humor All the Way

RETIREMENT

Congratulations if you are retired.
It's a special time in your life. You now qualify
to follow your spouse to the grocery stores and
inform them that they are doing everything wrong.
You might have to UBER home.
It's always the mouth that can trip you up!
—Bob Bartlett

DATING

Girls, having dating problems, no prospects?
I'm here for you and will share the BIG secret.
Cruise the waiting rooms of UROLOGY Doctors.
They are always full with mostly men, OVER
FLOWING to be honest. I'd say the ages are
anywhere from 20 to 100.
Great assortment! Just saying from one who
OBSERVES.

A MUST for exciting places to visit!

> I look in the mirror and all I see are brown spots.
> It appears that I have become a banana!
> —Dallas Peterson

Humor All the Way

EXPLOSION

I was cooking on my stove and heard a
tremendous blast, almost like a shot had been fired.
I jumped so high that I was nearly on the roof!
Luckily the stove shut down automatically but
it's not that easy for MY recovery.
Does this kind of thing happen to Martha Stewart?
—Linda Gruber

SPRING

Finally, it is spring. The only thing I see
blooming is our driveway.
Every species of weeds are proudly
sprouting up in every crack.
Neighbors have blooming
flowers. We have
blooming weeds.

MAKE UP

Ladies, all we need to do is look in our mirrors
In the a.m. to appreciate why makeup was invented!

Reneé Servello

UPDATES

I don't know about you, but whenever my computer or phone wants to shut down for UPDATES, I'm terrified!
I feel sure if I press O.K. I'm letting the Russians in again.

My husband and I married when we both had HAIR!
Will someone please tell me what happened?

VIDEOS FOR YOUR HEALTH

Due to watching helpful videos on my phone
I now enter the grocery store with trepidation.
Why? I wonder which fruit or vegetable is
about to kill me as the videos suggest. Guess
I'll never know because I click on all health
videos which promise to enlighten us on
healthy foods for our bodies and what will
destroy us.
However since these videos never end I'm in
the dark and in danger I guess.
Has anyone ever reached the end of one of
these videos?

CIA

This government agency needs ME!
New, updated method of torture…
Yank a strand of hair out of your head and tickle
the prisoners' nose.
Trust me, they will be driven crazy.
Well, it sure drives me crazy.

TECH TEAM

I now have a TECH TEAM to keep my
phone and computer running. You too can
have a TECH TEAM! My team is anyone
that rings our doorbell.
I now owe the world!

ANCESTRY

I had no idea of mine until freezing weather arrives. I found out instantly that I must be descended from the green sea turtles. I absolutely do not move in cold weather, not even an inch. Not even for food!

WORK DAYS/RETIREMENT

For the working public they assure us that
Friday is the best day of the week. The worst
day they say is Thursday because it is still
Thursday and the hours seem to be longer.
I say enjoy retirement. Seven days a week of Fridays!

SENIOR SLEEPING

It's really just speed napping

PANDEMIC

I never thought the comment "I wouldn't
touch him/her with a 6-foot pole" would
become a national policy!
I need to practice social distancing from the refrigerator.
Hope the weather is good tomorrow for my
trip to the BACKYARD. I'm getting tired of
the LIVING ROOM.
Never in a million years could I have imagined
I would go up to a bank teller wearing a mask
and ask for my money.
Never in a million years would I have thought
my hands would consume more alcohol than
my mouth.
-Submitted by Lynn Slaney Siguero, Ebby
Halliday Real Estate, Frisco, TX

PANDEMIC

Why is it that when you wear a mask during
COVID you then CANNOT hear?
Just saying.

Reneé Servello

PANDEMIC

During the pandemic we could have used drive-by haircuts plus nails.
Our son is up to 7 meals a day. We are holding the line at 3.
Kroger's has blocked us from the store on the basis of "Get a life, you cannot live here!"

Humor All the Way

PANDEMIC QUARANTINE

Exercise Program
O.K. I'm home. I'm being safe.
To really be safe I am exercising not only at
home but in my own bed.
If I get tired, I'm already THERE!
Believe me, I know all about safe shortcuts.
—Linda Gruber

QUARANTINE

Times must be hard in the gasoline
marketing business.
I pulled into the Exxon station today to fill the
tank and the clerk ran out and hugged me!
—Phil McCann

Humor All the Way

QUARANTINE NEWS

Trapped for weeks in your home?
You scroll through your T.V. channels for a
5-star movie.
A good amount turns out to be garbage.
The question becomes… what is a 5-star movie
and to whom?
Think I'll reconsider and look for a solid
2-star!
—Kelli Servello Holloway

PANDEMIC LONG DAYS

Instead of three loads of laundry washed
weekly, we're up to eighteen!
Every afghan in the house has now been washed so
frequently they are now shreds!
All silver has been polished... again and again.
Runs and runs to Walgreens to pick up critical
stuff... SENIOR PILLS.
Three meals a day plus snacks - we used to
provide this routine for our kids... OMG, WE
are the kids now.
Averaging two movies per day. Four books per
week read.
We crash Kroger's three times a week.
We are now contemplating crawling on the
roof and washing THAT!

Humor All the Way

PANDEMIC NEWS

It's been nearly a year folks.
Daily average of movies watched: One per day
in the beginning and sometimes two per day.
Well over three hundred have been viewed in
our home.
The day will begin with a simple question
from hubby… "What type of movie would
you like to watch today, war or comedy?"
My reply for three hundred plus days has been
COMEDY. With the exact same answer
everyday, my husband then proceeds to find a
WAR movie.
We have been to war ALL over.
Germany, Great Britain, Holland, France,
North Africa, Spain, Italy, Pearl Harbor, Philippines,
South Pacific and Malta!
I now suffer from a serious case of
BATTLE FATIGUE.
Not to make light of our brave warriors
including family and friends who fought for
Our freedom… however, going into battle
daily will drain a person.
I have now declared our home to be a
BATTLE FREE ZONE. Puhleeze…
Bring on comedy

Reneé Servello

PANDEMIC
REAL ESTATE HUMOR

Dumbest thing I ever bought was a 2020 planner.
I was so bored that I called Jake from
State Farm just to talk to someone.
He asked what I was wearing.
2019: Stay away from negative people
2020: Stay away from positive people
The world has turned upside down.
Old folks are sneaking out of the house and
their kids are yelling at them to stay indoors!
Every few days try your jeans on to make sure they fit.
Pajamas will have you believe all is well in the kingdom.
Does anyone know if we can take showers yet,
or should we just keep washing our hands??
This virus has done what no woman has been able to do.
Cancel sports, shut down all bars, and keep men at home!
Submitted by Lynn Slaney Siguero

MORE PANDEMIC REAL ESTATE HUMOR

The hardest thing about being a real estate agent is:
You're on call 24/7 but no one is dying.
Waiting for the septic tank cover to be lifted…
and a big wind happens to hit then.
When you need to tell your client, the deal will not close.

Realtors are part repair specialists, marriage counselors
and house cleaners.
Realtors retire when they become LISTLESS
(from Lynn's Mom, Alice of Dallas).
—Lynn Slaney Siguero

Reneé Servello

I
GERMS

I came down with COVID.
Not to worry, we live across the street from
Kelli Servello Holloway who knows
that machines cure all.
She dropped three germ machines
on our front porch.
When I recovered and returned her machines
I told her I had lost
thirty pounds of Germs.

Kelli was happier that we've ever seen her!
—Carl Nelius

WHO?

I'd like to see who I have been
talking to in 2020.
Haven't been sure of that since wearing a mask
and others doing the same.
Who really knows?

Reneé Servello

PANDEMIC

One day I needed a cashier's check.
Being fully checked out on banking rules
during the pandemic I KNEW they would want
me inside, not the drive-through for this transaction.
So, I headed inside the bank with mask in place.
There was a lady in the rear of the lobby seated at a table.
I walked directly to her and extended my forehead for
a temperature check.
She looked alarmed and said
"What are you doing?"
I explained what I was there for and
waiting for my temp check.
She assured me she didn't do that
and to please leave immediately.
Did she think I was there to hold the bank up?
However, we have ALL known for the last year…
person seated at table means only one thing:
TEMP CHECK
Maybe not in banks?

Humor All the Way

PANDEMIC/TESTS

Thank goodness my hubby is so alert.
One day, he was out running errands.
When he returned, he told me to hurry,
Get in the car that they were giving the
COVID tests at the high school.
I asked how he knew this and he told me
there was a long line in front of the school and
people with clipboards were coming to the cars.
Off we rushed. A lady immediately came to
my husband's side of the car.
He offered to give them his insurance cards.
They looked puzzled.
Then they told us they were
giving out free cat and dog food
which required no cards.
Folks... DO NOT follow my husband!

Reneé Servello

PANDEMIC CHILDBIRTH

We have waited years for our first grandchild.
It will actually happen a little different from what we imagined.
Instead of flying over to Australia for the birth,
it will all be on Zoom.
While that sounds like a good alternative,
Does this mean we cuddle our computer?
—Claudia and Mike Noonan

SCARY

Who else besides me has noticed their phone
is trying to take over?
I may type in "How are you?"
What appears on my screen is "Just returned from vacation."
So, my question is: When did our phones try
to take over our brains?
Folks, I have enough stress without
my phone getting into the act!

Reneé Servello

NO EXCUSES/ ENCOURAGEMENT

What does it take to be a college graduate?
My college days flew by so fast that I barely
knew I was there.
Here are my stats:
Years to complete: 35
Number of counselors: 12
Number of campuses: 5
Approximate number of teachers: 48
Approximate number of miles driven:
400 to 400,000?
Approximate hours of homework:
4, 224 to infinity
How often I called in sick: Only when there
were a few parties to plan.
Zoom often ruined my plans.
How many projects completed:
Your guess is as good as mine!
How many times did I consider quitting:
Every registration day after the
first semester, at least 47 times?
—Claudia Noonan

Humor All the Way

This inspiring story proves that SENIORS
are capable of anything! Claudia during her 35
years of college, married, raised a family and worked!
Luckily, Mike, her husband played a large part
in helping run the household, carpools, meals…
while HE was working.
We salute you both, MISSION COMPLETED.
SENIORS really do ROCK.
No excuses, go out and make your dreams happen!

Reneé Servello

WORN OUT AND STILL IN LOVE/ ENCOURAGEMENT

When one has an injury such as Jane's that is so catastrophic,
it is hard to know how to process.
One goes through so many emotions.
It always happens to the other person, never in our
wildest dreams did we ever think our later years
would be like this. You look so forward to retirement
and then eight months before you retire, your world stops.
There is hope at first, you think there is going to be an improvement
and at first there is. Just raising your arm a few inches after not being
able to move at all for months brings a smile to your face,
but it turns out to be like a bell-shaped curve.
You get to a certain point and then your body just starts
to give out and hope fades. Depression, which neither of us
has ever had, sets in. You try to keep a happy face in front
of family and friends, but you lie awake at night and quietly listen
to the tears fall from your cheeks onto the pillow. The next night the
tears are from your spouse… You look over at your mate of a
lifetime and think to yourself, is this really happening? You wonder
why your prayers are not answered. You watch most of your friends
slowly stop calling and coming by, as caregiver, you get tired. You
just get tired. You look after your partner in life, you dress and clothe
her every day, fix her meals. You get frustrated because you get
angry and snap at her at times, but you are really snapping at the pain
of the situation, not your mate, and sadly, you just go on. There is
something else in being able to do and say that which makes you feel
good inside. Would we have liked to retire and see more of the world
together? You bet your sweet applesauce, but it wasn't in the final
draw of cards. I don't know that we overcame the life challenges,
because as we get older, they only become more challenging. We can
only look back and be thankful for the memories, and each other.
That is something…
—Jane and Ben

Humor All the Way

These good friends were thrown a large curve
ball years ago.
Accidents happen.
Jane was not expected to live, but guess what?
Heaven was not ready for her. She came back.
She and Ben faced the biggest challenge of
their lives. They have dealt with it by many
feelings along the way. They are still dealing
with it, still together, still in love and pain.
At times depression has set in and sometimes
jokes and laughter arise. Occasionally, Ben has
put her shoes on the wrong feet and away they went.
The catheter was not always inserted correctly.
Jane has blocked people from exiting elevators
with her very large wheelchair
(more like pinned them in!)
The list goes on and so do they!
Anything is possible in this life.
Jane and Ben are living proof of this and that
life may change. We may be called upon to
learn coping skills along the way.

Reneé Servello

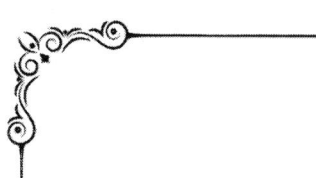

ACKNOWLEDGMENTS/ CONTRIBUTORS

Bob Bartlett
Jane and Ben B.
Brenda Briggs
Ron Briggs, Phil McCann
Joanne Cotton, Lynn Slaney Siguero
Phil McCann, Dolly, and Walter Womack
Carrie Russ Gimmestad and the Memorial Athletic Club
Linda Gruber, Ty Servello
Jo Fuchs Luscombe, Jeanette Sellier
John Luscombe, Judy Campos Scott
Carl Nelius, Carol Robinson
Claudia and Mike Noonan
Dallas Peterson, Lillian Roberts
Tom Peterson, Jean, and Ed Reynolds

SPECIAL THANKS AND ACKNOWLEDGMENT TO OUR FAMILY AND FRIENDS WHO ARE VETERANS WITH OUR SINCERE GRATITUDE FOR YOUR SERVICE

Jane M. Cox
Paul Cotten Jr.
David Cotten
Danny Peurifoy
Gerald Peurifoy
Tom Peterson
Don Peterson
Robert Ostrander
Robert G. Ostrander
Robert Fuchs
Jeanne Fuchs
Logan Mims
Ben (Corky) B.
Michael Noonan
James Rutland Procter
Robert Walker
William A. Cameron
Don Bechtol
Jimmy R. Kirk
Jerry Darrow Jr.
Thomas V. Wilson
George Markey
Gale Bloomer
Sim E. Woodham
Robert E. Dasch
Jim Allen
Ed Reynolds

Gus and Cooper Fuchs swear that naps give them boundless energy!

OMG…those muscles!